ABOMINATION IN THE BOG

ABOMINATION IN THE BOG

ACADEMY OF NECESSARY MAGIC™ BOOK EIGHT

MARTHA CARR

MICHAEL ANDERLE

LMBPN Publishing
PMB 196, 2540 South Maryland Pkwy
Las Vegas, NV 89109

Version 1.00, August 2021
eBook ISBN: 978-1-68500-411-8
Print ISBN: 978-1-68500-412-5

THE ABOMINATION IN THE BOG TEAM

JIT Readers

Thomas Ogden
Dorothy Lloyd
Diane L. Smith
Dave Hicks
Jeff Goode
Zacc Pelter

If I missed anyone, please let me know!

Editor

Skyhunter Editing Team

From Martha

To everyone who still believes in magic and all the possibilities that holds.
To all the readers who make this entire ride so much fun.
To Louie, Jackie, and so many wonderful friends who remind me all the time of what really matters and how wonderful life can be in any given moment.

From Michael

To Family, Friends and
Those Who Love
To Read.
May We All Enjoy Grace
To Live The Life We Are
Called.

CHAPTER ONE

On the southern coast of South America outside the small
Chilean hamlet of Villa Puerto Edén, Amanda Coulier sat in
front of the blazing fire in the center of the Coalition-funded
expedition camp and sighed heavily. She couldn't help but lean
toward Fiona sitting next to her and tried one more time to get a
good look at the tracking unit in the red-haired woman's hand.
"Get anything yet?"

Fiona glanced at her sidelong and smirked. "Not anything
more than the last time you asked, kid. Or the time before that.
Or the time before that. What are we up to now, Bill?"

"Twelve." The shifter man glanced at his watch and shrugged.
"In the last hour."

"That's what I thought." Fiona stuck the device into the pocket
of her field vest and gave it a loving pat.

"Wait, what are you doing?" Amanda looked her mentor up
and down. "You can't put it away. If something comes up—"

"If something comes up, we'll hear it. Like we heard it the last
four times those tech nerds sounded the alarm, okay?"

"Yeah, but the last four times, we were too late." The shifter
girl gazed around the dark camp lit by three other fires and the

1

constantly blinking lights of all the gear Dr. Caniss had sent with the team down here to South America. "Maybe something will come up in the system *before* they sound the alarm."

"Oh, yeah?" Fiona pulled a protein bar from a different pocket in her vest and ripped open the cellophane wrapper. "Like what?"

"I don't know. Like a…blip or something."

Bill snorted and immediately fought to hide his smile. "A blip. Very scientific."

"Oh, come on. You know what I mean."

"Listen, kid." Fiona chewed her first bite of chicken-flavored protein brick and waved the rest of the instant meal at the shifter girl. "These guys know what they're doing, okay? They're the ones who found the first wave of unidentified magic down here. Hell, they're the ones who made the system in the first place. We're not heading out again to try to nab this thing because of a *blip*."

"We don't even know what this thing *is*." Amanda stared at the half-unwrapped protein bar. "I don't think they know what they're doing at all."

"*Oh*. Listen to you." Fiona chuckled and ripped off another bite. "You think you can calibrate their entire network better than they already have? Go right ahead. I'm sure that'll go over well with the shifters who've been doing this for *decades*."

"I, uh…" Bill cleared his throat. "I might have to agree with her on this one."

Amanda spread her arms. "*Thank* you."

"Et tu, Bill?" Fiona pinned the resident zookeeper of Omega Industries with a scathing glance. "You two wanna team up and start a mutiny over this? All the way down *here*?"

With a chuckle, Bill shook his head. "You know that's not what I meant."

"Then by all means, Beastmaster. Enlighten us." Fiona raised the protein bar to her mouth again, paused when she saw

Amanda eying it, then sighed and pulled one more from yet another pocket of her vest. "Here."

She tossed the package toward the shifter girl, and Amanda snatched it out of the air. "I'm not hungry."

"No, you're hangry. You're also starting to get on my nerves, which is exactly the opposite of what we need while we're waiting for this thing to rear its ugly head so we can move in and grab it. Eat."

Giving her mentor a deadpan stare, Amanda ripped open the side of the protein bar and tore off a large chunk of the meaty nutrient block between her teeth.

She's not technically my mentor anymore, is she? I got promoted and told to build my team for these missions, which technically makes me Fiona's boss. I'd bet everything in my bank account she wouldn't be talking to me like this if I were older.

The thought made her snort as she chewed the snack bar.

Who am I kidding? She talks to everyone like this.

"What's so funny?" Fiona took another bite of her food and folded her arms.

"Nothing."

"Calling it ugly sounds like jumping to conclusions, if you ask me," Bill muttered.

Fiona washed down her mouthful with water from a tin cup, then smacked her lips and widened her eyes at him. "What the hell are you talking about?"

"You said 'before it rears its ugly head again.'" He shrugged. "We haven't gotten a glimpse of this thing even from a distance, let alone up close."

"Ha. Well, *excuse* me for insulting the most dangerous, super-powered magical beast we've ever *not* seen." Fiona shook her head. "Knowing you, you probably think they're *all* beautiful."

"No, I didn't say that." Bill cracked a small smile as he stared into the fire. "I mean, yeah. Every creature has a kind of beauty, in a way. But trust me. Some of the divergent species we have

3

back at the lab? I wouldn't call them beautiful by any stretch of the imagination."

Amanda almost choked on her protein bar when she laughed, and Fiona instantly thrust another tin cup of water into her hands. She drank deeply, then chuckled. "Like the quorgill."

Bill threw his head back and roared with laughter. "You're right about *that*."

The shifter girl fell into another fit of laughter with him, and Fiona scowled at her companions around the fire. "Okay, fine. I'll bite. What the hell is a quorgill?"

"Think of…" Amanda laughed again and shook her head, trying to get herself under control. "Think of a hippo. Then shrink it down to two feet tall."

"A hippo covered in mud," Bill added. "Only the mud is its skin…"

"And its head and its butt got switched around!"

Fiona's dubious frown and furious blinking as she stared into the crackling flames and tried to imagine such a creature set Amanda and Bill off again in another fit of laughter. "That's disgusting."

"*That's* an ugly head." Bill slapped his knee and hooted. "Thing's as gentle as a lamb, though. You haven't seen it at the lab?"

"Do I *look* like a woman who wants to spend my time surrounded by mutated buttheads?"

"Ever think they don't wanna spend their time with *you*?" Bill said through another chuckle.

Amanda nearly fell backward off the low bench as she howled with laughter and gripped herself around the middle.

Fiona snorted. "Amateurs."

"Unbelievable." One of the other scientists paused on his rounds through the camp and shook his head at the three shifters sitting around the fire and laughing. "We're out here in the middle of the damn jungle with these—"

He slapped at a massive bug buzzing through the air toward his neck. "These monster mosquitos. Sweating through our clothes. Chasing this invisible monster that keeps giving us the slip, and *you* think it's funny?"

Amanda pressed her lips together and tried not to laugh again. "It's not funny. You're right."

"Uh-huh." The guy slapped his arm this time with a snarl, then quickly wiped away the sweat dripping from his forehead with the back of a hand. "I didn't sign up for this crap."

"You sure about that?" Fiona tilted her head. "Kinda comes with the territory."

"Just...mind your own business." The man stormed away, slapping at more bugs and spinning to swat them as he kept moving through the camp.

Amanda snorted. "I guess bugs aren't a thing in Colorado, huh?"

"Inside a giant self-contained lab in the Rockies with a closed air-filtration system and completely invisible to the rest of the world?" Fiona raised an eyebrow. "Probably not."

"Got a few in two of the biodomes, though," Bill added, wiping tears of laughter from the corners of his eyes.

"Of course you do."

"It's part of the ecosystem, Fiona. The creatures in there might be Oriceran, but they still have to—"

"Yeah, yeah. I get it." The red-haired woman cut him off with a dismissive wave. "Spare me the biology lecture."

Amanda took another bite of her protein bar and slowly chewed as she eyed the rest of the camp around them.

Okay, fine. Maybe I did need to eat something.

"They look miserable." She lifted her tin cup to her lips again.

"Huh." Fiona studied the dozen other scientists and field operatives who'd joined them on this little expedition and shrugged. "Guess it's hard to get around and see the world when you're stuck in a lab all day every day. You think any of them expected they'd have to make their lab come to *us*?"

"I seriously doubt it." Bill looked up at a massive moth fluttering in ragged circles around the fire. "I never thought I'd be out here either, but here we are."

"You can thank Amanda for that." Fiona smacked her young team leader's arm with the back of a hand. "I bet everyone else is thanking her for the bugs and the heat too right about now."

The girl rolled her eyes. "I'm not the one who brought us all out here. We can thank the giant magical creature who keeps avoiding us for that." A slow smile twitched across Amanda's lips. "Think I should tell them South America in December isn't anywhere near as bad as the Everglades in July?"

"Ha. Only if you wanna get tied up and left in a tent until we get another hit from this monster on the loose."

The mention of the creature they'd been chasing for the last five weeks brought the mood down again.

Because none of us know when this thing's gonna show up again, or what it wants, or even what it looks like. How are we supposed to go after something like that?

Bill's loud *slurp* from his tin mug broke the silence.

"Oh, come on." Fiona leaned forward to prop her forearms on her thighs and stared at him. "Is that necessary?"

He tore his gaze away from the fire to look at her. "I'm thinking."

"Uh-huh. A universally *quiet* pastime."

"About what?" Amanda asked as she popped the last bite of protein bar into her mouth and stuffed the cellophane wrapper into her pocket.

"Only that I feel like I've missed something."

Fiona scoffed. "Stop giving yourself so much credit, Bill. We've *all* missed something. Obviously. That's why we're still here."

"No, I know." The man sighed and returned his gaze to the

fire. The moths intermittently thumping against his head or brushing across his arms didn't seem to faze him at all. "I'd give myself more of a break if this creature didn't leave any trace of itself behind whatsoever. That's not what's happening."

"Right." Fiona bumped her fist and snapped her fingers in sarcastic defeat. "Damn thing keeps swimming away in the ocean, and all we have to show for it is a whole lotta nothing and a steaming trail of magical goo floating around with the seaweed."

He wrinkled his nose. "Steaming?"

"It's as close to a pile of crap as we've seen in the last month. Oh, come on. I'm going with euphemisms here."

"Okay..." Bill scratched the side of his head and frowned at the fire. "Still. A kind of trail like that should mean something. I should be able to analyze some of this thing's behavior patterns by that alone. Then maybe I could find out what it wants."

"It's not your fault we can't get a sample," Amanda added. "It's not like we have an instruction manual for this thing."

"Ha. Right. Turn to page forty-three for an in-depth explanation of why this unknown creature with an insanely powerful magical frequency can never be spotted or captured. Page fifty-seven explains why it leaves behind massive trails of concentrated magic that instantly disperse in saltwater, and we can't trace."

Fiona turned toward Amanda and pointed at the dejected zookeeper. "There isn't already a book on this thing, right? 'Cause I can't tell if he's joking. Is he joking?"

Playfully rolling her eyes, Amanda shook her head. "We'll figure it out, Bill."

"Sure. Yeah. I know." He scratched his head again and gave her a self-conscious smile. "After the last few times moving out to snatch up a critter wreaking havoc with *you* at the helm, I'd be stupid to think you don't know what you're talking about."

"Thanks." She grinned back at him, but her smile faded quickly when a subdued argument broke out between three of

Caniss' scientists poring over the data from all their portable readout machines and who knew what other kind of expedition tech. "I'm not sure anyone else here would agree with you."

"Forget about them." Fiona tilted her head and snickered when one scientist threw his hands up in exasperation and stormed away from the computer setup outside one of the tents. "Like I said, kid. They don't get out much. Plus, if you didn't know what you were doing, you wouldn't be here in the first place. The doc isn't exactly a fan of dead weight."

"She still keeps *you* on retainer," Bill muttered.

Amanda laughed.

Fiona's mouth popped open in mock insult. "*I* happen to be an asset, thank you very much."

"Yeah, a real pain in my asset."

"Somebody woke up on the wrong side of the cot, didn't he?"

Bill straightened on the bench and chuckled. "Oh, yeah. Eighteen hours ago. And forty-two. And sixty-six—"

"Okay, okay." Fiona cracked a crooked smile. "Cut it out with all the math before you hurt yourself. I don't wanna have to break out the calculator when you get past a hundred."

"Nine hundred and one."

"Gesundheit."

Bill snorted. "That's how many hours we've been out here on this mission. Five weeks, two days, and thirteen hours." He glanced at his watch again. "Fourteen."

"Jesus, they should've put you in accounting instead of mucking out creature cages."

He tapped his temple. "How do you think I handle feeding over three hundred different species across four biodomes?"

"Don't ask *me*." Fiona spread her arms. "I don't do math. Or feeding."

Amanda snorted and drained the rest of her water.

At least they can sit out here waiting for another hit from the radar without tearing each other apart. I'm supposed to be back at school in a week. Fat chance of that *happening anytime—*

A blaring siren cut through the camp with a high-pitched *whoop*. Red lights flashed on top of several machine units placed in front of the tents, and everyone stopped what they were doing to turn toward the main collection of computers in the center of camp.

The shifter woman monitoring the gear leapt from her folding chair and scanned the readouts. Then she slammed a hand down on a large black button set in the control panel to cut off the alarm and looked up at the rest of the expedition. "Not a false alarm! Let's go!"

The camp burst into action as the scientists rushed to their stations to send coordinates to all the handheld trackers before getting down to business analyzing the readouts flashing across countless screens. The four other field operatives assigned to accompany Amanda and her special team of three grabbed their gear and headed toward the fire.

Amanda, Fiona, and Bill leapt from the benches.

"Finally." The shifter girl grinned at her mentor turned subordinate as Fiona tugged the tracking device from her vest pocket.

"You can say *that* again." The woman scanned the device, then snatched her pack off the ground and hauled one strap over her shoulder. "This thing's moving fast."

Bill shouldered his pack and grabbed his tracker from where he'd tied it to his belt with six inches of thick cord. "And it's…it's out of the water."

"What?" Amanda tried to get a good look at the device in Fiona's hand, but the woman was already stalking away from her. "Wait a minute—"

"You're the one who said you wanted to get a head-start on this thing, kid. Less talk, more moving out." The woman nodded at the four other shifters who accompanied them on every other close-call chase of the new, uncatchable creature and twirled her finger. "That means all of us. Let's go."

Bill kept staring at the tracker in his hand, his frown deepening. "I don't get it. It hasn't breached dry land in five weeks."

"Plus two days and fourteen hours." Amanda grabbed his arm to shake him out of his confusion gently. "But now it is. Maybe it's slower on land than it is in the water, right?"

"Amanda, there's no possible way to know when we haven't—"

"Sorry, Bill. That was a rhetorical question. But we should—"

"Get a move on, you two!" Fiona called as she stormed off into the thick foliage surrounding the camp. "If you think No Shifter Left Behind applies right now, you're wrong."

Amanda huffed out a laugh and raced to catch up with the shifter woman leading the team to what would hopefully be a successful discovery this time.

Like she's the one running this whole thing. I'd be at the front if someone remembered to bring another tracker for the shifter girl. I bet they left that one out on purpose.

CHAPTER TWO

The expedition camp outside Villa Puerto Edén was only two miles off the coast. It would have taken them forty minutes tops to reach the shoreline, but they weren't heading for the shore. Instead, the coordinates of the last major frequency readout led them another mile and a half west through the mist-flooded jungle and added another half hour onto their trek.

By the time they breached the tree line and stopped at the exact place they were supposed to have found the cause of so many massive waves of magic driving Caniss' technology crazy, though, it was clear they'd reached another dead end.

Even if Amanda hadn't been at the front of the team with Fiona to see it for herself, the disappointment was written all over everyone else's faces too.

"Great." Fiona tossed her hands up and scanned the dark landscape beyond the forest. "Just the kind of morale booster we needed."

Bill grimaced and ran a hand through his hair. "So much for moving slower on land. Nice theory, though."

Amanda slowly stepped forward, eyeing the dark silhouettes

of spiky bushes and thin-limbed trees dotting the open land before they eventually gave way to the shoreline again. The moonlight rippled across the South Pacific Ocean in the distance, though groups of other islands still lay between Amanda and the open water. Other than the wind rustling through the foliage and a few nocturnal birds occasionally chittering behind them, everything was still and silent.

"Keep looking," she whispered. "If it came onto land, it has to be here for a reason, right?"

"A reason we can't even begin to predict," Bill muttered.

Fiona turned to eye the four other shifters loaded with their packs and each carrying creature-hunting weapons augmented to stun and capture instead of maim and kill. "Fan out. Take a look around. If you see anything at all, call it in."

"Don't shoot it," Amanda added. The shifters eyed her with matching expressions of disbelief. "Unless it gives you an actual reason to. Like an attack."

"An attack means you're in actual physical danger." Bill pointed at them. "Not just that the thing's coming toward you."

"We know how to do our job, thanks," one man muttered as he turned and headed back through the trees. The others rolled their eyes and shook their heads before branching out in different directions to scout the area.

Amanda sighed. "You know what? This should be a new rule. Only give guns to shifters who don't want to use them."

Fiona turned in a slow circle, squinting as she searched the dark landscape for any sign of their target. "That's how you lose an entire team in South America, kid."

Amanda lowered herself onto the rough ground where the forest's thick undergrowth and emerging tree roots gave way to sparse grass and eventually sand. "Yeah, but knowing how to shoot something and not wanting to are two completely different things."

The redhead looked over her shoulder at the shifter girl and raised an eyebrow. "Okay, Socrates. Point taken."

Bill hunkered down beside Amanda and opened his pack to pull out more of his gear. "If that thing left any waste samples behind again, I seriously hope they react differently to open air than saltwater."

Fiona scoffed. "Only *you* would be excited about adding to a magical shit collection."

He gave her a glance of distaste, then returned his attention to setting up his supplies. "I'll stay here with Amanda."

"Yeah, you do your thing, kid. I'll call it in if I see anything."

Amanda's eyes were already closed as she lowered herself onto her back, but she nodded and was only vaguely aware of Fiona's footsteps moving quickly away.

If there's anything out here, I can find it faster than they can. I won't shoot it first, either.

She drew a deep breath and felt the ripple of the warm breeze wash across her skin and lift her hair slightly away from her shoulders. Then she reached out to her magic, and her ghost-wolf emerged to join in the hunt.

The connection with her magic like this was as natural and easy as breathing now. Amanda padded across the ground, her awareness and all her senses intensified in the form of the white, shimmering wolf that moved like smoke.

Bill let out a long, slow breath. "Never gets old watching you do that."

Never gets old doing it.

Of course, he couldn't hear her like this, and she didn't bother turning around to look at her body lying on the ground.

Time to find the thing leading us on a wild creature chase for the last five weeks.

She and her ghost-wolf moved swiftly across the ground, sticking close to the tree line but not disappearing through the foliage yet.

This thing can probably smell me like it smells everyone else. Especially if it's leaving so much magic behind it all the time. But I want it to see me too. Just in case.

The edge of the forest curved with the coastline, and in less than five minutes, Amanda had gone far enough that a quick look back showed nothing but a stretch of open land blending into the beach and the ocean.

Nobody's called anything in yet. Which means it's either still out here somewhere or—

A soft squeak up ahead made her stop. Another followed it, and she tilted her head, her ghost-wolf's ears swiveling to catch the source of the sound. At least three small, weak voices cried out and carried toward her on the ocean breeze. Amanda sniffed the air and found a completely new scent.

Not human or magical. Not any kind of creature I've smelled before either.

She did, however, recognize a single strain of that scent that would have made her stomach drop if she'd been in her physical body.

It was the smell of fear and pain laced tightly together, the stench of it growing even stronger on the wind as the tiny squeaks grew into squeals.

That's not good.

She raced across the sparse vegetation, not feeling any of it beneath her ghost-wolf's paws and not disturbing a single grain of sand or plant frond shuddering in the breeze. The cries of at least three unknown creatures grew even louder, and Amanda stopped quickly to reorient herself to the sound before a small wave of intensely strong magic rippled across her incorporeal pelt.

Where are they?

As she followed the scent and the sounds, the intensifying strength of new magic in the air made her hackles raise.

That only happens when something's getting ready to explode or attack. I think...

That wasn't enough to stop her, and she darted back into the trees, leaping from root to jutting tree root and over low-hanging branches. Whatever she didn't avoid went right through her as she hurried toward the source of so much fear and pain and magic. Then she came upon a brightly glowing light nestled under the emerging network of an enormous tree's roots.

She'd found them.

Three small creatures the size of newborn kittens struggling in a heap, their fur covered in dirt and leaves. The squeaking only grew louder. Then the creatures *changed*.

One of them pulsed with orange light and shrieked when its long, thin tail split in two. Another rubbed its head against an unearthed tree root, struggling to stay on its feet as a crown of tiny silver horns grew through the flesh of its scalp. Blood splattered the leaves beneath it.

Then it scraped those new horns against the root, leaving behind sharp gouges and more streaks of blood. The third creature writhed on its back, shuddering and panting as patches of its purple fur fell away, replaced with shimmering purple scales.

They're changing. They're mutating right here, and there's no way they want to be here.

The divergent critter wriggling on its back let out a fierce snarl for such a tiny thing, and its wide eyes blazed with purple light before doubling in size with a sickening squelching sound.

The next second, Amanda gasped where she lay on her back and sat bolt upright on the ground.

"Whoa!" Bill lurched away from her where he'd been kneeling and fell backward onto his backside. "What? Did you find it?"

She shook her head, drew a deep breath, and tapped the comms unit in her ear. "I found something."

"It's about damn time," Fiona said through the comms. "Please

15

tell me you pulled your weird little Dr. Doolittle thing and told our friend to stay the hell where it is."

"No, it's not the creature we're after." Amanda pushed herself to her feet and headed back down the tree line the way she'd gone as her ghost-wolf.

Bill puffed out a sigh behind her and pushed himself to his feet. "Amanda—"

"I found three others in the trees."

"Kid, that's not why we're—"

"They're mutating. Like, in real-time." Amanda picked up the pace. "I think they were already divergent species, but now they're…they're changing again. I'm pretty sure it's torturing them."

"Three divergent species all morphing at the same time?" Bill snatched up his supplies and hurried after her.

"That time of the month, huh?" one of the other operatives muttered.

Fiona hissed. "Real mature, Frank."

"No, it's not three different species." Amanda scanned the curving tree line and the coast line beyond, looking for the spot she'd reentered the forest the first time. "They were all the same to begin with. But they're not changing into the same thing anymore."

Bill sucked in a sharp breath. His heavy breathing as he picked up the pace to run after her came through the comms unit in her ear and directly behind her now. When he caught up to her, he looked at her with wide eyes. "You mean an already divergent species evolving *again*? Into three other—"

"Yeah, we all get the idea, Bill," Fiona interrupted. "They're double-mutants."

"Anyone think that's *not* related to seeing a giant spike of magic right where this thing we're tracking down is supposed to be?" Amanda asked.

No one said a thing.

Yeah, that's what I thought.

"Everybody has visuals on Amanda and me, yeah?" Bill panted.

"We'll meet you there."

CHAPTER THREE

It took Fiona and the four other shifters four minutes to meet Amanda and Bill at the base of the tree where the agonized critters still shrieked and snarled and writhed about on the ground. Two of the horns on the one creature's head had tripled in size. The orange-glowing one had sprouted seven more tails. And the poor thing losing its fur to scales lay nearly motionless beneath the roots, panting and mewling as it stared with massive purple eyes at absolutely nothing, clearly exhausted.

"This is new," Fiona muttered. "I'll give you that."

"What happened to them?" one of the other shifters asked.

Bill squatted two feet away from the horned creature that looked like a miniature black and green tiger from a nightmare and tried to get a better look. "They were forced into mutation. Look at this. Blood everywhere. Tufts of fur. This had to be excruciating."

The horned critter hissed and tried to leap toward him, but it wobbled on unsteady legs and dropped onto its back haunches with a sharp yelp.

"I think it still is." Amanda gritted her teeth. "What could do this to them?"

"Something I'm guessing we don't wanna mess with, kid." Fiona glanced at the four other shifters on their team.

Three of them paced around the area, brandishing their gadgets that let out short *beeps* and *ticks* as they took readings of the area. The fourth stood back with his weapon trained on the three double-divergent creatures trying to both protect themselves from a perceived shifter threat and manage the pain of their ongoing transformations at the same time.

"Oh, come on." The woman snorted. "You're scared of a few wild kitties glowing different colors?"

"You seen any cats lately that grow scales and horns?"

"Fair enough. Still, at ease, all right? These things don't have it in them to give you a run for your trigger-happy money."

The man frowned at her and only slightly lowered the barrel of his weapon.

"Wait, wait. Hold on." Bill pointed at the purple thing with more scales than fur now as it rolled over and tried to rise on shaky legs. "What's that?"

Amanda stepped slowly toward him and bent to get a better look. "A…glowing rock?"

"That's not a rock. Divergence like what we've seen doesn't extend to inorganic material."

"As far as you know." Fiona folded her arms. "Which is diddly squat in this scenario, like the rest of us. Or maybe we should convince the good doc to open up a mutating rock museum—"

"I found something." The shifter's voice came through the comms unit loud and clear, but he hadn't gone more than twenty feet away from the tree and the struggling evolving critters. "Looks like more glowing rocks."

"Oh, for crying out loud." Bill slowly backed away from the creatures, then stood from his crouch. "They're not rocks."

"You can say that again." Another shifter had joined the first and now looked back at Amanda and the others to wave them forward. "The readout on this thing is insane."

Everyone else made their way toward the two operatives on the other side of another massive tree. When Amanda rounded that tree, she stopped and blinked against the sudden glow between the two shifters' feet.

A large mound of what looked like shattered crystals almost a foot high rested on the forest floor. It pulsed with a brilliant white light that refracted through each piece and only intensified the glare. One of the operatives pointed another device at the pile and swept it up and down, back and forth. The gadget let out a swiveling *whoop* of high tones dropping into low again every time it moved.

"Um…Brandon?" Amanda pointed at him and wrinkled her nose.

"Who?"

"Sorry. You're—"

"Brian."

"I'm Brandon," said the man standing beside him.

I need to get better at remembering who's who. Five weeks should've been long enough if we weren't so busy trying to catch this thing.

"Right. My bad. It's just…really dark out here."

The men frowned at each other and shook their heads.

"What's it saying?"

"Insane levels of magic coming off the rocks," Brandon said. "Almost as strong as the signals we've been getting in the water but not quite. Same magical signature, though."

Bill raised both hands and gestured for the other shifters to step aside. "Okay, then they're not rocks, so stop calling them that."

Fiona snorted. "Again. Would you prefer we call it a massive pile of sh—"

"Waste." Bill nodded and stepped toward the mound. "Yeah. Perfectly intact on land. I gotta get a sample."

"Yeah, yeah. Sure. Whatever floats your boat."

He ignored the verbal jab and opened his pack to get to work collecting the glowing crystals.

"So the thing we're hunting just...what?" Amanda stepped back and wrinkled her nose despite there being no stink whatsoever. The pile of glowing crystals didn't give off any scent at all. "Left a giant dump in the forest?"

"It sure left *something*." Fully gloved now, Bill reached toward the closest crystals with a pair of tweezers and a glass vial poised in his other hand. "I won't begin to guess as to which end of the thing this came out of. It could be a crystallized shedding of some kind."

"A what?"

"You know, like how a snake sheds it skin." Two hard bits of glowing crystal *plinked* into the vial. "Only in a pile of..." He paused, studied the base of the mound, then immediately stood and backed away. "Did anybody touch this?"

"We're not idiots," Brian muttered.

"I know that. I mean... Look, maybe you knocked it aside with a boot? Brushed up against it somehow?"

Frank clicked his tongue. "We've been doing this long enough to know walking over a pile of glowing rocks is a stupid move."

"Not rocks." Bill shot the other man a scathing glance, then pointed at the ground again. "Something disturbed this pile. And there was another piece of this...substance over there with the creatures."

"Great." Fiona shook her head. "Now we have double-divergent species who hoard magical crap too."

"I don't think they were hoarding it." Bill stalked back toward the tree and the squeaking, mewling creatures still trying to get their bearings beneath the tree roots. "Hey, one of you get over here and take a reading of these things."

"We already know what *they* are," Brandon replied. "Kind of."

"I'm serious. Just do it."

With a sigh, the operative *crunched* across the undergrowth before stopping and taking a quick sweeping read of the tiny creatures with his gadget. "There. Come on. We should be looking for that thing and not—"

"Look at the signature." Bill frowned at the three critters still wobbling around and trembling from their mostly finished transformation. "I'll bet you the rest of my Snickers bars that reading's the same as the one you took of that substance over there."

Fiona spread her arms. "You brought Snickers?"

"I have a sweet tooth. Big deal."

Brandon looked down at his device and cocked his head. "You're right. Same frequency."

"I know." Bill turned to meet Amanda's gaze and nodded as he raised the vial of glowing crystals. "Whatever this is, it's what forced new mutations on these creatures."

Amanda looked back and forth between the glowing vial and the poor divergent animals who still couldn't walk straight under the tree roots. "So...what? They got too close, and the magic made them transform like that?"

"Yeah, pretty much." Bill tucked the vial into his pack, then drew out a flat square of metal mesh before opening the collapsible and highly portable critter cage. "I'll have to run some more tests, obviously. Keep a close eye on these little guys to see what else they might be able to tell us. I think they stumbled onto that mound over there with no idea what it was and got a little too curious."

"Sure." Fiona gestured toward the creatures. "A fun little roll on a glowing pile of...whatever turned into a complete makeover. A painful one."

"They could have rolled in it, sure." Bill set the cage on the forest floor before inching toward the creatures. All of them were too exhausted to try fighting him at this point.

"A transformation as quick as this, less than an hour after the alarms went off and we headed out here? I'm not sure external contact would have this kind of an effect in such a short amount of time. My guess is these little guys ingested the stuff."

He reached for the tiny green-and-black-striped critter with horns first and gently ushered it into the cage. "Bet you wish you were a little more discerning about your meals, huh, little guy?"

"You mean they ate it," Frank said flatly.

"Yeah. Usually that's how anyone ingests something." Bill rolled his eyes.

"They ate the magical poop." Fiona turned in a slow circle and tossed her hands up. "This night keeps getting better and better, doesn't it?"

The four shifters snickered and shook their heads as Bill carefully handled the other two creatures and got them safely into the cage.

"It will once we get these guys safely back to the lab and figure out how to help them. That'll give me a much better idea of what we're dealing with in the creature who left that magical waste behind in the first place."

"And we're left with another no-show on the big bad monster's part, aren't we?" Fiona asked.

"We'll do another sweep," Brandon offered.

Everyone turned to look at Amanda, and for a moment, she had no idea why.

Right. I'm the one leading the team through the woods. And they're only looking at me for direction now?

She cleared her throat. "I think we should get those creatures and the glowing…samples back to camp. Maybe running a few tests will help us figure out how to, you know, track this thing. Better."

Nobody moved.

Fiona clicked her tongue and clapped, startling the already

terrified creatures in the cage. "You heard her, fellas. Let's get a move on!"

"Hey, maybe keep it down." Bill glared up at her as he ejected the handle at the top of the cage. "These little guys have been through enough already."

"It's not my fault they can't tell the difference between food and shit, Bill."

Amanda glanced at the woman in warning, and Fiona rolled her eyes. "Fine. I'll be *quiet*. But if those things start screaming again and keep me up all night, I'm blaming the zookeeper."

She pointed ahead of them through the woods and took off. "Keep up. I'm not turning around to look for anyone 'cause they wanted to try out the glowing rocks for themselves."

The four other shifters on their team shook their heads and stuffed all their gear back into pockets and packs before heading after her.

Amanda waited with Bill until he'd picked up the cage with three terrified, blood-smeared critters shivering inside. "You want any help with that?"

"No, no. I got it." He drew a deep breath and gave her a pained smile. "I'm glad you found these guys. I mean, yeah, they'll be able to give us a little more insight into this other creature we're trying to find, but..."

"You can help them, right?"

"I'm gonna try. It sucks they had to go through this. The other species we pick up and bring to the lab... I don't think any of them have been through this kind of dramatic change. These guys'll need a lot more intensive care than even *I'm* used to giving."

"Well, good thing you're the one who's taking them in." She gave the man a reassuring pat on the shoulder and turned to head back to the camp. "Once we get more information from that glowing stuff, we'll find the creature leaving it all over the place,

and we'll make sure it doesn't put any others through the same...
rough patch."

"Rough patch." Bill let out a weak chuckle and followed her, stepping as gingerly as he could so he didn't jostle the poor little critters too much. "I seriously hope so."

CHAPTER FOUR

None of the scientists back at camp were happy about three new mutated Oriceran creatures among their ranks needing to be examined, studied, and fed. Especially without any sign of the highly powerful beast they'd been trying to get their hands on for the last five weeks.

Once Bill got the mewling divergent wildcats settled at the edge of camp so they'd bother the exhausted team as little as possible during the night, he handed over the vial of glowing magical waste. The two shifters who had the knowledge and technology to analyze the samples practically fell all over him in their excitement.

"This is excellent!"

"We can work with this. Finally."

"Yeah, hand that over."

"Be careful with it," Bill warned. "It made those things change almost instantly."

"Please." The shifter woman who'd chosen to keep wearing her white lab coat in an expedition camp in South America snatched the vial from him and held it up to the bright lamp hanging over the desk inside her tent. "We know how to handle this."

"Feel free to get those things to shut up, though," the other scientist muttered as he sat beside the woman and stared at the sample with wide eyes.

"Right. Because I'm only the guy who handles the animals." With a sigh, Bill stalked out of the tent and almost ran into Amanda standing outside the entrance flap. "Whoa."

"Sorry." She backed up and gave him a sheepish smile. "I was trying to, you know…"

"Eavesdrop?" He chuckled. "Pretty sure you don't have to be this up close and personal to overhear a conversation. Not like anything those two say will make even a little sense until they come back with their *analysis*."

"Yeah. I'm pretty sure nobody wants to see the shifter girl's magic running around through camp."

When most of the shifters here can't even do half of what I can with their magic.

"Who cares what they want?" They turned to walk down the line of tents. "If you ask me, you're the only reason we found those creatures in the first place. I mean, sure, all these fancy devices would have picked up the magical signature off the glowing pile eventually. I bet it reads like a beacon." Bill ran a hand through his brown hair and sighed. "We wouldn't have any idea what to do with it if you hadn't seen those poor things going through…what they went through."

Amanda shrugged. "I guess I got lucky."

"Ha. That's a load of bull, and you know it." His crooked smile widened as he glanced down at her. "No one else heard a thing out there. They were all looking for the source of the big giant ripple that came up on all these screens. You found the missing piece. Well, *a* missing piece, anyway."

"Yeah, I guess I did." She stuck her hands into the pockets of her light zip-up hoodie and couldn't figure out what else to say.

He doesn't sound too happy about any of this. I guess I wouldn't be either if it was my job to make sure the creatures we find are taken care of while we study them.

"You don't like being out here, do you?"

Bill stopped and raised his eyebrows. "What makes you say that?"

"You just…seem a little angry, I guess."

"Oh. That. You know, I do what I can in the lab. I do more than I have to for the creatures that get brought in. It's…different out here. I mean, so those little guys like that? If I wasn't here, I'm pretty sure whoever came out with a cage would've chucked them in and tossed them with the rest of our gear crates.

"Don't get me wrong. I'm glad I'm out here to handle them the right way. Still, it makes me wonder about all the others that come into the lab. I get them when they've had a chance to get used to the cage. Maybe not in the best way, either. Judging by all the weapons everyone still likes to carry around to make them feel safe. Or…whatever it makes them feel."

"Yeah, I'm not a big fan of all the guns, either. Pretty sure that's part of why Caniss fired the last ones she sent me out with."

Bill snort-laughed. "It's a good thing you're out here too, Amanda. I got to teach you everything I know about handling divergent beasties, and now you're heading a whole team who's trying to bring in the biggest, baddest of them all."

"Doesn't feel like I'm heading anything, honestly." They stopped in front of the tent Amanda and Fiona shared, and the redheaded woman's remarkably off-pitch humming rose loud and clear on the other side of the entrance flap. "I guess I can't complain, right?"

"Hey, you can complain to me whenever you want. Neither one of us is completely happy with the way things are run." Bill stuck his hands into his pockets and shrugged. "Don't get me wrong. Dr. Caniss is doing her best. We all are. It's a lot better than any other organization's been able to manage."

"But it could still be better."

"Yeah." They stood outside the tent in silence. Then he nodded toward the entrance. "Get some sleep. No telling when the mad scientists'll wake up the entire camp screaming, 'Eureka!'"

Amanda laughed and grabbed the entrance flap before pausing. "Hey, Bill?"

"Yeah."

"If those things ate that stuff and it made them…mutate *again*, you think that's what's been happening with *all* the Oriceran creatures we've found? You know, like…is this thing we're trying to find the reason all these species are changing in the first place?"

He shook his head and shrugged, the corners of his mouth pulling down in contemplation. "No way to tell right now. It's possible. I hope not."

"How come?"

"That would mean the creature leaving behind this highly potent waste has been here for a lot longer than we originally thought, without giving away the kind of signals it's been throwing out for the last month. That begs the question I'm way too tired even to consider right now."

"Why now, right?"

The corner of Bill's mouth turned up in a tired smile. "Exactly. If we have to answer that question, I don't know if the answer's gonna be something we can handle." He wrinkled his nose with a grimace and waved her off. "Don't worry about that now, though, huh? I'm not going to. I'm gonna pass out on my oh-so-comfy cot that squeaks if I draw a deep breath. You should do the same."

"Yeah, okay. Goodnight."

"Night." He lifted his hand in a casual wave as he walked toward the tent he shared with two other members of their Coalition team, and Amanda drew the entrance flap of her tent aside.

Fiona's humming had stopped because now she lay on her cot

with her hands folded on her chest and a purple satin sleeping mask over her eyes. "Can't stop asking questions, can you?"

Amanda jolted and stumbled over the edge of her pack. "Jeeze. I thought you were asleep."

"Come on, kid. It takes me thirty seconds to pass out, but not with two animal nerds chatting away right outside my tent."

"Sorry."

"Don't be." The woman drew a deep breath through her nose but didn't move. "You did good work back there."

"Uh-huh." Amanda stepped out of her shoes and crawled onto her squeaky cot after brushing aside the flaps of the mosquito net hanging over it from the tent's ceiling.

"I mean it. Did we finally find this thing that's been jerking us around like a repeat episode of *Lost* for the last few weeks? No."

The girl snorted and peeled back the light blanket before nestling down under it.

"Still, you found some critters that looked like they went through hell. All for a little snack." Fiona chuckled. "Can't exactly say they're the smartest furballs in the barrel, but at least we know what happens when you eat the glowing crap."

Rolling her eyes, Amanda settled her head on the pillow and reached over the side of her cot to turn off the electric lantern on the floor. "How much longer do you think it'll take us to find this thing?"

"Who knows, kid?" The woman cleared her throat and smacked her lips before nestling more comfortably on her cot. "Took it five weeks to crawl out of the ocean and onto shore. Compared to the evolutionary process of this entire planet, that's nothing. Might be another five weeks for us, though. Give or take. That's me making sloppy guesses, so don't hold me to it."

Five more weeks?

Amanda rolled onto her back and stared at the dark outline of the mosquito net frame looming over her. "It can't take that long. Fiona, I can't be out here for another five weeks. I have school—"

The woman's long, growling snore cut her off, and Amanda turned her head to stare at the cot beside hers. Fiona hadn't moved an inch, her hands still folded on her chest exactly where she'd left them.

Right. Of course, she *doesn't care that I have my second semester of senior year to get back to. Graduating's no big deal, right? Because I already have a job, so why even bother?*

Puffing out a heavy sigh, she shifted around on her cot to get into a more comfortable position and didn't care even a little if the noisy squeaking disturbed her tentmate's sleep.

There's no way this is going on for another five weeks. I won't let it. I have to figure out how to catch this stupid monster that an entire lab of hardcore scientists can't find on their own.

CHAPTER FIVE

Despite having stayed up almost a full twenty-two hours at this point, Amanda couldn't get to sleep. She'd already gotten used to the constant drone of insects this far south, where the end of December didn't mean anything more to the wildlife than lower humidity and maybe a little more rain.

She'd been able to sleep for weeks with the rhythmic *beeping* and *whirring* of all the labs' portable gear running the never-ending system to look for more giant blasts of magical frequencies. Yes, even Fiona's obnoxious snoring had only taken the girl a week to be able to sleep through.

Amanda laid wide-awake in her cot, thinking about the three terrified creatures in Bill's cage who'd gotten way more than they'd bargained for when they'd decided to take a few bites out of that magical pile of ...whatever.

They're fine. Bill's taking care of them. He knows what he's doing.

Mostly, she couldn't get the image of those glowing white crystals out of her mind.

There has to be something in those we can use to find this monster and stop it. I can't believe I'm saying we have to stop it. It was another divergent species blasting off insane levels of magic before tonight. Now it's creating totally new species, and nothing's supposed to change that fast. That's not evolution. It's...a magical science experiment.

That thought made her heart race, and she finally threw off her thin blanket before sitting up on the cot with another bouncing squeak of the hinges. Fiona didn't stir.

Then she heard footsteps approaching her tent, joined by the voices she instantly recognized as those of the two scientists who'd been laboring over "sample data" since they'd brought the crystals back to camp.

"This isn't anything like what I expected," the woman said tersely.

"Seriously? You expected something?"

"Absolutely. Something. *Anything.* That's why we're here. To get absolutely nothing off those readings? It's a pulsing chunk of —" The man cut her off with an obnoxiously loud yawn, and the woman scoffed. "Am I boring you?"

"Yep. Until the sequencing program finishes running on that thing, there's no point in sitting in that tent waiting for grass to grow. No point in standing out here arguing over not having found any immediate results, either."

"I know how this works, Dylan. Don't talk to me like I'm a *child.*"

"Then stop whining like one." The shifters passed Amanda's tent and stopped before both of them broke out into subdued chuckles.

"You're right," the woman conceded. "I need sleep."

"We both need sleep. And a decent breakfast in the morning."

"Well, we're guaranteed at least one of those." More laughter. "See you in the morning."

"Bright and early, Dr. Pillard."

The tent flap whipped aside with a heavy *thump*, then the man's footsteps continued down the line until he entered his tent and flopped down on yet another squeaky cot.

Amanda rolled her eyes.

All this high-tech gear and probably millions of dollars poured into the lab, and they can't get us something to sleep on that doesn't make this much noise?

She sat there in silence for another three minutes, listening to the sounds of the two dozen shifters around the camp snoring, muttering in their sleep, swatting at bugs through the mosquito nets, and shifting around on noisy cots. There was no more conversation and no sign of anyone else still awake and trying to work through all hours of the night.

Why would they? It's not like we're any closer now to catching this thing than we have been since we got here.

Amanda couldn't even consider lying back down and trying to get some sleep. The unknowns were too much. The questions crashed through her head without any sign of quieting down anytime soon.

Those two scientists had left a perfectly good sample of magical waste unattended in their science tent. Without anyone watching over it. Completely unguarded.

Yeah, there's no way I'm not going in there.

Amanda flopped back down onto her cot, which creaked as she bounced a few times. Then she closed her eyes, drew a deep breath, and left her body with her ghost-wolf.

She'd been right about all the other expedition members turning in for the night. The only thing that moved around her as she padded silently across the trampled grass of the camp was the shadows cast by the three fires in the center and the torches staked around the perimeter to ward off wildlife.

Sure. They can fuel a bunch of endless fires with their tech, but they can't track down a creature shooting off way more magic than it would take even to cast fires like this. They're probably pumping gas through everything anyway.

Sniffing at the light, warm breeze blowing between the tents up ahead, Amanda quickened her pace toward the tent where Bill had dropped off the sample. The canvas flap didn't move an inch when she and her ghost-wolf phased right through it. Then she was inside. Alone with the sample.

Curious as ever.

I need to get a good look at it. Maybe I should've done that when we found those creatures, but now's a better time anyway.

She reared up onto her hind legs and caught herself with the ghostly-white forepaws of her magic propped up on the edge of the desk. The computer system in front of her blinked with dozens of tiny lights, and some kind of program code flickered across the screen. She wasn't interested in any of that and probably couldn't have figured out what it meant even if she'd tried to read it.

All Amanda could focus on now were the two lumps of glowing magical waste resting on a panel at the edge of the desk. No one had even bothered to secure the stuff with a strap or put it in a box. They'd left it there out in the open and assumed it wouldn't do anything to their computers.

I guess they'd know, right?

Almost as if the glowing crystal had heard her thoughts, it pulsed twice with brighter white light before fading into its natural brilliance again.

Don't be dumb, Amanda. This thing can't read your mind.

She sniffed at the edge of the panel and slowly poked her misty-white snout closer to the sample.

I mean, sure. I had an underwater conversation with the divergent mermaids. And yeah, I walked into *the Coulier Bear to pull that giant power-egg out of it. Those were creatures. This is a lump of magic. Can't have a conversation, and it can't do anything to me because I'm not physical here.*

The crystal pulsed one more time, and that same wave of incredibly strong magic that had raised the hackles of her ghost-wolf in the forest washed over her again. The sample still didn't give off a scent, and it didn't react to her magic's presence right here next to it.

Of course not. It's a rock. Or a crystal piece of—

Two snaking tendrils of light burst from the sample and hovered in the air, wavering above the glowing crystal like two misty tentacles.

Okay... Maybe I was wrong.

Amanda sniffed again, trying to find some odor or sound or sensation let off by the new behavior of the magical waste.

Wow, I really do need to get to sleep. This thing doesn't have behavior. *It's leftovers. Snakeskin, like Bill said.*

After a few more seconds of eyeing and sniffing the sample, Amanda was ready to give up on the investigation. It was late. She'd probably have better luck trying this again when she wasn't so exhausted and getting way too jittery because of it.

Before she could pull her ghost-wolf's paws away from the edge of the desk, the two flickering tendrils of light darted toward her and struck her right between her nonexistent eyes.

Ow! Hey! What the—

She tried to pull away but discovered she was rooted to the spot by two spears of glowing light attached to the crystal on the table.

Fine. I'll leave you alone.

Trying to pull away and return to her body didn't work either. She tried two more times to return to her human form lying on the cot in her tent, but the tendrils wouldn't let her go.

They wouldn't let her *magic* go.

Not good. Come on, this never happens. Concentrate.

That was the last thought she had before a blazing white light bloomed in front of her and consumed everything else.

It was all she saw. All she felt. If she'd heard anything in the tent or the rest of the camp, that would have been gone too. Because Amanda Coulier didn't exist anymore.

Only the thousands of images pouring out of that glowing sample of magical waste and into her mind—into her entire *being* —existed.

The darkness of space and all its billions of stars. Planet Earth, half-covered in darkness while the other half soaked up the light of the sun. A second much larger planet aligned perfectly with Earth in its orbit, its distance impossible to tell before the next image took its place.

Shimmering walls of light connected the two planets through the Oriceran gates. The figures of magicals moving back and forth between those walls of light, disappearing and reappearing on the other side. Dark, shadowy forms captured halfway between.

The next images were entirely foreign. Neon jungles that looked like they were growing upside-down. Purple oceans. Strange plants opened and closed to the wind and the starlight. Glowing creatures and magicals of every race Amanda was aware of—even more of those she wouldn't have recognized. Magic being used and guided to create civilizations at record speeds, hundreds of thousands of years squashed down to mere images in the blink of an eye.

Then a blood-curdling scream broke through the silence of the vision.

After that, the images came much faster and with a dizzying urgency. Shifters used their magic the way Amanda used it. Figures made of light stood in the center of rings of magicals, their oblong heads disappearing into the brilliance as their mouths opened impossibly wide. The scream came again, and all the figures of light winked out.

In the darkness, fiery explosions emerged. Thousands of voices rose, wailing and screaming. Magic flew everywhere, crumbling buildings, destroying cities and homes, taking lives. Everything burned. When it stopped burning, the screams were still there.

Magicals huddled in dark rooms, their arms wrapped around each other for comfort until people and forces ripped them away from each other. Magicals trapped in laboratories and forced to endure the agony of being torn apart and put back together again, studied with magic and technology combined.

Oriceran creatures chased, hunted, and killed for nothing but sport. Humans and magicals fighting each other and themselves with weapons and dark magic.

So much death and destruction and war, all of it flashing through Amanda's mind faster than it took her heart in her body lying on the cot to beat more than twice.

Then a final image drowned out everything else.

It was Earth again, viewed from space and spinning much faster than the planet's natural rotation. Dotting every continent were hundreds of glowing white lights, pulsing faster and faster with even brighter light as the planet spun. It picked up speed, and the dots of light flared to the same blinding brilliance as the first flash that had separated Amanda from her consciousness.

That light overwhelmed everything again, and the second it faded, she bolted upright in her cot again with a massive, ragged gasp.

"Holy shit!" The sound of her raw voice startled her, and she cleared her throat before turning toward Fiona's cot. "Fiona. Get up! I just—wait. Fiona?"

The cot was empty, crisply made, and Fiona wasn't in the tent.

Crap. She woke up and realized something was wrong. And now she knows I went spying on the magical turd in that tent...

Only then did she realize why she was alone in the tent. Sunlight through the thick canvas had lit everything up without the need for a lamp. Purposeful footsteps, casual conversation, and the *clink* of tin plates and cups rose from outside.

Loud yawns and a few growls rose from the other expedition members as they went about their morning and got ready for what they all expected to be another day of sitting around and waiting for one more magical surge from the creature they hadn't caught yet.

No way.

Amanda blinked and widened her eyes.

I was in the other tent. If that...whatever it is held me there overnight, somebody would've noticed me. So...what? It shot me back into my body when it finished, and I passed out for the whole night?

The tent flap whipped aside, and a smirking Fiona entered with two trays of breakfast in hand. "Morning, sunshine. Hungry?"

CHAPTER SIX

"Fiona. Listen to me. I—"

"Yeah, I'm listening." The woman approached the cots and handed one tray down to her mentee turned team leader. "You're starving. *I* got up at a decent hour to make sure I got my hands on the coffee. Go ahead. I got you some."

"No, I don't want coffee." Amanda jumped off her cot and scanned the ground for her shoes. "Look, I—"

"Whoa, kid. Take it easy, huh?" The woman barely managed to pull the trays out of the way while Amanda stuffed her feet into her sneakers. "I wanna *eat* my breakfast. Not wear it. You...do whatever you want with yours, I guess." She set the tray on the ground as she sat on her squeaky cot, hungrily eyeing her meal. "I'll be—hey. Where are you going?"

"The tent."

"Kid, we're *in* a tent."

"No, the other one. Just listen to me. I went out to take a look at that sample thing for myself. No, wait. I didn't *just* go out, I guess." Amanda eyed the tent. "It's morning, right?"

"Sunlight, breakfast, me not passed out and dead to the world." Frowning at the girl, Fiona leaned forward to grab the tin mug of coffee from Amanda's breakfast tray and set it beside her feet instead. "I don't think you need coffee this morning. Because I thought I heard you say you went to go look at the glowing poo these scientists have been drooling over since last night."

"I did."

"Amanda." Fiona tilted her head and fixed her with one of those condescending looks that normally didn't last very long. "Please tell me you didn't touch it. *Please.*"

"I didn't." The girl whipped aside the tent's entrance flap for a quick peek at the rest of the camp outside.

Everything looks normal. Nothing's blowing up. Nobody's screaming. Yet.

"I mean, I *kind* of did..."

"Oh, for crying out loud. That's what the science nerds are for, kid. Is this why you're freaking out? You went in there and grabbed the thing without putting on any gloves, and now what? You think *you're* gonna start mutating?"

"No. I went with my ghost-wolf."

Fiona shoveled a forkful of runny scrambled eggs into her mouth and raised her eyebrows.

"My magic. I mean, I never left the tent."

"Yes, I remember the cute little pet name you gave your magic."

"Okay, whatever. Look, I wasn't trying to touch it. I wanted to—"

"Sit down and eat your breakfast. Trust me. It tastes like hell if you let it get cold."

"Just shut up and *listen to me!*" The surge of Amanda's magic racing through her—plus an understandable level of rage—made her snarl. Her skin prickled with the flash of magic before an oncoming shift, and she stood there glaring at the redhead while trying to catch her breath.

Fiona glanced at the tent's entrance, then set her tray down

41

beside her on the cot and lowered her voice. "You wanna flash your eyes at someone, kid, do it after breakfast."

"Sorry. I just—"

"You want me to listen. Okay, fine. I'm listening."

Yeah, and she had to interrupt me again *to let me know.*

Drawing a deep breath, Amanda smoothed the loose hair away from her face and stared at her empty cot. "Okay. Last night, I went out to one of the science tents and—"

Fiona snorted. "Good name." When the girl glared at her, she mimed zipping up her lips and thrust her hands into her lap.

"To see if I could find anything that isn't…you know, normally seen. Or heard or smelled or whatever. 'Cause I can… do that sometimes."

"Uh-huh."

"But that crystal thing. I didn't touch it, I swear. I was careful. I wanted to look. And it…it *shocked* me or something."

"You don't say."

"I'm serious, Fiona! This isn't good! That thing got inside my head and showed me a bunch of—"

A group of shifters outside the tent burst out laughing. "Figures. Teenage girl can only handle getting crawled on by giant bugs for so long."

"What?" Amanda scowled and turned toward the tent entrance.

"Hey!" Fiona stood from her squeaky cot and glared at the canvas flap. "Why don't you come on in here and say that to her face? I got a giant bug for you right here!" She brandished her fist despite no one being able to see it. The shifters who'd laughed at Amanda's urgency kept laughing but took it farther down the line of tents.

"Freakin' ingrates. I swear, if any branch of the military got their heads out of their asses and took on shifters in the first place, I'd tell Caniss we need to quit hiring soldiers. Huh. You know, I've seen a few shifter armies in my day. Or attempts to make them. Didn't work out."

"Fiona."

"What?"

"This is serious, okay?"

"Yeah, yeah. You got zapped by a glowing pile of poo, and it gave you hallucinations. You feeling funny?"

Amanda wrinkled her nose. "No."

"Then big whoop, kid. Eat your breakfast—"

The tent flap fluttered aside, and Bill took one step in, his eyes wide. "Please tell me you two aren't talking about what I think you're talking about."

"Whoa, whoa, whoa." Fiona raised a hand toward him. "Please tell me you didn't walk into a girls-only tent without knocking first."

"What?"

"I mean, it's fine. We're both dressed."

"Oh my God." Amanda groaned in frustration. "Why is it so hard for you to take me seriously?"

"I *am* taking you seriously, kid. I don't see what the big deal is."

"You don't see—" Bill scoffed and slapped a hand to his head. "Amanda, you can't go around touching foreign magical waste products with your bare hands. Especially after what we saw it do to those—"

"I didn't! I didn't touch it at all. It started glowing, then that *thing* latched onto my magic and gave me a bunch of…I don't know. Visions or something. And they weren't good."

"Jesus. Come on." Bill stepped into the tent and reached for Amanda's arm but stopped himself before pulling the sleeve of his light pullover down around his hand to use as a glove.

"What? What are you doing?"

"We need to get you looked at."

"Bill, I'm fine." She tried to jerk her wrist out of his grasp, but he held on tight and tugged her out of the tent. "Seriously. You're worried about the wrong thing."

"That doesn't exist when we're dealing with a completely new substance no one on this planet has ever studied before. We don't even know what it's made of or why it was left behind, and we have no idea what it might have done to you. That was…a stupid call on your part."

"I didn't touch it!"

"Dr. Baker," Bill shouted, jerking his chin up at one of the scientists standing in a group around one of the sturdier computer setups. "Dr. Baker, can we talk to you for a minute?"

"Bill, seriously." Amanda rolled her eyes and tried to peel the man's fingers off her wrist.

Dr. Baker frowned at them both and gestured toward the computer system, her frown deepening. "I'm a little busy right now, Bill. I'll find you when—"

"Yeah, this can't wait. We have a…a Code…" Bill looked over his shoulder at Fiona, who stood in front of her tent with her breakfast tray in hand, shoveling more eggs into her mouth. "What is it?"

The woman snorted and shook her head at Amanda. "You stepped in it this time, kid."

"Fiona!"

"Code 32."

"Yeah. Code 32." Bill stared at the scientists crowded around the system display. "Did you hear me? I said Code 32!"

"Yep." Dr. Baker rushed away from the table and pulled a pair of gloves from her back pocket before urgently tugging them on. "Where?"

"Right here." Bill looked at Amanda with a panicked frown. "She touched the sample from last night."

"I didn't—"

"Wow. That was dumb." Dr. Baker looked Amanda up and

down, then called over her shoulder, "Dylan, we need a hookup in Lab 5—Sorry. The tent pretending to be Lab 5."

"For the kid?"

"Yes, for the kid. Move."

The scientists hurried away from the computer in every direction to hop on the emergency, shouting directions at each other and moving with only slightly less precision in the camp than they would have back at the Canissphere.

"Oh, come on." Amanda grimaced and tried to pull away from Bill again. This time, he let her go, but Dr. Baker grabbed her with a gloved hand instead and started pulling her toward whatever tent was pretending to be Lab 5. "I don't need a hookup. Or whatever. Listen, that thing showed me a bunch of—"

"Hallucinations, huh?" Dr. Baker looked her over. "Not a good sign, but we can deal with that."

"What? No. Listen to me."

"You probably shouldn't talk. No idea how this stuff affects bodily functions of *magicals* instead of divergent critters. So...try to relax."

I take back everything I said last night. This whole thing runs like crap. No one even thinks to slow the hell down and listen to what I have to say!

"Fiona," Amanda called. "Fiona! Tell them to stop freaking out!"

The redhead strolled casually across the camp as the rest of the team that wasn't busy setting up to run Amanda through a bunch of tests stopped what they were doing to watch the excitement. "First rule of working with scientists, kid. Don't ever get between them and their tests."

"Oh, come on!"

Dr. Baker hauled the girl into the next tent and pointed at the single chair in the center surrounded by half a dozen black crates with their hinged lids already opened. "Sit. Don't move."

"No." Amanda stepped back toward the tent's entrance and

folded her arms. "You can do whatever tests you need to do after everyone stops running around like lunatics and somebody *listens* to what I have to say!"

The shifter who'd been handling the specimen tent the night before—Dylan—crouched beside one of the open crates and lifted a fully loaded syringe. "If you want to join us for this, I'd sit. Otherwise, keep fighting it. I have no problem knocking you out for a few years if I have to."

"Are you insane?"

"What do you think?"

"Yes! This is ridiculous." Amanda spun and tore the tent flap aside before storming back out again. "Fiona. Oh, come on. Fiona!"

"Get her back inside," Dr. Baker shouted. "She mentioned hallucinations. If that's true, we need to contain this before we end up having to navigate psychosis too."

"What?" Amanda spun to see Dylan emerging from the tent with a concerned frown and the syringe still in hand.

"Sorry, Amanda. I told you to—"

"No way in hell are you sticking me with that thing. Fiona!"

The rest of Dr. Baker's closest scientist friends raced toward her now, one of them with two leather straps meant to hold Amanda down. If they could catch her first.

She raced around the closest table that held a massive computer and a bunch of black briefcases with probably more gear inside as the scientists circled her and closed in.

"It's okay, Amanda. We're not going to hurt you."

"You're experiencing hallucinations. Just listen to our voices."

"We'll help you out. But we need you to come with us so we can run some tests."

"No, you need to listen to me." Amanda snatched up one of the black briefcases and held it out like she meant to throw it.

The scientists paused and shouted in wordless protest.

"Put down the case."

"Anyone touches me, and I'll put it down, all right." She tried to catch her breath as she turned her back toward the computer table and counted six scientists trying to pin her down and study her. "Just *listen* to me. That thing—"

"What is *taking* so long?" Dr. Baker burst from the lab tent and scowled at Dylan. "Bring her in here already. What are you doing?"

The man shrugged. "She took a hostage."

"I emptied those a week ago. Let's go."

With a low growl, Dylan headed straight for Amanda, trying to keep his loaded syringe from touching anyone else.

She chucked the empty case at him with a snarl, which he dodged, then grabbed the edge of the table. "I know what we have to do!"

"Yeah, and you can tell us all about it once we make sure you're not putting yourself or the rest of us in any more danger," Dylan spat.

"Jesus, what do I have to do to…" With a growl, Amanda tightened her grip on the edge of the table and let her magic surge through her. She couldn't shift and do what she was trying to do, but the extra boost of strength from *almost* shifting gave her exactly what she needed.

White light blazed around her hands as her magic responded, the paws of her ghost-wolf seeping out of her to lend a proverbial hand, and she let out a roar of frustration and effort.

"What are you—No, no, no, no!" Dr. Baker raced forward, but it was already too late.

Amanda overturned the entire table—computer equipment, empty cases, neatly coiled cables, and all—and sent it flying toward the woman and the lab tent behind her. The system broke apart midair and peppered the lab tent, making it shudder and wobble while smaller pieces flew through the tent flap and crashed against the single chair and all the equipment inside.

Dr. Baker let out a horrified cry, her arms outstretched in a useless attempt to keep the entire setup from falling in multiple pieces to bounce across the ground with sparks bursting from broken panels and ripped wires.

"You need to listen to what I'm telling you!" Amanda screamed, her voice echoed by a terrifying growl she didn't think came from her throat but from her ghost-wolf instead. Another burst of magic flooded through her, this time lining her entire body in an aura of silver light.

The scientists who'd closed in on her staggered backward, and the entire camp fell silent. She drew a deep breath and added, "I think that thing we picked up last night told me what it's trying to do. So instead of running around trying to strap me down for a bunch of *tests,* somebody needs to get inside my head and figure this out!"

Nobody moved. Someone on the other side of the camp coughed loudly, but that was it.

Amanda fought to catch her breath as she gazed around at all the adults making up this expedition, every one of them staring at her in mute horror.

Great. Either I'm too young to pay attention to, or I'm the freaking boogeyman. At least I got their attention.

CHAPTER SEVEN

"So." Amanda spread her arms and looked around the camp. "Anyone have something to say, or do I have to figure out the rest of this on my own too?"

Dr. Baker's mouth silently opened and closed before she drew in a ragged breath. "Do you have *any* idea how much this equipment costs? Look at this! We only had *one* machine like this on site, and you destroyed it. I can't even begin to—"

"Quit your whining, will ya?" Fiona emerged from the rations tent three spots over and sipped from her tin mug, probably slurping as loud as she did on purpose. "Every piece of data in that thing is backed up to the system even from out here. You're not the one who paid for it."

"Did you see what she did?" Dr. Baker pointed at Amanda. "She's obviously contaminated, and now it's affected her amygdala response."

"No, Doctor. I think *you're* the one affecting her amygdala response." Fiona snorted and headed toward the mess Amanda had made of all the gear. "So *this* is what it takes for a bunch of know-it-alls to finally listen to the head of strategic operations on this thing, huh?"

"You weren't even here."

"I'm talking about the girl, and you know it." Fiona studied the wreckage, then looked at Amanda with a raised eyebrow. "Somebody pissed you off, huh?"

"Yeah, everybody. Where were you?"

"Getting a refill." The woman raised her mug to her lips again, took another loud slurp, then sighed. "It's good this morning. Or maybe I'm losing my tastebuds." She fixed her gaze on Dylan and grimaced in disgust. "What the hell are you doing with a tranquilizer like that?"

"I…" Dylan looked down at the syringe in his hand, then shoved the cap back onto the top and thrust it into his pocket before lifting both hands in surrender. "Okay, we can try it her way. No tranqs. But we need to test—"

"You and your tests. Come on. Did none of you hear what she said?" Fiona chucked her mostly full coffee mug aside, spraying the wall of the lab tent with black sludge in the process. "She said the sample gave her all its plans. Why aren't you hopping around like good little scientists to figure out how the hell to get it out of her?"

"Oh, *now* you believe me?" Amanda snarled.

"You should've started with that instead of trying to make a big reveal out of it, kid."

"You—" The girl clenched her fists and took a deep breath to calm herself. "Or you could listen to me without making a joke out of every little thing."

"Hey, now we know."

"Fiona, they were about to jab a needle into me and run a bunch of tests! In a camp in South America!"

"They most certainly were not." Fiona snarled at Dylan, who backed away with his hands still raised. "And they're not gonna keep standing around here like a bunch of trees. Do your jobs!"

The scientists jumped into action again, only this time, they all moved away from Fiona and Amanda and the wreckage the girl had made of their extremely expensive computers. Dr. Baker was the only one who didn't hurry away to do something else. Instead, she folded her arms and glared at the girl. "We still need to run those tests."

Fiona scoffed. "Why?"

"Because we don't know what contact with the sample might have done to her. Honestly, after what I saw, I'm still leaning toward hallucinations and an increased amygdala response. You know, rage."

"You hallucinating, kid?"

Amanda shot her mentor a deadpan stare. "Seriously?"

"I'll take that as a no. If the kid says she's not hallucinating, Doctor, that's good enough for me. Should be good enough for you too. So come on. Chop, chop. Get her what she needs to let us…read her mind or whatever. I guess." Fiona leaned toward Amanda and muttered, "That's what you wanted, right?"

Amanda widened her eyes. "Yeah."

"We don't have anything here that can do that," Dr. Baker muttered. "So we'll have to think of something else."

"Doesn't sound like she *wants* anything else—"

"Wait." Amanda spun in a circle, then pointed at Fiona. "That thing they built by the lake."

"The what?"

"The machine. To talk to the divergent mermaids. You know, the weird helmet he put on to… Oh, come on. What's his name?"

"Mel? Yeah, that's not a catch-all for mind-reading, kid. Sure, maybe someone *else* could read your mind if they made a second…head-thingy. I don't see how that's gonna help the rest of us see what's going on in that scrambled brain of yours."

Amanda gritted her teeth and muttered through them, "Calling me 'kid' and saying I have a scrambled brain isn't exactly helping."

"Oh, yeah? Sorry, I didn't think you were that sensitive."

"I meant with everyone else taking me seriously."

MARTHA CARR & MICHAEL ANDERLE

"Again, who cares what anyone else thinks?"

Amanda rolled her eyes and let out a big sigh, puffing out her cheeks.

"It could work," Dr. Baker muttered.

"Not giving a shit?" Fiona chuckled. "Listen to you. Finally coming out of your science-nerd shell to—"

"The machine, you blithering moron."

"And…I take it back." Fiona folded her arms.

"What do you mean?" Amanda asked, ignoring her mentor's aggravating quirks.

"I know the equipment you're talking about," Dr. Baker continued. "Mel found a way to translate brainwaves into sound through the helmet. If the brainwaves—*yours,* obviously—were translated into images instead, we might have a better idea of what you think you saw."

"What I *know* I saw." Amanda shook her head. "I promise I'm not hallucinating, okay? That thing showed me…"

Showed me what? Death and destruction on two planets in the past or in the future? I don't even know what half of that meant.

"I think it was a map."

"Of what?"

"I don't know, Fiona. That's why I want to get it out of my head so everyone else can see it and we can figure it out together."

"Wow. Going heavy on the sarcasm today, are we?"

"Whatever it was," Dr. Baker added as she stepped over the wreckage and cast it a pained glance, "we still have to address the biggest obstacle."

"Which is what?"

"The fact that we don't have Mel *or* his communication machine out here with us."

Fiona snickered. "This is your very first time stepping out from behind your fancy lab desk and all the stainless steel, isn't it?"

The other woman scowled. "I don't see what that has to do with anything."

"That has everything to do with everything right now." Fiona slapped Amanda's shoulder, then pulled her phone from a vest pocket with her other hand and grinned. "I gotta make a call. Try not to unleash hell on these poor, unsuspecting test-nerds again, okay? I mean, unless they give you another good reason."

Without waiting for a response, she trudged off across the camp and pressed the phone to her ear.

Amanda swallowed and scanned the destruction between herself and the lab tent.

Okay. Not that they didn't deserve it, but I might have to work on managing my anger a little better from here on out.

She looked up at Dr. Baker, whose lower jaw jutted out in irritation as she searched the scattered pieces of her gear. "Sorry about...your computer."

"Uh-huh." The woman bit down on her bottom lip and blinked rapidly. She didn't look up at the shifter girl when she added, "Sorry about threatening to sedate you so I could run a few tests."

Amanda snorted. "Yeah, we both know it wasn't a threat."

Finally meeting the girl's gaze, Dr. Baker cracked a small smile. "Right. You know, all the table-throwing aside, you're handling this a lot better than most kids your age. Most adults too, now that I think about it."

"I get that a lot."

"I'm sure you do."

"Okay!" Fiona came waltzing back toward them and rubbed her hands together. "We've got incoming in two hours. I'd say break out the champagne, but I don't think they'll be staying that long. And no one thought to bring champagne. Which is a pretty dumb move out here, if you ask me."

Dr. Baker shook her head. "What are you talking about?"

"Just got off the phone with the Grand Poohbah back home.

She's sending Mel *and* his super fun little mind-reading…whatever out here to join us. Then we can yank this map out of Amanda's mind and start solving a completely new puzzle that'll probably take us way longer than it should."

"Wait." Amanda tilted her head. "She's sending him out here?"

"Huh. Didn't expect an echo in the middle of the Chilean rainforest."

"That'll take forever."

"Not in the jet." Fiona pointed at her. "You know, I've always wanted to take a ride in that thing. Kinda stings that you got to do it before me. But hey, I won't hold it against you if—" She patted down her vest and pulled out her buzzing Coalition phone before turning away. "Excuse me."

"Do you have any idea what she's talking about?" Dr. Baker asked.

"Yeah." Amanda smoothed her hands down the side of her light hiking pants and shrugged. "If it's the same jet I took out to Pennsylvania with a totally different team, it'll probably only take them two hours."

The scientist pursed her lips and looked the girl up and down. "How long have you been doing this?"

"Chasing down magical creatures everyone else wants to shoot but being the only one who can handle them?" Amanda shrugged. "About a year. A little less than six months if we're only counting, you know…paid work."

Dr. Baker huffed out a disbelieving laugh and shook her head. "You're how old—"

"Yeah, yeah. Keep your pants on." Fiona thrust her phone under Amanda's nose. "It's for you."

"Who is it?"

"Take a wild guess."

Crap.

Amanda took the phone and raised it to her ear. "Hello?"

"You realize this is millions of dollars' worth of equipment you're asking me to jettison down to South America all on a hunch, correct?" Dr. Caniss' sharp, clipped tone through the speaker made Amanda grimace. "Not to mention the small fortune I heard you destroyed in a fit of rage."

Don't bite. Just ignore that last part.

"It's not a hunch, Dr. Caniss."

"Really? Wanting to play arts and crafts with my equipment has a perfectly rational explanation you're more than willing to back up with hard facts and concrete data? Or did I miss something?"

Amanda closed her eyes and drew another deep breath.

The worst part is she's not even sarcastic.

"Even if it was a hunch," she said slowly into the phone, trying to keep her voice even, "have my hunches ever been wrong?"

Dr. Caniss clicked her tongue. "No. But if they are this time, I hope you're prepared to face the repercussions."

"Fine. When will—" The line went dead with a sharp click, and Amanda pulled the phone away from her ear to stare at the blank screen. "Never mind."

"Don't you hate that?" Fiona snatched her phone away before pocketing it again. "I swear, it's like the woman grew up without anyone around to teach her basic manners."

Amanda decided to ignore the irony of that statement coming from Fiona Damascus and let out another long, slow exhale. "Okay. So they're heading down here with everything we need to do this. I tried to ask how long it'll take, but apparently, she didn't think I'd have any questions."

"Everyone has questions, kid. That woman with a computer for a brain doesn't care."

"A few hours." Dr. Baker met Amanda's gaze with a hopeful and still apologetic grimace. "I'm going to take a wild guess here and say you probably don't have anything better to do while we wait. Right?"

After a glance at Fiona, who didn't give any response besides a careless shrug, Amanda closed her eyes and sighed. "Fine. We can run the tests."

"Great."

"No needles. Like, at all."

"I want to take a few blood samples—"

"No needles putting anything *into* me."

Dr. Baker gave her the first real smile she'd seen since they'd landed in South America. "That I can promise you one hundred percent."

"Good. Thanks."

"Better hop to it, pincushion." Fiona patted her mentee on the shoulder. "Those tests aren't gonna run themselves."

"Go annoy someone else."

CHAPTER EIGHT

Amanda had no idea it was possible to run as many tests as Dr. Baker ran on her in the span of two hours without any fancy equipment or injections or strapping her up to magical testing machines. The woman took her vitals, way more blood samples than seemed necessary, and followed it up with incredibly odd requests.

"Pat your head and rub your stomach."

"Try to make yourself sneeze."

"Can you hear this tonal frequency? What about this one?"

"Follow my finger."

"Walk in a straight line, then jump quickly five times, turn around, and walk back."

"Tell me what you see in this picture."

Finally, the girl had enough. "Okay, taking blood is one thing. Now I feel like I joined the circus."

"I want to test all your senses. Check your balance. Look for any tiny detail that seems off, no matter how insignificant—"

Shouts of surprise and curiosity rose from the other side of the camp as the rumble of mostly silent jet engines filled the sky overhead.

Amanda jerked the pulse oximeter off her finger and dropped it onto the chair as she stood.

Why does she even have one of these out here in the first place?

"Wait. Where are you going?" Dr. Baker held up a hand to stop her. "We haven't finished—"

"Yes, we have. Time's up." Amanda pointed at the tent's entrance flap as she hurried toward it. "Our special mind-reading computer's here, huh?"

The woman's agitated sigh followed Amanda out of the tent, and the girl heaved a sigh of relief.

Most boring, totally useless two hours of my life. But I didn't get injected with a tranquilizer, so I guess there's that.

Beyond the camp's ring of iron torches staked into the ground, the trees shuddered under the force of the fancy Coalition jet landing as easily on the coast of South America as it had in an empty parking lot in Pennsylvania a year ago. The craft's rear cargo door dropped open with a low *hum*, and the only shifter who emerged was Mel, loaded down with a heavy pack and pushing a dolly with three large black crates stacked on top of each other.

"Damn." Fiona grinned as the bay door ascended again, then glanced at her watch. "That *was* fast."

"I can't believe this," Mel muttered, turning around to lug the dolly backward over the terrain that was much bumpier than the inside of a Coalition super-jet. "You know there's an actual reason I didn't come out here in the first place, right?"

"Can't take the heat?" someone shouted.

"I don't want anything to—" He almost dropped the dolly when whoever piloted the jet took off again without warning, blasting everyone who'd gathered for Mel's arrival with a gust of hot air and bits of leaves stripped from the surrounding trees. Their newest team member growled again and lugged the dolly after him.

"I didn't come out here five weeks ago because I *don't want to be here*. Simple. The rest of you voluntarily put your names down for this one, but *I'm* the one who has to pack everything up and ship out to the middle of nowhere to read some stupid kid's memories of a—"

Fiona cleared her throat. "I'd watch it with the name-calling if I were you." When Mel turned to glare at her, she stuck her thumb out toward Amanda. "She's already made one statement today. You don't wanna see her when she's angry."

Then Mel realized the entire expedition team had come out to greet him, including Amanda. He dropped the dolly to set it upright, ran a hand through his hair, then looked Amanda in the eye and nodded. "Sorry. You're not a stupid kid. I'm just—"

"Tired and pissed." She smirked back at him. "Join the club."

Most of the shifters around them chuckled, and Mel stared at her with a mixture of amusement and disbelief. "Well, okay. Where do I get to set up shop?"

"Take your pick." Fiona gestured toward the camp. "Anywhere she'll fit."

"Awesome." He rolled his eyes and grabbed the dolly's handle to continue dragging it into the circle of torches.

"Did Dr. Caniss tell you what we're trying to do with your machine?" Amanda asked.

"No one's trying anything. It'll work."

"Okay, do you need any help getting it to…you know. Translate images instead of—"

"Listen." Mel stood the dolly upright and grabbed the first giant crate before setting it gently on the ground. "I came here to get a job done. The sooner we do that, the sooner I can make that jet turn back and come pick me up while the rest of you keep playing hunter-explorer in the Amazon."

Fiona snorted, and even when Mel gestured toward the other two crates in a clear offer to let her help him unpack, she didn't move.

"It'll go faster if you have help, right?" Amanda said, looking back and forth between her mentor and the shifter who'd built the only machine with a chance of helping them now.

"It'll go faster if I don't have to stop to answer questions. No, I don't need help. I already recalibrated the system to produce images instead of sound."

Fiona chuckled. "What, you get some kind of premonition that'd come in handy?"

"I did it on the flight down here." Mel shook his head and bent to start unlocking the crates. "Give me half an hour. Then we'll see what you're trying to get out of your head."

"Oh. Okay. Um…yeah." Amanda turned jerkily away from him and headed back toward the center of camp.

He's literally the only one of us who can do anything quickly. We've been here for five weeks, and he recalibrates *a mind-reading machine on a two-hour flight. I wonder if he and Johnny know each other.*

With nothing to do but wait—and she wasn't going back into Dr. Baker's lab tent to spend the time doing more ridiculous tests —she headed toward the closest fire and plopped down onto the bench. Two minutes later, Bill shuffled toward her and took a seat on the next bench over.

"Amanda—"

"I'm fine. Really." She looked up at him and plastered a tight smile onto her lips. "Not crazy. Just…sick of everybody thinking I don't know what I'm doing."

"I mean, I wouldn't call sneaking into a tent to interact with a foreign magical sample, completely unsupervised, not to mention unauthorized, knowing what you're doing."

"Look, I get that it wasn't the best choice, okay? But I *knew* there was something weird about that stuff, and now we're about to pull a map out of my head. Which that *sample* put there, so it worked out."

"Right. I know. I wanna say—"

"Bill."

He blinked quickly and looked away from her like he thought she'd explode at him and flip his bench over like the computer table.

"We finally have new information, and I'm not trying to sit around here for another five weeks hoping that creature walks right into camp to say hi. I have to get back home. If that means I get a little magical jolt to my head...or my *magic's* head..." Amanda snorted and closed her eyes. "It's worth it."

Bill scanned the camp activity for a moment, looked over his shoulder at Mel setting up his machine, then scooted down to the end of his bench toward Amanda's and clasped his hands in his lap. "I wanted to apologize."

"Oh." She swallowed. "Okay..."

"I shouldn't have freaked out like that when you were trying to tell Fiona what happened."

Amanda huffed out a laugh. "You were the one talking about eavesdropping last night."

"I know. I know." He shook his head. "It's hard not to hear when you're right outside the tent in question. I am sorry. Really. I should've given you the chance to explain before jumping to the worst-case scenario. I..."

With a small chuckle, Bill lowered his head. "I guess I'm used to dealing with creatures in cages. You know, the kind that can't talk back or tell me what's wrong or even if there *is* anything wrong. Most of the time, I'm the one who has to figure it out with a bunch of tests and observation."

"I get it." She nodded. "Good thing you didn't try to put me in a cage, then, huh?"

They both laughed, and Bill followed it up with a groan before dropping his head into both hands. "I don't even wanna think about what would've happened to the poor cage. Did Dr. Manzury really try to sedate you?"

"You mean Dylan?"

"Uh…I think so."

"Yeah, he tried. Kinda."

"Amanda, I'm so sorry. I didn't think they'd pull something like that on *you*—"

"It's okay. Really." She gave him two thumbs-up and tried to make her smile look less forced and more hopeful. "We have a new plan now. I'm not passed out in a tent, so we're all good. Honestly, I'm kinda glad that whole thing went down the way it did."

"Why's that?"

Amanda glanced around the camp and noted almost half the team trying to sneak glances her way. She leaned toward Bill and whispered, "I think flipping over a table and damaging a small fortune in fancy computer gear will finally get everyone to take me seriously."

He grinned. "I already take you seriously."

"Yeah, 'cause you've already seen what I can do."

"Good point. Luckily for me, I got to see it without you breaking any of my stuff."

Half an hour later, as he'd said, Mel stalked toward the low-burning fire and jerked his chin up at Amanda. "Are we doing this or what?"

Wow. He's a way bigger jerk out here than he was at the underground lake. I'd probably kill all my emotions too if I had to spend all day every day with Dr. Caniss breathing down my neck.

"Yeah. We're doing this." She stood from the bench and followed the man toward the setup erected inside the camp's perimeter. It looked the same as when she'd seen him wearing that helmet at the underground lake as he'd tried to communicate with the divergent mermaids. Except he'd added one extra panel on the side of the hulking metal box standing almost six feet tall.

"All right." Mel pointed at the panel. "This right here is—"

"Where the images will show up." Amanda nodded. "You have a way to save them too, right? So we can look them over afterward?"

He leaned away from her and frowned, clearly unamused. "Maybe I should've let *you* build a new one."

"Sorry. I didn't mean to—"

"Sit." He grabbed a folding chair and swung it beside the machine before jamming it into the ground with both hands. "Yeah. I have a way to save the images."

"Right." With a final glance at Fiona and Bill approaching the setup behind her, Amanda spun and quickly sat in the provided chair.

Fiona jerked her chin up at the girl and winked. Bill shoved his hands into his pockets and rocked back and forth on his heels, clearly out of his element with so much machinery instead of the company of newly mutated Oriceran critters.

This isn't exactly my *element, either. Or at least it didn't use to be. Looks like I'm turning into one giant case study anyway.*

"All right." Mel cleared his throat as he lifted the bulky metal helmet over Amanda's head. "You ever played with one of these before?"

She stared at him. "You're kidding, right?"

"Yeah. I make jokes that aren't funny. I think it's funny." His complete lack of a smile didn't particularly mesh with his statement, but he was pissed and tired like the rest of the team.

Mel secured the helmet on her head, then quickly fastened the strap under her chin and shifted the bulky headgear back and forth to make sure it was firmly in place. "I've only tested this out on myself, and it didn't exactly provide conclusive results."

"Great. Anything I should know before going in?" Amanda rubbed her hands on her pants and tried not to fidget.

"Yeah. No matter how bad it gets, keep focusing on the image you want to pull up."

"What do you mean *how bad it gets?*"

Mel straightened and stepped beside her to press buttons, flip switches, and poke around on the controls on the machine's side. "Just a little pinch. You've teleported before, right?"

"Not on my own."

"Same thing." He sniffed and spun a dial without looking at her. "The pressure in your lungs. Only it'll be inside your head this time. Shouldn't last too much longer than a teleport."

"Shouldn't. Awesome." Amanda shot Fiona and Bill a bitter smile. "I thought science was supposed to be more scientific than this."

Fiona laughed and folded her arms.

Mel stepped around her chair again and squatted in front of Amanda to double-check the headgear. "There is nothing more scientific than trial and error. Especially the error part."

"See?" Amanda grinned at Bill, who looked like he was about to be sick. "My bad choice to check out that tent and get zapped by a glowing rock is a *good* thing. Scientific, even."

Bill bit his bottom lip and didn't say a word.

"Are you done?" Mel grumbled.

"Yep." She nestled her hands in her lap and leaned back in the chair.

"Don't move." He punched a final button. Then the helmet started humming.

The vibrations felt like they were going through her skull and eardrums to rattle around in her brain. Another flick of some other switch, and nobody needed to tell Amanda when she was in.

She gritted her teeth against the jolt of energy rushing through her and clenched her eyes shut.

Breathe through it. It's a little pinch. Like teleporting. Think of the map.

In the next five seconds, it became clear that this wasn't anything like a little pinch. It wasn't anything like being teleported by Fiona or Rick or even the cute little device Fiona had given Amanda to do it herself.

It was so much worse.

The pain grew almost unbearable, and she forced herself not to start screaming at Mel to take the helmet off her that instant. She wasn't even sure if she would've been able to scream anything.

She focused on the memory of the visions the crystal had given her, still so fresh in her mind. Not the horror and destruction and war and so much pain but the map.

The more Amanda tried to focus, the more the images of everything else she'd seen before that map grew stronger in the forefront. This time, though, they flickered from one to the next in a disorienting blur, mashing all the colors together and creating blurry, formless shapes.

This isn't working. Why can't I focus?

Another strong jolt of energy burst through her head, and she thought she felt all her muscles tensing at once.

Maybe this is what it feels like to be electrocuted. Nonstop. Where's the map?

The other images blended into one constant stream of garbled, incomprehensible memory that didn't belong to her. The next stinging jolt shooting through her made her panic.

So the shifter girl did what she'd taught herself over the last three years to do when she panicked.

She called on her magic.

It wasn't exactly like drawing out her ghost-wolf to bring her awareness into that form because this work was now all inside her head. The second she thought of her magic, the blurred images that felt like they were trying to fight back—like they didn't want to be rediscovered and thought about at all, let alone shared—faded away beneath instant darkness.

Then Amanda was staring at the face of her ghost-wolf—the same muzzle and glowing eyes she would have seen in her reflection during a shift. A halo of swirling white mist bloomed from the top of her ghost-wolf's head as it stared back at her.

The map. I need to find the map...

The white mist in her mind's eye instantly burst apart, and there it was. She'd locked onto the memory of what she'd seen. The image of Earth as if looked down upon from beyond the atmosphere. Thousands of bright pinpricks dotted the globe on every continent.

A low, whirring *hum* rose in her awareness, like a massively heavy aircraft with eight roaring engines had taken off somewhere very far away and was heading right toward her. It grew louder by the second, and she struggled to keep her focus on the vision of that map and all the points of light around Earth.

The pinpoints of light flared all at once with a blinding intensity—blinding if she'd been looking at them with her eyes, at least. Then there was a sharp *crack*, a *sizzle* like drops of water flung onto a pan of hot oil, and everything disappeared.

"Okay, get it off her." That was Fiona.

What's Fiona doing in my head?

"I said get that damn thing off her head, Mel!"

"What do you think I'm doing?" the man shouted back. "Shut up and let me—"

Amanda smelled the acrid tinge of burning wires and plastic, then he lifted the heavy giant metal helmet off her head, and she sagged forward in the chair.

"Whoa, whoa. Okay." Fiona's soft, gentle voice was in her ear, then Amanda realized the warm pressure on her shoulders was the woman's hands keeping her from falling out of the chair and onto the trampled dirt. "Come on, kid. Say something. Amanda!"

She drew in a searing gasp, and her eyelids fluttered open to see nothing but a glinting halo of the same wild red curls that were tickling her face. "That was…"

"*There* you are." Fiona barked out an uncertain laugh and pushed the girl back to sit upright on the chair again. She lowered her head to meet Amanda's gaze with wide green eyes. "Pretty intense, huh?"

"Yeah…" A wave of dizziness overwhelmed Amanda, making it look like the entire expedition team was crowding around her and Mel's machine until the dozens of bodies slowly coalesced into only three—Fiona, Bill, and Mel.

Bill ran a hand through his hair and puffed out a sigh. "That was pretty reckless."

"When I had to repurpose the machine I built for a single objective to do something completely different?" Mel scoffed. "Yeah, it's reckless. I'm doing my job."

"How you feeling, kid?" Fiona asked.

Amanda swallowed and blinked with wide eyes, trying to force the blurriness out of her vision so she could focus on one thing at a time. "Thirsty."

"Not what I expected, but okay." The redheaded woman released her mentee and stood to call over her shoulder, "Hey! We need some water over here ten seconds ago!"

Bill tilted his head and studied the shifter girl with a concerned frown. "That looked a little rougher than it should've been."

"How do *you* know what it should've been?" Mel whirled to face the zookeeper, the helmet still clenched in his hand while the connecting cables dangled a foot above Amanda's head. "You couldn't tell me the first thing about how this device works."

"It looked…painful. That's all." Bill didn't look away from her. "You sure you're okay?"

"Yeah. I'm…" Taking a deep breath, Amanda pushed herself to her feet and gazed around the camp. "I'm fine."

One of the scientists marched purposefully toward them with a tin cup of water in hand.

"Ah." Fiona gestured toward the water-bearer. "Here you go. Get hydrated, kid. One of the first rules of staying alive."

"Thanks." Amanda took one step toward the scientist with the cup, but another wave of dizziness made her pause. Still, she licked her dry lips and reached for the water anyway. "Did it—"

The last thing she saw was her outstretched fingers missing the cup completely and brushing against nothing but air before everything went dark and she dropped to the ground.

CHAPTER NINE

Water. How hard is it to get some water around here?

Amanda slowly opened her eyes and immediately shut them again beneath the agonizing glare of the blinding light shining down on her face. She groaned and tried to swat at the light.

"She's up."

Who's that?

Muffled voices and hurried footsteps grew closer. When Amanda raised a hand to shield her face and open her eyes, the first thing she saw was a furious-looking Fiona whipping the canvas flap aside and storming into the tent.

"Of course she's up. Quit hovering. She's fine."

The woman who'd alerted everyone to Amanda's current state stepped aside with a frown as Fiona approached the bed. The woman snatched another tin cup off the table beside the cot and held it out to Amanda as the girl slowly pushed herself up into a sitting position.

"Wanna try this again without passing out?"

Blinking quickly, Amanda reached for the cup and downed the entire thing in one breath. "More."

"One more. Then I'm cutting you off."

MARTHA CARR & MICHAEL ANDERLE

The splash of water pouring made Amanda feel even more parched, but when she finished the second cup, that seemed to do the trick.

"Okay. Good. Now." Fiona slammed the tin container back down on the table and drew a folding metal chair up beside the cot before plopping down into it. "If you feel like you're about to lose it again, say something, okay? I mean, at least you're already sitting down. How's your face?"

"My…" Amanda gingerly prodded her face and sucked in a sharp breath through her teeth when a burst of pain shot through her nose and up between her eyes. "Ow."

"Yeah. Who knew you could break your nose hitting the ground face-first, huh? Good thing we have at least *one* scientist here who isn't completely useless when it comes to medical procedures."

"Excuse me?" The other woman who'd apparently been monitoring Amanda in the tent folded her arms.

Fiona turned her head to look the woman up and down. "Do you mind?"

Rolling her eyes, the scientist turned medic marched out of the tent without a word.

"I mean, come on. It shouldn't be that hard to get a little privacy even out here. There aren't that many of us."

Amanda grimaced and experimentally touched her face again. "I broke my nose?"

"Yeah, but Miss Huffypants out there set it again pretty quickly. Hey, you were already unconscious. Might as well get the job done while you couldn't feel it."

"I passed out."

"Yep."

"I've been lying here for…"

"Almost twenty-four hours, kid." Fiona raised her eyebrows and failed to make her smile look entirely reassuring. "Whatever happened in your head packed a punch, huh?"

"My…" Amanda's eyes flew open when she remembered what had gotten her here in the first place. "The image. The map. Did it work?"

"You know, that's what I *thought* you were trying to ask before you hit the dirt. Literally."

The tent flap opened again, and Bill stood there with his arm raised to hold it aside. His urgent concern melted instantly into overwhelming relief, and he shook his head. "You woke up."

"Um… Did you think I wouldn't?" Amanda pointed at the tin cup again. "Can I get more water?"

"If you can talk, I guess you can drink." Fiona filled the cup, and the girl forced herself to drink it more slowly this time.

When she finished, she looked back and forth between Fiona and Bill. "Well? Did it work? The map."

Bill stepped farther into the tent and let the flap fall shut behind him. "It worked."

"Great." Amanda swung her legs over the side of the cot. "So as soon as you guys tell me what it means, we can get—"

"No, no, no. Hold on." Fiona clamped a hand down on the girl's thigh as Bill rushed around the other side of the cot. "You're not going anywhere."

"I'm fine. Seriously." Amanda looked up at Bill standing in her way and sighed. "Please tell me you guys aren't gonna ignore everything I say again. 'Cause as much as I like throwing tables and destroying giant computers, I don't wanna have to do that again."

Fiona snorted. "You enjoyed it, huh?"

"Not really. I'm trying to make a point."

"Yeah. Shifter kid Hulking out on a bunch of dumbass scientists who won't shut up and hear you out. I get it."

Bill pressed his lips together to hold back a laugh. "I'm pretty sure she's talking about us too."

"Obviously. I'm not a scientist. And *you* need to stay on this cot." The redheaded woman snapped her fingers and pointed at Amanda's legs. "I mean it."

When fixing her mentor with a deadpan stare didn't get her any response except the same expression right back at her, Amanda sighed and drew her legs back up onto the cot to cross them beneath her. "Fine. For how long, exactly?"

"For as long as it takes the swelling to go down." Fiona studied the girl's face and smirked. "Not that long. We heal pretty fast, don't we? Hey, too bad you won't still have that gnarly shiner when you go back to school, huh? Would've been a hell of a story to tell your friends."

"I thought I wasn't supposed to talk about Coalition stuff."

Even though I've pretty much broken that rule a hundred times already, but she *doesn't know that.*

"You're not." Fiona patted the girl's thigh and sat back in her chair. "You have an imagination, kid. Comes in real useful for war stories."

"Here." Bill pulled a wrapped protein bar from his pocket and tore it open before handing it over. "You need to eat something."

"Okay." Amanda took the bar, stared at it with no appetite whatsoever, then brandished it at her team members. "I'll eat this. You guys can tell me about the map and what it means now that we got it out of my head."

The two adults hovering over her shared a hesitant glance, then Bill slipped his hands into the pockets of his khaki shorts and shrugged. "Well, it's definitely out of your head."

"And?"

"And nothing. Yet." Fiona pointed at her. "Eat."

Amanda took a quick bite to hold up her end of the deal and only chewed once before forcing it down. "What do you mean nothing?"

"They're still working out what all those points of light signify," Bill replied. "You were right. It's definitely a map."

Fiona snorted. "Didn't exactly come with a key, though, did it?"

"Wait, so you guys have had this thing for almost twenty-four hours, and you don't know what it means?"

"Hey, this whole mission is a shot in the dark, even with all these specialists and experts and algorithms. We're doing what we can." The woman shrugged and eyed the mostly uneaten protein bar in Amanda's hand. "Keep eating. Then when you finish, go ahead and tell us what happened that night."

"I already told you I went to go check out the sample—"

"I mean in detail, kid. Every little step. Everything you saw. Don't get me wrong. Talking to magical animals and doing a bunch of weird crap the rest of us wouldn't even believe is possible, let alone consider doing ourselves… I mean, that's kinda your thing now."

"I guess…" Amanda looked up at Bill for reassurance, but the man only shrugged again.

Great. That's totally my thing now. Not like I wasn't already thinking it about myself.

"Getting zapped with visions from a hunk of magical poo?"

"Waste," Bill corrected. "We don't exactly know what it is beyond that."

"Fine, whatever. That's a whole different animal, kid." Fiona snorted. "Well, not literally, obviously. You get my drift."

Amanda peeled the cellophane wrapper farther down around the protein bar and shook her head. "You mean why am *I* the one who gets to communicate with glowing *waste* that made three divergent creatures…diverge again?"

"Exactly. Hell, we all know you're special. Nobody's arguing against that. It could be a fluke too."

"Right place at the right time kinda thing," Bill added. "So we need to hear everything before we can come to any conclusions about this."

"Or not."

"Yeah, yeah. I get it." The girl took another big bite of food-brick, then another, and didn't taste a thing before she'd finished her quick and easy meal. She downed another cup of water before drawing a deep breath and told them what she'd experienced.

At least these two don't have a problem listening to a teenage girl without thinking I'm too young to be worth their time.

It took Amanda almost an hour to finish the entire story of what had only taken about five minutes to occur the night before. Fiona and Bill kept interrupting her to ask questions, but the part that took the longest was trying to remember as much detail as she could about all the visions that had come before the glowing map of Earth so she could accurately describe them in words.

When she finished, both her teammates looked thoroughly flabbergasted.

"Okay, so you're either staring at me like that because none of this made any sense, or because all of it does, and you put a bunch of pieces together that made you realize something seriously awful."

Fiona cleared her throat. "Nope. Not awful, kid. Just... You know, it's a little hard to wrap my head completely around all the things you saw."

"I told you it would be hard to explain."

"You did your best." Bill's statement sounded more like a question. "It's hard to imagine everything in as much detail as I think you were trying to get across."

Amanda rolled her eyes. "I'm not getting back into that stupid machine if that's what you're thinking."

"Wouldn't even ask, kid." The woman looked at her watch, and her eyes widened. "Hey. Anybody notice what day it is?"

Bill's eyes widened, and he offered Amanda a crooked smile. "Well, look at that."

"What? What's today?"

Now they're screwing with me.

"Something about December thirtieth rings a bell, doesn't it?"

Amanda froze, then she barked out a laugh and clamped a hand over her eyes. "You're kidding."

"Happy birthday, kid. Hey, sorry we didn't get you a cake."

Bill chuckled. "Guess you'll have to settle for some water in a tin cup and that protein bar you inhaled."

"Um...thanks, I guess."

"Look on the bright side." Fiona elbowed the girl in the ribs. "Now you're officially old enough to carry a driver's license with that scooter."

Right when they all found a reason to laugh during this insane mission that had already gone on way too long, someone outside across camp started shouting.

"Oh, come on." Fiona rolled her eyes. "It can't be that—"

"I got it! I figured it out! Where is she? Fiona!"

Bill turned toward the tent entrance. "Sounds like Dr. Manzury."

"What the hell does he want with me?"

"What did he figure out?" Amanda asked.

"Hold on." Fiona stood and hurried toward the tent flap. It whisked aside before she could grab it herself, and Dylan poked his head through, brandishing loose papers in his hand like a sword. "Whoa! Jeeze. If you're trying to take me down with a papercut, you seriously need to—"

"I figured it out." The man's eyes were wide beneath his disheveled hair. "I know, I know. It seems like a long shot, but I checked it four times with all the other coordinates to make sure. And I'm *sure*—"

"Slow down." Fiona clapped a hand on Dylan's shoulder, and he jumped away from her. "You get any sleep last night?"

"No. I was running these coordinates on the map Amanda…" The scientist found the girl in question sitting upright on the cot in front of him and swallowed. "You did it. This map you pulled out with Mel's machine? This is what the creature showed you."

"Spit it out already," Bill barked, his face growing red in the excitement.

"Every single point of light on this thing corresponds with a kemana. The same spot on every continent. The subject put this in your head, Amanda!"

"Wait a minute." Fiona snatched the papers from his hands and rifled through them, her frown deepening. "This thing knows where all the kemanas are? And it gave up all that information to *her*?"

"Why would it have a map of Earth's kemanas?" Amanda watched Fiona studying the papers, then realized she wasn't strapped down to the cot and finally slid off the edge to stand. "Fiona?"

"Wait a minute." Bill wagged his finger at no one in particular and stared at the floor. "High levels of concentrated magic in the waste sample. Which was apparently digestible by those unknown divergent species we found the other day, horrible side effects notwithstanding."

"But kemanas?"

"How have I not thought of this?" Bill raced across the tent.

"Hey!" Fiona shouted after him. "Wanna share with the rest of the class?"

"If I'm right again on this one, the makeup of that waste sample will be surprisingly close to if not the same as the crystals powering the kemanas. Maybe slightly altered as a byproduct of the creature we've been looking for, but I can almost guarantee the similarity's there. I have to test it." Bill launched himself out of the tent.

Amanda and Fiona stared at the scientist who'd tried to jab the shifter girl with a syringe full of sedatives the day before. He gave them both a weak smile and backed toward the tent's entrance. "Can I...have those back?"

"You didn't make a copy?" Fiona rolled her eyes and slapped the papers against his chest. "Here."

Dylan spun and raced out of the tent without another word.

"Kemana crystals." The woman shook her head. "How does that even make sense?"

Amanda stared at the ground as the memory of all her visions started piecing themselves together in a completely new light. "It does. It makes total sense. Listen, all the images I saw were about magic. Earth, Oriceran, and everything in between. All the...the bad stuff that's happened because of magic."

"Say what?"

"Fiona, if Bill comes back and tells us that sample *is* the same as the kemana crystals, I think..." She let out a long, slow breath. "I think the creature's going after the kemanas *because* of magic."

"To do what, kid? Eat the damn things?"

"I don't know. Maybe. Or maybe destroy them."

Fiona chuckled. "Maybe you need to get a little more sleep too."

"No, I'm serious. It makes sense. If this creature thinks everything bad that's happened over who knows how long is because of magic, and it knows what's *fueling* magic on Earth, I think it's trying to get rid of it."

"By eating kemana crystals."

"Oh, come on. Pretend that you're making the connection." Amanda stormed past her mentor and whipped aside the tent flap to hold it open for the woman. "Or at least tell me where the closest kemana is."

"The second half's easy enough. Closest one to where we are now is right under Puerto Natales, a few miles..." Fiona stopped outside the tent and leaned backward in realization. "Oh. Shit."

"It's going after *that* kemana." Amanda nodded. "I don't care if you don't believe me or you think it's too farfetched of an idea because I *know—*"

"I believe you, kid." Fiona laughed and thumped Amanda on the back, making the girl stumble forward. "You got one hell of a brain. Now we gotta bag this thing in the Puerto Natales kemana. Then we can all go home and pretend like none of this ever happened. Ha! Happy birthday!"

CHAPTER TEN

Once Bill came back with the confirmation of his hunch—that the waste sample did have almost the same chemical and magical composition as the kemana crystals—his entire theory had to be circulated among the camp's scientists and verified before they could act on it. When combined with Dylan's discovery about the map from Amanda's head being a map of Earth's kemanas, nobody disagreed with *her* theory either.

They'd find the creature at the closest kemana to their little camp in South America, and that was when they'd finally be able to catch the thing.

It took the team two hours to gather everything they needed, including more tracking systems reset now to sweep the area around Puerto Natales for the creature's magical signature. They made calls to the local magical network to alert them of the emergency need to clear out the kemana as soon as possible. When they finished, they had a ridiculous amount of combat gear, stun weapons, cages, creature-catching apparatuses, and a bunch of new stuff Amanda hadn't seen in five weeks of being stuck at this camp.

The only magical who argued with her when she said she

wanted to be there at the kemana was Dr. Baker. "If this creature has a connection to you now, you could endanger this entire operation by being on-site. It might sense you—"

"It won't." Amanda strapped on a vest that was supposed to protect her from deadly surges of concentrated magic and nodded at the doctor. "I don't think the connection went both ways. I didn't see the creature, only its…waste. I'll be fine."

"But—"

"Not your call, Doc." Fiona guided Amanda toward the pair of utility terrain vehicles parked on the other side of camp. "She knows what she's talking about."

Amanda and her mentor headed toward the vehicles. The four combat operatives on the team were finishing stashing all their gear into the racks. The few other scientists who'd insisted they tag along—having claimed they could take better readings with a lot more accuracy if they were onsite, now that a site had been confirmed—climbed into the back seats.

"So whose call is it?" Amanda asked with a small smile.

"Yours, kid. Don't get me wrong. If you were making stupid calls, I'd be the first one to tell you. And the first one to stop you. But this? This is what we need to be doing right now. Good work."

"Thanks." Amanda patted down the bulky vest over her clothes and wrinkled her nose. "This thing is supposed to protect against…magical surges or whatever?"

"That's what they tell me." Fiona thumped a fist against her vest and chuckled.

"So why haven't any of us worn these things before when we went out to follow the magical trail?"

"Hmm?"

"Five weeks, Fiona. We've spent five weeks trying to track this thing down, and I'm only now getting protective gear."

With a snort, Fiona opened the back door to one of the vehicles and gazed around the camp. "I don't know, kid. Guess nobody thought we'd manage to pull this off until now."

"Oh, yeah. That's great. Real confidence-booster."

"Get in the UTV."

———

Twelve hours to get from one minor island to a slightly larger port city was way longer than Amanda expected. However, the team had to stop twice to put together temporary bridges from one island to the next before they reached the mainland.

The sun was setting by the time the two-vehicle team had parked inside the official city limits of Puerto Natales, where a Wood Elf in brightly colored clothing who introduced himself as Ignacio greeted them. In thickly accented English, he thanked Fiona for calling him and briefly summarized what they were doing to clear out the kemana beneath the city as soon as possible. It wasn't an easy thing to do, especially when there were no official warnings through any kind of magicals-only network to alert regular citizens to the danger.

"We can handle anybody who doesn't wanna listen," Fiona muttered before nodding for Ignacio to lead the way into the kemana.

The closest entrance he led them to happened to be through one of the underground crypts in the cemetery behind one of Puerto Natales' oldest churches. Fiona seemed to think that was particularly hilarious, but Amanda felt like she was trespassing.

It's a kemana. That's it. The church was probably built on top of the entrance way after the kemana was here in the first place. No big deal.

There had to be another entrance, though, because the magicals in the massive underground city built for them in South America had already cleared out. Mostly.

"Like I say," Ignacio muttered as he gestured toward the small pockets of magicals congregating around the few storefronts and

MARTHA CARR & MICHAEL ANDERLE

restaurants that hadn't taken the warning seriously enough to close up shop. "Some *paisanos* no wanting to leave."

"Uh-huh." Brandon nodded and grabbed his stun-rifle with both hands. "Some *paisanos* are about to want something completely different in a minute."

"Go on." Fiona nodded at the other three operatives. "Make sure we clear this place out top to bottom. Explain as much as you have to, but for the love of your jobs, don't get nasty with anyone, all right?"

The shifters filtered out through the kemana to strike up firm conversations with the magical citizens who didn't want to conduct their business elsewhere in safety.

"*Gracias*, Ignacio. We'll take it from here." Fiona shook the Wood Elf's hand, and he nodded before booking it back up the wide staircase leading back into the crypt and the cemetery above them. Then she studied the five scientists who'd lugged all their gear down here to set up monitors and magical-frequency radars and all their tracking technology. "You got what you need?"

"We're good," one woman flatly said as she plugged thin cables into a large black box inside one of the crates.

"You sure? Nobody wants an *empanada* or anything?"

"What?"

Fiona waved the scientists off and rolled her eyes. "Forget it. I'm not buying snacks down here right now. Come on, kid. Let's go make sure there aren't any stragglers."

Amanda couldn't stop staring at the dark green crystal pulsing in the center of the kemana as they descended another flight of old, worn stone steps to the main avenue. With most of the magicals down here now evacuated to the surface and the usual din of a busy underground metropolis cut by at least three-quarters, it was too hard to ignore the low hum of concentrated magic rising off that crystal in constant waves.

This is what the creature wants to get rid of. The sources of magic on Earth. Why does it think that's gonna change anything?

"Whoa, whoa, whoa." Fiona raised both hands toward a group of young witches and wizards who couldn't have been much older than Amanda and shook her head. "Fun's over. We need everybody out of here."

The kids frowned at each other and clearly didn't understand a word the red-haired woman said. So as Fiona practiced her broken Spanish and tried to get the gravity of the situation across, Amanda made her way along the outer walls of the kemana to search for any other stragglers.

Can't blame them for not taking us seriously. Sure, maybe a few shifters down here know about the Coalition. Maybe they don't. I'm pretty sure everyone in the Everglades kemana would laugh and call us crazy if we showed up and told them to clear out. It's not like there's a mayor in these places or anything.

She peered through the front windows of storefronts, relieved to find most of them empty. The low conversations of Fiona and their four combat-experienced operatives gently trying to guide the remaining magicals through the entrance on the other side of the kemana echoed within the massive cavern. Still, fewer people made listening for footsteps and other pockets of hiding magicals a lot easier.

After walking at least a third of the way around the perimeter of the kemana walls and seeing nobody, Amanda stopped to watch the others ushering the last few magicals away from the oncoming danger none of them had the time to explain. Most of them were confused and curious. A few tried to argue back until Frank ended up screaming at an immensely hairy Kilomea in Spanish. That got everyone else's attention. Then the remaining magicals who didn't want to leave started streaming out of dark alleys and storefronts that only looked closed up and emptied.

Fiona barked a laugh as she approached Frank. He stared down the Kilomea without any expression whatsoever before the belligerent guy finally snorted and stomped away toward the main exit to the surface. "What did you say to him?"

"That if he wanted to worry about superstitions, he shouldn't be underground right before the New Year in a country that has active volcanoes *and* penguins."

She snorted. "What's that supposed to mean?"

"Guess it's a Kilomea thing. I don't know."

Amanda kept searching the alleys between shops and buildings, her focus split between searching for magicals who weren't supposed to be there and listening to the almost mind-numbing hum of the giant green crystal jutting from the center of the kemana floor.

There's no way the kemana in Florida pumps out that much power. Not that I've ever been down there when it's empty, but this feels way more intense.

It smelled more intense too. The scent of so much concentrated magic powering an entire underground city for magicals had always tickled Amanda's senses. It made her a little light-headed if she got too close to the giant crystal. This one had something different. A new scent that for some reason didn't seem like it belonged down here, under a city in Chile. Or anywhere.

She stopped to sniff the air and frowned.

What is *that? I know I've smelled it before, but...*

A knot of dread tightened in her gut a second before the memories crashed over her in a horrifying wave.

Quick, meticulous footsteps raced toward the front of the house as she lay in her bed. Claire's wide eyes stared at her from the opposite side of their shared bedroom because her sister had heard them too. Their dad's urgent shout for both of them to stay in their room no matter what. Their mom's scream when the front door burst open and strangers with guns flooded into the living room. Amanda and Claire trying to help their parents. Trying to fight back.

The deafening roar of gunfire.

The sound of bodies hitting the floor and never moving again.

Amanda's entire world darkening in an instant, and the last thing she'd heard as she tried to crawl back to consciousness beneath the agonizing pain shooting through the back of her head.

Their vicious, snarling laughter...

She drew in a shuddering gasp and shook her head, trying to direct her focus onto the massive green crystal in the center of the kemana.

Holy crap. That was...weird. Why the hell am I thinking about all that now?

"Hey!"

She spun and found Brian standing at the mouth of the next alley in front of her, with his weapon aimed halfway between the ground and at whoever he'd discovered hiding between buildings.

"Everybody out." He swung his rifle toward the kemana's main avenue and repeated various urgent iterations of the same command. "Frank. Come over here and tell these guys they need to leave, will ya? Would've been nice to know from the beginning you speak Spanish."

"We speak English too, okay?"

The low voice echoing from the alley made Amanda break out in goosebumps.

What?

"Oh, you do, huh? Great." Brian waved the hidden magicals forward. "Then I shouldn't have to tell you this many times to come on out of there. This kemana isn't safe, and everyone needs to evacuate. That means you too. Let's go."

"Okay, okay. Just had to finish a little business."

"Uh-huh. Now we need to finish ours." Brian stepped aside as four men emerged from the alley, smirking and raising their hands in concession.

The two Kilomeas wore matching business suits. The Crystal missing two fingers on his right hand wore bright local colors and a serape like Ignacio.

The fourth man, a tall wizard with a streak of white down one side of his otherwise pitch-black hair, wore jeans and a maroon polo shirt. He chuckled and gazed around the empty kemana. "Seems a little over the top to bring weapons down here for everyone's *safety*, don't you think?"

"Not if you try to get smart with me." Brian nodded toward the main entrance across the cavern. "This isn't a joke. Let's go."

"So it's…what?" The wizard scanned the cavern. "Five shifters clearing the place out all on your own?"

One of the Kilomeas snorted when he saw Amanda standing there a storefront away and staring at them. "Five and a half."

The men snickered, and Amanda's pulse pounded in her head as her breath quickened.

No. No, no, no. I'm going crazy.

The wizard turned halfway around and looked her over from head to toe with a sneer. "What, you're giving out free passes to kids?"

Brian let out a low, warning growl. "Why don't you worry about yourself and let us handle everyone else, huh?"

Everything in Amanda's awareness slowed to a timeless crawl when she saw the wizard's face. His hair. His twitching upper lip. The way he rolled his eyes when he turned away from her to follow the other three magicals across the kemana.

Like he didn't even see me. No. Like he didn't even recognize *me.*

She recognized *him*.

She should've guessed who it was the second she caught his scent wafting out of the alley. Still, there'd been no way for her to know. The smell that brought back all her memories of the worst night of her life could've belonged to the kemana, not one of the bastards who'd been there.

One of the bastards who'd murdered her family, kidnapped

her, and sent her across New York to be auctioned off to the highest-bidding crime lord.

"Stop." Her one-word command croaked out of her as she clenched her fists and stared after the magicals walking away from her.

Brian was the only one who turned to look at her. "What?"

"No." Amanda snarled and stormed forward, her skin tingling with all her magic coursing through her before an oncoming shift. She didn't want to shift. She wanted to rip that wizard's throat out. "Hey! I said stop!"

"Amanda, what's—"

"Shut up," she snarled at Brian as she stomped past him before breaking into a run. "Turn around and look at me, asshole!"

"Whoa." Fiona jogged toward her as the wizard stopped and turned again to look at the shifter girl racing after him.

His stupid sneer was the same.

"You *bastard!*" Amanda shouted. "I know who you are!"

"Somebody get this crazy kid out of here too, okay? And away from *me.*" The wizard chuckled. "She's completely lost it."

Amanda screamed in fury as she ran toward him, all rational thought obliterated beneath her rage and the instinctive urge to hurt him as much as she could as quickly as possible.

"Amanda!" Fiona barked. "What are you—"

A deafening *whoop* blasted across the kemana and hadn't finished echoing before one of the alarm sirens on the scientists' setup of creature trackers blared nonstop.

"I'm getting massive readouts beyond the kemana walls," someone shouted. "It's here!"

CHAPTER ELEVEN

"Everybody out *now*!" Brandon roared as he urgently waved the last remaining magicals toward the exit.

The siren kept blaring, the wizard with the white stripe in his hair spun to break into a quick jog, and Amanda was on the verge of shifting right then and there and launching herself at his back.

Before she could take another step, Fiona caught her by the wrist and yanked her back. "What the hell do you think you're doing? Do you hear what's happening right now? That thing's here, and whatever that guy did to piss you off, you need to let it go." Then she turned to shout at the other operatives, "Jesus, why is everyone so slow? Get them out of here!"

"No!" Amanda snarled and tried to jerk out of her mentor's grasp. "Not him. Not *him*!"

"Listen to me, kid. I don't care about one wizard down here while we have an alarm blasting through the place telling us we need to get our shit together. That includes you. We have a job to do."

"You don't understand! He's one of the—"

A horrifyingly loud rumble shook the kemana walls, followed by the sharp *crack* of solid stone breaking in half. A massive slab of rock broke away from the ceiling above the cemetery entrance. It hit the ground and crumbled, sending a tremor through the surface. The last magicals who still hadn't evacuated shouted and screamed and scattered toward the main exit, finally picking up the pace.

"Let me go!" Amanda snarled, trying to keep her eye on the wizard as he was swept up in the group of panicking magicals trying to squeeze through the tunnel that would take them back to the surface. "I have to—"

"Jesus, kid. That thing's trying to tear this place apart. Come on!" Fiona finally released her, but only to race back toward the scientists and all their gear as she shouted directions and asked for updates.

Another tremor racked the kemana, and Amanda stumbled sideways, her chest constricting to the point of suffocation when she saw a final glimpse of the wizard's white-striped hair disappearing through the tunnel.

He's getting away. Again. How did I let him get away?

The siren cut off a second before a massive explosion at the opposite end of the kemana sent chunks of stone and thick clouds of dust spraying across the main avenue. The shifter team shouted at each other. The operatives aimed their weapons at the giant hole in the side of the kemana and tried to shield themselves from the shockwave of debris still hurtling across the cavern. Amanda couldn't look away from the dark mouth of the tunnel where one of her family's murderers had disappeared.

She hardly noticed the ringing in her ears from the next massive explosion. The intensified pulse of humming magical energy bursting from the kemana crystal barely registered. She felt like she'd been socked in the gut, trampled, and tossed off a hundred-foot cliff into freezing water all at once.

I can't...

Then all the sounds and smells and magical vibrations disappeared.

Her head was buzzing now with the same energy as the crystal, and she felt something coming closer, sneaking up right behind her.

Not behind me. It's already here.

A surge of righteous fury burned inside of her, and she knew without a doubt that it didn't belong to her. It belonged to someone else. Some*thing* else. Some new presence in her mind had locked onto all her pain and rage and was both feeding off it and fueling it.

Trembling from head to toe, she slowly turned to see the entire kemana filled with billowing dust and smoke, cracked stone, crumbled boulders, and her team getting ready to face the creature who was coming for the crystal powering the place.

The same creature that was now in her head.

How did it find me? How does it even know I'm here? This isn't supposed to—

A thick, heavy pressure pulsed through her mind and rippled down across her body. It filled her with heat and purpose and even more rage.

Tear it all down. Release it. Everything had to go.

Half of her knew these weren't her actual thoughts, that the creature that had blasted massive holes through the kemana wall to get to its prize had somehow hijacked her. The other half of her didn't care. Because all that rage and longing to destroy—to finally take what others had abused for so long—felt *right*.

She didn't want to take the crystal's magic for herself. That would have been too much for even her, and she knew it. Still, if she got rid of the crystal here, it would damage magic on Earth. It would strip away the energy powering this kemana and keeping Oriceran magicals on this planet nice and cushy and believing they were unstoppable. Maybe it would stop them.

Maybe it would stop *him*. The wizard. The murderer she'd let escape because she'd been too focused on stopping the creature now telling her it was perfectly okay to act on her hatred.

This is justified.

Amanda stalked toward the center of the kemana, zeroing in on the energy pulsing through the dark green crystal hovering in perpetual stasis less than two inches off the stone floor. She had no idea how she would destroy the thing, but somehow, she knew she could. This was supposed to happen. She was *supposed* to do this.

"Amanda!" Fiona barked. She'd grabbed a weapon from their pile of gear and now backed away from the smoke and settling rubble. "Target at *my* twelve, not yours! You hear me?"

The shifter girl heard everything in the massive chamber. She didn't care.

Everything that had formed her conscience for all sixteen years of her life lay buried beneath the justness of the wrath and destructive intent she shared with a creature she'd never seen.

"Hey!" Bill took off running after her, his eyes wide as the small sixteen-year-old girl stopped two feet from the kemana crystal and ignored everything else. She clenched her hands into fists, oblivious to the next crash of more broken stone crumbling off the cavern walls and to the ground. A halo of silvery mist grew around Amanda's body, pulsing outward as her magic emerged not in a shift but as her snarling ghost-wolf pulling itself out of her toward the crystal.

"Amanda, what are you *doing*?" He skidded to a halt beside her and grabbed her arm. "Hey! That creature's coming in whether we like it or not, and we don't have time for—"

She snarled and jerked her arm away as she whirled toward him, her eyes wholly silver and blazing. Bill stepped back in surprise. Amanda didn't look like a sixteen-year-old girl anymore.

She doesn't even look like herself. Like she's not even in there...

"Snap out of it!" He grabbed her shoulders and risked the magic seeping out of her to shake her a few times. "We have a job to do. Amanda!"

"Incoming!" Frank yelled.

Bill stepped away from the girl and turned to stare at the largest gaping hole at least twenty feet high in the kemana wall. The rain of debris had almost cleared away, but the smoke and dust still hadn't settled. That didn't mean it hid the creature heading toward them now.

A bright light pulsed behind all the smoke, making it impossible to catch the details but outlining a shadowy figure stepping forward out of the debris.

That thing has to be huge if it made a hole that size to get in here.

"There. Right there." Bill pointed at the oncoming silhouette stepping out of the dust cloud. "Amanda, that's why we're here." When she didn't respond, he grabbed her shoulders again and forcefully turned her toward the hole at the far end of the cavern. "We need you!"

When Amanda spotted the figure stepping out of the thick smoke and settling dust, what she saw snapped her immediately out of whatever connection the creature had made with her mind. The rage that doubled hers disappeared. Her fury aimed at the murderous wizard and herself for letting him get away dampened beneath a surge of disbelief.

"What?"

The creature stepping out of the debris to fully reveal itself wasn't a giant monster like they'd all expected. It didn't even look like a creature from Oriceran or Earth or anywhere else.

It looked like a girl.

A small, fierce, determined girl every Coalition operative and scientist in this kemana recognized. Even Amanda recognized her.

That's me.

Except it wasn't. Not exactly.

Of course, it was impossible for there to be two Amanda Couliers simultaneously, even if they were in the same kemana. This one looked like it had stepped out of a nightmare. All the light and warmth of an actual magical living and breathing and existing on Earth was missing from this golem with Amanda's face. Instead, a darker version had replaced it—a more insidious version.

Is this what I look like when I'm angry?

"What the actual fuck?" Brandon backed away from the Amanda-creature with slow, careful steps, leveling his firearm squarely at the thing's chest. He glanced over his shoulder at the real Amanda to double-check he didn't imagine the whole thing. "Somebody better explain why this thing looks like *her*!"

The other operatives joined him in stepping away from the newcomer. Their fingers rested on triggers as they tried to cast aside their surprise and focus instead on being prepared for whatever happened next. Still, none of them wanted to stay in one place and risk getting too close to the thing pacing forward on two legs and snarling at them with Amanda's mouth.

"You need to get out of here," Fiona shouted. "This is all kinds of wrong. Bill, get her out!"

"Are you serious?" he yelled back.

"Until we know why the hell this thing looks like her, you bet your ass I'm serious. Go!"

"I'm not going anywhere," Amanda protested.

"This is one of those times I'm calling you out on your terrible ideas, kid. We'll take care of this. Get out!"

"Come on." Bill tried to grab her arm again, but she leapt away from him and raced forward toward the dark, vengeful copy of herself pulsing with even more concentrated magic than even the kemana crystal was putting out. "Amanda, you can't—"

"I got this. That thing was in my head, remember? I'm the one who knows how to get to it."

"You're the one who gave it a shape," Fiona snarled. She and the other four operatives tried to form a boundary around the Amanda-creature to stop it from getting any closer to the crystal, their weapons fully powered up and ready to be used. "This isn't a suggestion, Amanda. Get your ass up to the—"

The Amanda-creature tossed a hand up and sent a blazing streak of opalescent light right at the center of the operatives' formation. The shifters leapt aside at the last second, shouting and firing warning shots that didn't do a thing to stop the creature's straight path toward the crystal.

Stunning bolts of electric green and blue burst from the weapons and ricocheted off an invisible shield erected around Amanda's black-eyed, snarling doppelgänger. The shots *cracked* against the walls and floor of the kemana, and Amanda quickened her pace toward the creature.

"Shit!" Fiona dropped to one knee as she skidded out of the way. "Hold your fire!"

Amanda stepped right into the creature's path and spread her arms. "I got this."

"The hell you do! You have no idea what you're doing, and we have no idea how to take it down!"

"Get her out, Bill!" Brandon roared as he adjusted the settings on his weapon.

"I..." The zookeeper's mouth silently worked as he struggled between listening to the shifters with battle experience and trusting that Amanda did have a plan.

"*Now!*"

Amanda glared into the dark, lightless eyes of the creature stalking toward her, and her anger cracked wide open again.

Even Fiona thinks I'm useless. Why doesn't anyone listen *to me? I shouldn't have to spell it out every single time!*

The second she turned her frustration onto the adult shifters of her team all around her, she knew she'd made a mistake. The Amanda-creature snarled and spun, changing course from its straight shot toward the kemana crystal to now head for the other magicals. Another burst of opalescent light shot from its outstretched hand right at Fiona.

The redhead leapt aside with a snarl and spun to aim. She couldn't swing the barrel of her weapon up fast enough to get off a decent shot before another blast of light cracked against the stone floor mere inches from her feet and sent her flying backward in a spray of shattered rock and more dust.

Now it's feeling my *anger.*

Amanda stared in horror as Fiona landed on her back and slid away across the ground before trying to blink herself out of her dazed shock.

"No!" The girl raced toward her darker double, completely aware now of how they'd connected and what the creature was trying to do because it thought it was *helping* her. It thought it could make both their anger justified and right if they shared it. "No, this isn't how we *fix* things!"

The blazing tingle of her magic raced through her, and she didn't think about what might happen if she let herself shift. The only thing she cared about when she leapt in front of Fiona to head off the mirror image of herself was that she had to make this right.

With a snarl, Amanda leapt through the air, her clothes left behind in a pile on the floor, and sailed toward the sixteen-year-old girl with all-black eyes that flashed silver like hers.

By the time the young gray wolf would have reached her target to knock the creature over, the fake Amanda had shifted too. Only it left no clothes behind like the real shifter girl but morphed its entire form into an exact copy of Amanda's wolf.

At least, it would have been the same if a haze of dark, smoky light didn't surround the second gray wolf.

Amanda landed on her paws behind the creature and scrambled to get her bearings once she realized she'd missed. She spun and snarled at the smoky gray wolf baring its fangs at her and stalking forward with its head lowered in warning.

Gives a whole new meaning to the definition of shapeshifter, but fine. If this thing won't listen to me on its own, I'll have to make it.

She leapt toward the creature again, and the two small wolves crashed together in a violent whirlwind of snapping fangs and slashing claws and bristling fur.

"What the hell is it doing?" Brian shouted.

Frank backed away from the growling, snarling pile of two wolves attacking each other blow for blow. He raised his weapon's scope sight to peer through it and hissed. "I can't get a good shot."

"Shot?" Bill's jaw dropped. "You can't take a shot. That's Amanda!"

"That's our *target*," Brandon barked. "We came here to—"

"Do *not* take a shot!" Fiona roared as she pushed herself to her feet and retrieved her weapon. "The first idiot to fire spends the rest of this mission unconscious and the next fifty years in a cell! You hear me?"

The operatives exchanged uncertain looks as they backed away from the violent fight between the girl who'd told them she knew what she was doing and the creature who mimicked her every move. However, they all slowly lowered their weapons but kept them ready and prepared for the moment when they could take the shot they needed.

Fiona tightened her grip on the firearm that was completely useless now and scowled at the teenage wolf locked in battle with a thing none of them understood.

You better be right about this, kid. I'll be damned if I have to explain to anyone how I let you get yourself killed down here.

CHAPTER TWELVE

Amanda yelped when her double tossed her across the kemana floor and leapt after her with a snarl that sounded way too much like hers. The next second, she was on all fours again, snapping and clawing at the face of the wolf that matched hers in almost every way.

It doesn't only look like me. This thing fights like me. It thinks like me.

They exchanged equally forceful blows, clamping jaws down around chunks of fur and sinewy ankles and ears. Amanda launched herself at the darker wolf, trying to take it down, and they both toppled to the ground in a flurry of scrambling limbs and furious growls.

Why does it keep fighting me? I'm trying to—

The dark wolf hurtled toward her through the air. Without any conscious thought of drawing out her magic in a completely different way for this mind-numbing fight, Amanda's awareness surged out of her gray wolf's body and leapt toward her attacker to meet it head-on as her ghost-wolf now.

She didn't feel when her physical form collapsed to the ground mid-battle and immediately shifted into a small, battered, naked girl. She wasn't aware of anything at all but a horrified fascination. As the creature headed toward her to continue the fight, a second ghost-wolf emerged from the Oriceran double, whose body fell but retained its dark wolf form. The other ghost-wolf caught her mid-air, and the desperate, scrambling fight continued.

Are you freaking serious?

Their incorporeal bodies clashed together with a burst of light and eerily matched growls. Gravity, mass, and density didn't matter anymore. The two wolves made of magic and smoke grappled with each other in the air over their fallen bodies, snarling and clawing at each other without inflicting any pain or serious injury.

Amanda felt the surge of magical energy race through her when the dark wolf's misty form shuddered and pulsed with dim, smoky light.

Stop! This has to stop!

That was precisely what happened next.

Instead of being pummeled by another ghost-wolf as impossible to injure as she was in the same form, the creature disappeared. So did Amanda's unconscious body on the floor, Fiona, Bill, the operatives shouting and gripping their weapons, and the team of scientists scrambling madly to get enough readings and data that would highlight the key to any of the creature's unknown weaknesses.

The entire kemana disappeared.

Now it was only Amanda standing there alone, surrounded by an endless white nothingness.

"What the heck?"

She turned—or at least she thought she did. There was no sensation under her feet, nothing around to orient herself to the certainty that she was moving.

Great. Either I got sucked up into some kind of different dimension, or this is all in my head. Again.

For a moment, she fully expected to receive another surge of images and emotions like the vision the glowing waste crystal had implanted in her mind. Instead, an amorphous blob of shimmering opalescence burst into existence in front of her, rippling and morphing like quicksilver. She tried to step back, but there was nowhere to step back *to*, and the twitching, pulsing mass followed her.

So she forced herself to stare it down and muttered, "What do you want?"

"You know what I want." The creature's voice was a rumbling growl and a lilting, gentle chime all at once, and its amorphous form rippled in time with its words. *"You have seen it. I have seen that we want the same thing."*

"Yeah, I saw what you're trying to do." Amanda thought she'd be frowning right now if she could feel her face.

"Then why did you stop me?"

Seriously? This thing made a map of every kemana on the planet, came down here with all this magic to tear apart the crystals, and can't figure out why I don't *want it to rip Fiona apart before destroying all magic on Earth?*

"I stopped you," Amanda said slowly, "because attacking my friend and the magicals I work with won't fix what you think is so broken here."

The creature's floating form shrank into itself before ballooning back out again to its previous size. *"You agree with my conclusion. I felt your anger as much as you felt mine. We both know this is a broken planet."*

"No." She would've shaken her head, but she had a feeling the creature rippling in front of her could hear her thoughts—or at least feel them.

Not sure how I'm supposed to convince this thing other than knowing what I know. But I'm kind of out of options right now.

"It's not broken," she added. "It just needs some work—"

The creature *hissed* and flared to twice its size, tendrils of silvery sludge streaking out of it as if she'd punched the thing and splattered it against the floor. *"This planet had millennia to correct its wrongdoings. I have watched from my post. So much needless suffering beneath generations of cruelty. So much entitlement to the abomination of magic and the desecration of life with no regard for the cost."*

"Well…" Amanda paused.

What am I supposed to say to that? It's not wrong.

"I can't tell you those things haven't happened—"

"Then stand aside. I will cleanse this planet. I must eradicate magic to restore the natural balance."

"You can't do that."

"You know I can."

Amanda's mind raced with everything she could've shouted at the creature. That it wasn't fair to sweep down out of nowhere and condemn an entire planet of magicals and humans for the mistakes of only a few. That it had no right to make this decision in the first place. That she would do whatever it took to stop this thing because she couldn't imagine a world without magic, atrocities or not. That the lowlifes responsible for her family's deaths deserved punishment for what they'd done, but that didn't mean every other magical on Earth should pay the price.

Instead, she went with the deepest, most powerful truth inside her heart—the truth that remained despite losing Claire and their parents and wanting so badly to bring their murderers to justice.

"You're right. I know you can."

The creature jerked to one side, then the other before withdrawing its splattered tentacles and contracting into itself again.

"But you're only paying attention to all the horrible things without looking at the rest of it."

Another *hiss* came from the creature's nonexistent mouth. *"There is nothing else."*

"That's the problem with your *decision*."

"You would fight for those who turn a blind eye to your *suffering? Those who already have?"*

"No, I would fight for the people who helped me. And everyone else who doesn't misuse magic to hurt everyone around them. Yeah, there are a lot of shitty magicals who do awful things, but that's not all of us. There's still so much good in this world. On this planet. That's worth fighting for to stop you. If I have to, I will."

I have no idea how I'm gonna do that, but I'm better on the fly anyway.

Whether or not the rippling creature could hear her thoughts, it floated there in silence before slowly moving from one side to the other, as if it were studying whatever form of Amanda Coulier existed in this weird mind-connection plane.

"You know I'm serious," she added to solidify her point.

The creature pulsed twice. *"Then show me."*

"What?"

"Show me what you believe is so worthy of protecting."

"Um… Okay. We're kind of—"

The silvery mass lunged toward her, and there was no way for Amanda to ward off yet another jolt of energy flooding through her and the instant link the creature made with her mind.

Her memories surged forward in flickering images.

Johnny and Lisa putting their lives on the line to save her from the worst fate imaginable in New York. Their dedication to taking her in as their own, no matter how hard it might've been for either of them.

Fiona agreeing to help the youngest shifter in known history activate her magic and step into her ability, never leaving Amanda alone despite the woman's infuriating quirks.

Dr. Caniss taking a chance on welcoming Amanda into the Coalition and giving her a genuinely useful purpose at the lab.

All Amanda's teachers at the Academy, who didn't know what

to do with one shifter girl starting high school at only twelve years old but who'd agreed to let her prove herself.

Summer, Grace, Jackson, and Alex choosing to be her friends and standing beside her even when she couldn't tell them everything and had probably terrified them with what she *had* revealed.

Every single memory that held a glimmer of hope and gratitude and the good that had outweighed all the bad in Amanda's life—the creature sifted through them all. It even found her moments with Matt. Their time spent together, his confessions about who and what he was, and their joint decision not to judge each other for what neither of them could control about their lives. Including the magic that Matt had inherited from his transformed father.

With another burst of light and a *hiss*, the creature extracted itself from Amanda's mind and left her reeling as it rejoined her in the white nothingness all around them. *"None of this comes without a cost. This is why I must eliminate magic on this planet."*

"Wait, *that's* what you got from reading my mind?"

"The ones this planet calls the Dark Families did this to those you love. This entire world is tainted with the very affliction I mean to destroy."

"Dark Families." Amanda huffed out a bitter laugh. "They're gone. Mostly. They have nothing to do with this."

"The ripples of their greed and brutality remain. Remnants of it lie dormant even in a boy you think you know. Even you are afraid of being wrong. Of being turned against by dark magic—"

"No. I'm not." At that moment, the only thing Amanda was afraid of was the possibility that she'd failed to convince this thing of what she did believe. Or that it didn't want to consider anything she said or felt or remembered and was trying to screw with who she was. Who she wanted to be.

Then Fiona's simple words floated through her mind, and she

seized on them because they so perfectly made her point. Now she understood what her mentor had meant.

"It's not the magic that decides who we are or the kinds of decisions we make. It's the other way around. We're the ones who choose how to use it."

The creature shuddered and let out a warbling moan like one of Johnny's new inventions unexpectedly short-circuiting.

"Magic decides everything! You know this. I felt it when you saw the wizard who destroyed your life. All that rage in you turned against him. It is the only reason I have come to this planet."

"Don't put all that on me," Amanda spat. "*I* didn't ask you to leave…wherever you came from to show up here and destroy magic on Earth."

"Your fury is the same across the globe." The creature's quivering mass grew and shrank with jerky movements. Its voice lost the delicate chiming sound and pounded inside Amanda's head as nothing but a roar now.

"Magicals living in terror. Humans wishing the gates between two planets had never existed. Vengeance and spite and greed, no matter the root of it. Even the wild beasts in your world have had enough. They change their forms, their very biological makeup, to protect themselves against what they all know is coming. What I know is coming if Earth is permitted to continue in this way without consequence."

"Wild beasts?" Amanda forgot her lack of a physical body in this place and tried to back away from the creature again. Although now the thing seemed to rise higher above her all on its own. "You mean the divergent species are doing this to *themselves?*"

"They do not resist the transformation. Nor should you resist what must happen."

Crap. This thing looks like it's finished talking. I can't let it zap on out of here and finish what it started.

"You're right!"

The creature burst into its largest size yet with a trembling roar.

"You're right. There's a lot that needs to change here. Not only how we use magic and why but how we do pretty much everything."

"Then we are in agreement—"

"Only about the fact that we need to do better." They technically didn't physically exist wherever they were right now—most likely still in her head. Still, Amanda felt like the formless creature rising higher and expanding to even greater size now cast some dark, foreboding shadow over her.

In a figurative sense, maybe it was. She steeled herself and kept trying to reason with an Oriceran entity that didn't want to be reasoned with at all. "Ripping the literal roots of magic from every kemana on Earth isn't going to make that happen."

"It ensures nothing *will happen—"*

"It has to be done the right way!"

An eerie howl permeated the nothingness as the mass shrank back down and resumed its previous bobbing right in front of Amanda's face. *"You presume to judge right from wrong for yourself?"*

Wow, this thing has no idea how magicals with real bodies who can think for themselves work.

"Yeah." Another sharp laugh escaped her, filling her with more confidence now that she'd snagged the creature's attention again. "Yeah, I *do* know right from wrong. We all do. Well…most of us, at least. If you wanna see things change on this planet and with magic, it *has* to happen the right way. I'm pretty sure I have a good idea of what that looks like but trust me, I'm not the only one."

"You are the only one who attempted to commune with me."

"That was me being in the right place at the right time. There are still so many other magicals on this planet who know exactly how to do things the right way. Like Johnny. You saw my memories. You know who that is."

The creature slid from side to side in front of her again, pulsing and rippling but completely silent.

Please, please, please *don't let it freak out again.*

"He taught me a lot of things about doing whatever it takes to get something done the right way," she muttered. "That's why I'm at the Academy. That's why we're all there. Because yeah, I have to find the magicals who killed my family. But I'm not like them. I'm going to do *that* right too, and that means going to a school created to teach us how to do things the right way, no matter what. Otherwise…"

Otherwise, I'll end up like everybody this thing hates so much and proving its point. Then none of this would even matter anymore.

A soft *pop* emerged from the creature's floating mass, and it surged forward until its rippling, silvery form hovered mere inches in front of Amanda's face. *"There is already so much anger inside you. So much willingness to destroy whatever stands between you and what you want."*

"Maybe." She would have swallowed if she were in her body, but at least her voice held steady in this nonexistent place. "But I can control it."

"What makes you so special?"

The question surprised her, and for a fleeting second, she didn't think she could come up with an answer that would satisfy either of them.

"Nothing." The second she said it, she realized how true it was, and an overwhelming relief flooded through her. "I'm not special. Not really. Not enough to make me that much different than everyone else. I'm trying to be better. I deserve that chance, and so does everyone else."

The creature hovered in front of her for a moment longer, then shot backward through the nothingness. *"Then here is your chance."*

Holy crap. Did I really talk this thing out of destroying every last bit of magic on Earth?

"You are the only being on this planet to have stepped forward into communion with me. I find a new curiosity in your beliefs, and I will wait to watch them unfold."

"So…that means you're not going to tear apart the kemanas, right?"

"For now. All those you say deserve the chance to better themselves despite all evidence to the contrary will have that opportunity."

"Um…okay. Thank you."

"If nothing changes, neither will my judgment. Then I will return to finish what I started, and I will not consider your pleas for more chances *after such failure a second time."*

Amanda's newfound relief disappeared, replaced by a crippling sense of dread.

Did it really make me *responsible for righting all the wrongs of every single magical on Earth over the last few thousand years? How the hell am I supposed to do all that?*

"Right. Any chance you wanna lay out a time limit on this so—"

The creature exploded into a million fragments of blazing light. All of Amanda's senses rushed back into her, and a single spear of excruciating pain cutting through her head with agonizing precision drowned them out immediately.

Multiple voices shouted incomprehensible things somewhere far away. Then there was nothing.

CHAPTER THIRTEEN

"Don't tell me you have no idea how it happened. You were right there with us!"

"We haven't seen this kind of reaction before—"

"What are the readouts telling you?"

"Nothing. They don't tell us anything."

"You want me to believe millions of dollars worth of equipment stopped working for no reason?"

"They *do* work! It's not a problem with the machines. It's the data. It's not possible to extract a pattern from these results. They were all over the place. Then they stopped."

"What about a trail?"

"What trail?"

"The goddamn trail we've been following for the last five weeks! The waste. A magical frequency. The whole reason we're out here in the first place."

"That's what I'm saying. There *isn't* any trail. Not anymore. That thing...disappeared—"

"That's it. I'm finished! Be useless somewhere else. Preferably where I can't hear you. Don't come back until you've figured out how not to piss me off."

Amanda tried to wrap her mind around what she'd heard, but the pounding in her head and the burning in her dry, raw throat made it hard to think of anything else. The bustling chaos all around her didn't help much either—shouting, snarling, the clack of fingers typing furiously on keyboards and mechanical switches flipping, hurried footsteps, crates opening and shutting, vehicle doors slamming.

What's going on?

The shifter girl opened her eyes and found herself in yet another tent back at the expedition camp. Completely alone.

There wasn't even a table in this one with a cup of water or equipment set up beside her to monitor her while she was out.

"Fiona?" she croaked.

Of course, the woman didn't hear her. It was impossible to hear anything right now, and Amanda's voice didn't work nearly as well as it should have.

Grimacing, she pushed herself up to sit on the cot and blinked at the flickering shadows racing back and forth across the outside of the tent.

They have no idea what happened. That's why they're freaking out, and I'm in here sleeping!

It took her legs a few extra seconds to remember how to hold her up, but when they did, Amanda stumbled forward and ripped the tent's entrance flap aside to see what she'd imagined in the rest of the camp. The entire team scrambled around from computer to computer, checking and double-checking data, yelling at each other because none of it made sense.

Right. Leave it to a bunch of scientists to try figuring out something they can't explain with science.

Nobody noticed the bleary-eyed, wobbly shifter girl emerging from the tent and bracing herself on a stack of supply crates so she wouldn't fall over. Only when she'd made it halfway to Mel's machine did anyone turn to look her way. It happened to be Fiona.

"Jesus, kid. What are you doing?"

"Walking."

"That's another one of your bad ideas. Get back in that tent."

"I saw him. I need to—"

Fiona grabbed Amanda by the shoulders and thrust her face toward the girl's to get her attention. "Listen to yourself. You got hit with a massively lethal dose of magical energy, and now you're calling the thing that got a kick out of looking like you a *him*. This time, hallucinations aren't looking all that far-fetched."

Amanda tore away from the woman and stomped across the camp, only one thing in her mind.

I have to show them who he is. If I'm supposed to make things better here so magic doesn't get sucked out of everything, I have to find that wizard. Before I forget his face again.

"Amanda!" Fiona growled in frustration and whirled to shout at the closest shifters. "Don't stare at *her*. We're outta here in an hour, and this place isn't even close to halfway broken down."

"Should she be doing that?" One of the scientists pointed across the camp.

"Walking around like she's invincible? No. *You* should quit slacking off while we're on a strict time crunch to…"

The woman frowned when multiple scientists abandoned packing up the camp to stare at Amanda. Then she spun and found the girl sitting in the chair beside Mel's machine, the heavy metal helmet already strapped to her head as she flipped switches on the panel. "Oh, come on. She's completely lost it."

"No!" Mel raced toward his machine, dodging scattering scientists and their packed crates being hauled into a giant heap to wait for the jet to pick them all up. "No, no, no! What are you doing? That technology isn't a toy!"

Amanda ignored them all and flipped the last switch the way she'd seen Mel do it before. The pressure in her head from the machine reaching into her thoughts wasn't nearly as painful as the last time, and she zeroed in on the memory of the wizard's face.

The white stripe through his black hair. The lines at the corners of his eyes as he raised an eyebrow. The upturned nose. The constant sneer of his upper lip when he'd scoffed at the shifter girl he'd orphaned without recognizing who she was.

"Get her out of there!" Mel roared.

Not before I get his face.

It didn't take much concentration at all to bring the wizard's face into striking clarity in her mind. And it didn't take more than two seconds for the machine to translate Amanda's brainwaves into one more image before a deep *thud* rose from the base of the metal box.

That didn't sound good.

The machine *hissed* and *crackled*, then something inside the mechanism exploded and shot the entire front panel off the device. Sparks flew, a cloud of thick gray smoke spewed from the opening, and the closest shifters shouted and scrambled out of the way.

"Oh, *now* you've done it." Mel finally reached his machine and stared at the wreckage inside the frame. "I *told* Caniss this thing wasn't supposed to be tampered with, and now you've destroyed the entire thing!"

Amanda blinked quickly, then waved the smoke out of her face before unstrapping the helmet. "I needed it to work."

"You'll be lucky if I ever get it to work again after this!"

She stood, dropped the helmet on the chair, and scanned the screen on the machine's control panel.

The wizard's face—sneer and all—stood out in bright-blue pixels with full clarity.

I got him. I finally got him, and now I can find the rest of them and make them pay for what they did.

"Don't you dare touch anything else." Fiona grabbed the girl roughly by the shoulders and spun her around. "This is insane, kid. Even for you."

"*This* is more important than anything else right now." Amanda pointed at the screen. "Look. That's him. That's the guy—"

"Who said something insulting about you being a kid, so you thought you'd teach him a lesson in the kemana we were trying to evacuate?" The woman scowled and shook her head. "Whatever that creature did to you, Amanda, it obviously screwed with your—"

"This asshole was there the night my family died!" Amanda thumped her fist against the machine beside the screen, and another spray of sparks leapt from the hole in the front with another small puff of smoke.

Mel grabbed two fistfuls of his hair and stared in horror at the destruction. "Will somebody put a leash on this kid?"

"Can it." Fiona pointed at him, and he looked like he was about to lose it completely before she turned back toward her mentee. "Say that again."

"Fiona, he was there. He killed them."

"There's no way for you to—"

"I know it was him! I smelled him in the kemana, and I recognized his face. There were others too, but I can't find *them* without finding him, and I can't find him without getting a picture." Now that she had to stand here explaining her rash decisions and ignoring all the warnings not to do anything stupid, Amanda's eyes welled with tears, and her bottom lip trembled. "Fiona, I had to. I have to find him."

"Shit." The woman looked back and forth between the wizard's face on the screen and the teenage girl begging her with tear-filled eyes to hop on board and help her find the murderers who walked free.

"Okay. We'll look into it. Still, you can't walk right up to something like this and start using it all on your own. That was way too reckless, and you know damn well that's saying something coming from me."

"I know. Yeah. I'm sorry."

"We'll hash that out later." Giving Amanda's shoulder a gentle squeeze, Fiona spun to face Mel again. "Tell me you can still send that image back to the lab."

"Why the hell would I do that?"

"Because I'm telling you to."

"No."

"You have to!" Amanda lurched forward but stopped herself before completely going nuts on the pissed-off scientist. "Fiona, he has to."

"You broke the most complicated piece of technology I've ever put together," Mel snarled. "Maybe that goes over well at your school for delinquent morons, but I'm not lifting a finger to do anything for you."

"Do I need to confiscate the whole machine?" Fiona snarled.

"You're rewarding her for vandalizing private property!"

"I'm keeping a promise, and you're about to lose your damn job!"

"I'd like to see you make good on that threat, Fiona." Mel pointed at Amanda. "Someone needs to teach you how things work. You're not above making serious mistakes, and it doesn't look like you've figured that out yet."

Amanda glared back at him and clenched her fists.

He doesn't know anything about me.

"That is *not* your job," Fiona growled. "Amanda unlocked—"

"*Amanda* sent this entire expedition into a tailspin with her stupidity," Mel bellowed. "Now we're flying back to the lab with our tails between our legs and absolutely nothing to show for it."

All the willpower Amanda had left to keep herself in check completely snapped. "Of course that's what you think when you won't even listen to me! None of you will! I know exactly what's going on, and nobody can shut up long enough to give me a chance!"

The man straightened and looked her up and down with wide eyes.

"I'm so sick of everyone telling me what I can and can't do!" She stalked toward him, completely unaware of her feet moving beneath her. "You know what? Let's strap *you* to your stupid fucking machine. I bet it won't pull a single useful thing out of your tiny brain—"

"Amanda," Fiona snapped.

"*What?*"

The woman swallowed and lifted both hands as she backed away. "Take it easy, okay?"

"*Stop saying that!*" Amanda's voice cracked across the camp with way more force than a sixteen-year-old girl was capable of summoning. A flash of opalescent light pulsed around her body in a quivering halo, and the machine behind her sparked again and trembled.

Computer sirens wailed. Alarms *whooped* and *beeped* on dozens of devices. The metal helmet on the folding chair rattled where she'd left it, and a stream of smoke wafted from the underside of the headgear.

"What?" She looked down at her hands, which now glowed with the same light of the destructive creature's blobby form. "What's going on?"

"I don't know, kid, but you better turn it off. Right now."

"I…" She sucked in a sharp breath when the heat in her hands only intensified. "I can't. It's—"

The light around her pulsed again. Amanda doubled over under the searing heat pulsing from her core to shoot through the rest of her limbs.

"Contain it," someone shouted.

"We need to get this under control! Where's the emergency—"

Amanda screamed and dropped to her knees, holding herself

around the middle. The light surrounding her and building by the second washed out everything in her vision.

No, no, no. What happened? What did that thing do to me?

"Got it." Footsteps raced toward her as she fought to catch her breath.

Fiona snarled. "Put that thing away. You can't shoot her up with—"

"It's either this or she blows the entire camp!"

Amanda looked up in time to see a hand swinging down toward her and the tip of a syringe glinting in the light. She didn't feel the sting of the needle piercing her neck over the blazing heat burning her up from the inside out.

CHAPTER FOURTEEN

I really, really, really *need to stop passing out all the time.*

Amanda groaned and rolled over, unsure if she was about to be sick or if she needed to lie still and never move again.

When she opened her eyes, it took a minute to realize she hadn't imagined things. The curved ceiling was only eighteen inches above her face.

Seriously? The Canissphere? Man, that was some heavy-duty tranquilizer.

She gave herself another five minutes to let her stomach settle and to test out her ability to move her arms, legs, and each of her fingers and toes. Everything worked the way it was supposed to, as far as she could tell.

I'm fine. Okay. So now I can work on finding that wizard before anything else gets flushed down the toilet.

With her strength seeping back into her by the second, she hauled herself out of bed, narrowly avoiding knocking herself out again when she forgot how low the ceiling of the sleeping nook in her private suite was. Then she headed for the door and pressed the panel on the wall to let herself out.

The door didn't budge.

"Come on." She pressed the button again, but instead of the green light blinking beneath her hand, a small red dot flashed, and that was it.

Her Coalition phone wasn't in her pocket anymore. She hoped it hadn't fallen out during any of her recent bouts of unconsciousness. Thankfully, someone had been nice enough to put it on the large desk in her room instead of letting her sleep on it. When she tried to use that system instead of punching buttons, the door still wouldn't open.

"No!" She pounded the door with her fist, then spun and paced across the room.

They don't want me sticking around to fight off that creature. They don't want me to find my family's killers. They don't want me using what's right in front of me to get them a damn picture. Now they don't want me leaving my room. This isn't even my room. I'm supposed to be at school!

With a snarl, she spun and paced back across her newly updated suite.

I don't have time for this. Maybe it's a mistake. The system could be down. Some kind of malfunction. That's what happens when doors don't have actual handles anymore, right?

It took her another minute to calm down enough so she could sit on the floor beside her bed and close her eyes for a deep breath.

I only have to get somebody's attention. They'll come let me out.

Her ghost-wolf surged out of her as soon as she called it up. It raced across her room, phased straight through the closed door, and into the hall. Without having to slow herself on physical feet or paws, Amanda spun toward the central dome at the lab and stopped short.

Dr. Caniss stood right there in front of her in the middle of the hall. Her reading glasses dangled from a lanyard around her neck and her hands were in the pockets of her white lab coat. The woman looked the same as she always did—no expression whatsoever—but she saw Amanda's ghost-wolf trying to slip through the halls to grab someone's attention.

Guess that worked out pretty well. Except for Caniss isn't exactly the shifter I wanna see right now.

"We need to talk," Caniss said flatly. "However, there's no possibility of that if you're floating around this facility without the use of a physical mouth to explain yourself. Get back inside."

Jeeze, she's really pissed.

The lead scientist stepped forward, and her right hand moved inside her pocket.

Amanda and her ghost-wolf stayed where they were to see what the woman would do next.

I don't wanna talk to Caniss. I want Fiona.

With a sigh, Caniss removed a small device that looked like a key fob. "Have it your way, then."

What's she gonna do? Zap my nonexistent body into compliance? Oh, come on—

An electric blue light zapped out of the device and struck Amanda's magic as if her ghost-wolf *did* have a body. Webbing of the same blue light snaked across the wolf of white mist. The power behind it was enough to make Amanda feel absolutely all of it for a fraction of a second before it blasted her back into her body on the other side of the door.

Gasping, she lurched away from the side of the bed and pushed herself to her feet. At the same second, Caniss activated the hydraulic door, which *hissed* briefly before the woman stepped briskly inside.

"What the hell was *that*?" Amanda snarled.

The scientist thumbed the panel on the wall to close the door behind her without taking her eyes off Omega Industries' youngest employee. "Safety precaution."

"You're kidding."

"It's temporary. I will restore access to *all* of your room's amenities and readmission into this facility's mainframe once we

MARTHA CARR & MICHAEL ANDERLE

understand what exactly happened in the Villa Puerto Edén kemana and the expedition camp."

Amanda wrinkled her nose in irritation and glanced at the dark shape barely visible within the pocket of the woman's lab coat. "I meant your…magic clicker."

"That's also a safety precaution."

"What? You don't think I'd try to hurt you with my magic."

"What you would and wouldn't *try* is irrelevant at this point." Caniss approached the spinning desk chair behind the desk and turned it around to sit. "That was made clear before the expedition team cleared that site in South America two days ago."

"Two…days?" Amanda rolled her eyes. "I'm spending more time unconscious than conscious."

"And a lot more time exhibiting powerful magical surges at the same frequencies we've cataloged coming straight from UM-7000."

"Oh, sure." Tossing a flippant hand in the air, Amanda stalked across her room and snorted. "You give *that* one a number everyone can remember."

"It's important we all know what we're dealing with, Amanda. So start talking."

"How should *I* know what we're dealing with?" The girl spun again to pace in the opposite direction. "Even if I did, nobody wants to listen to me."

"I'm not in the habit of performing distasteful tasks without a moderate level of certainty that it will yield beneficial results."

Amanda froze and glared at the scientist. "Did you call me a distasteful task?"

"No, I was referring to the act of coming to your sleeping quarters myself to speak with you in person. *You*, on the other hand, are a pain in my ass and an incredibly expensive liability at the moment. I'm giving you the benefit of the doubt here and a chance to explain to me why I shouldn't walk away like *everyone else*.

"Unless, of course, your narrow escape from becoming a teenage explosive detonated by magic that doesn't belong to you was all it took to make you give up."

Letting out a bitter laugh, Amanda glared at the ceiling and picked up her pacing again.

I should've expected this. Two years coming in and out of this stupid lab. Of course, she figured out what my buttons are. She's not about to let up anytime soon, is she?

"Fine."

"Good. I want to hear everything you remember about your interactions with UM-7000."

"Not for free."

"Were your last two paychecks not enough—"

"I don't want more money, Dr. Caniss. I want the last image pulled from Mel's mind-reader to get used the way it was supposed to be."

Caniss crossed one leg over the other and leaned back in her chair. "You're in no position to barter for information that by all rights belongs to the Coalition of Shifters as a whole and Omega Industries in particular. You're an employed asset of this organization, Amanda. Which means what you know, what you do, what you say, and I might even go so far as to add what you *think* —all of it—belongs to *me*."

"You're insane."

"You're lucky I have no interest in one of those four line items. Don't underestimate my intentions and my ability when I tell you I *will* pry the other three out of you. One way or another."

She is *insane. That was as close to threatening me with torture if I don't give her what she wants.*

"The creature's—"

"UM-7000, I'm assuming."

Amanda gritted her teeth and stared at the wall behind Caniss' head. "Yeah. That one. It's gone."

"We have no data to confirm that claim."

"Right. Because you don't have *any* data."

The woman's single raised eyebrow and a slight shift in the office chair let slip one incredibly useful piece of information.

She doesn't think I know anything. Not so omniscient now, huh?

"That's right." Amanda stormed back across the room. "I heard everyone talking. I know there's no data to read. No trail. No frequency measurements. The thing we were hunting isn't a threat anymore, so it shouldn't still be the top priority."

"I imagine you have an alternate priority in mind—"

"Finding that bastard I blew up an entire machine to get you a picture of! *That's* the priority!"

Caniss sat perfectly still and held the girl's furious gaze.

"Oh my God." Amanda closed her eyes and shook her head. "Fiona didn't tell you who he is."

"I don't study wizards, Amanda."

"He killed my family."

The woman raised both eyebrows this time and folded her hands over her crossed thighs. "I see."

That's it? That's her only reaction? Of course, it is. She's a robot in a shifter's body.

Blinking back the tears threatening to overwhelm her again at the mention of the wizard, Amanda swallowed and lifted her chin. "So when you show me proof that you've run a search on that image and are using every single one of your resources to find him, *then* I'll tell you about 7000."

"It doesn't work that way. However, I'm more than willing to give you my word right now that when you tell me everything you know about UM-7000, I will initiate that search for you."

"No."

"All right." Caniss stood and headed calmly toward the door. "I'll give you some time to think about it. Maybe two days and what I imagine are the remnants of a grueling headache aren't enough to incentivize you."

"You can't lock me up in here against my will."

"Really?" The woman stopped at the door and turned to eye her youngest employee with no more emotion than if she were checking the time. "You're the one complaining about missing your last semester of school. I have nowhere else to be."

She thumbed the control panel beside the door, and Amanda growled in frustration as the hydraulic *hiss* filled the room. "Okay, fine. Fine."

"We'll try this again tomorrow, then."

"No, I mean I'll tell you. Everything. Just…" The girl sighed and gestured toward the door. "Don't keep me here any longer than I have to be."

Another push of the panel, and the door slid closed again before Caniss spread her arms. "I'm listening."

———

When Amanda finished her first account of everything she'd gone through since sneaking into that fateful lab tent to take a whiff of the waste sample as her ghost-wolf, Dr. Caniss bombarded her with question after detailed question. Once those had answers, she made Amanda tell the whole thing over again two more times. Three hours later, Caniss drew a deep breath and nodded. "We're going to run some tests."

"What? No, I don't need tests. I need to figure out who that wizard is so I can find him and the rest of the—"

"It's highly unlikely they'll disappear off the face of this planet before you and I are finished."

"They killed my *family*! What part of that do you not understand?"

"I understand you're upset."

"Don't…don't say that to me right now. Or ever."

Caniss stood from the office chair she'd settled into again for their discussion. "I understand that finding this as-yet-unidentified wizard is in fact *your* top priority. I don't think I have to remind you that we didn't create our technology to fulfill adolescent revenge fantasies, Amanda."

"Oh, for fuck's sake!" With another growl bordering on a scream, Amanda slapped the wall beside her, then turned and sagged against it. "This can't be happening."

"It can either happen right now, and I'll escort you to the medical wing for evaluation, or it can happen later. In which case, I'll still be the one escorting you to the medical wing for evaluation, and you'll be the only sixteen-year-old I've ever heard of who's missing her last semester of high school because she's too stubborn."

Right. I'm the only sixteen-year-old having to deal with any of this crap.

Amanda sighed. "Too stubborn to let you manipulate me into a bunch of tests and scans and probably sedating me again instead of going after *murderers?*"

"No." Caniss clasped her hands behind her back. "Too stubborn to acknowledge that I'm doing this to ensure your safety and because I do in fact care about what happens to you."

"You mean you care about what happens to that creature nobody can find."

The woman looked Amanda over from head to toe and blinked twice. "Right now, UM-7000 is not my top priority. You are."

That alone made what was left of Amanda's angry resistance fizzle out and die.

This is as warm and fuzzy as she's going to get, isn't it? She doesn't say anything she doesn't mean.

Drawing in a long, slow breath, Amanda peeled her back away from the wall. "Okay."

"Okay…"

"Fine. Tests. Let's get this over with."

"Excellent." Caniss opened the door and stepped into the hall.

"When we finish, you'll help me find that wizard, right?"

"I'll do what I can to find a positive match for that picture imprinted from your brainwaves. That doesn't mean the image you gave us is accurate enough to find your family's killers. Or to put them away."

"Trust me. There's nothing wrong with my memory."

The woman merely turned away from the open door to walk swiftly down the hall toward the medical wing. She didn't slow or turn once to make sure Amanda was following her.

She knows I don't have a choice. This sucks so much. I did not *sign up to be a science experiment, no matter how much they pay me.*

CHAPTER FIFTEEN

Amanda realized in the next hour that when Dr. Caniss had said they were running *a few* tests, she had wildly exaggerated. A team of four scientists who hadn't been on the expedition in South America surrounded her once they got to the medical wing. Soon after, the shifter girl was strapped into an exam chair as gently as possible.

Then they got down to all the poking, prodding, and questioning. They strapped electrodes to her arms and chest, drew more blood, and hooked her up to more medical devices than Amanda knew existed for use on a single person. Let alone all at once.

There were a *lot* of tests.

The hours dragged on, and Dr. Caniss stayed in the room to oversee all of it. She didn't ask Amanda any questions or comment on whatever the heck she was trying to find in the shifter girl, focusing instead on muttering directions and new tests to her employees scurrying around the exam chair and constantly checking machines.

It wasn't anything painful or overly invasive, all things

considered. When the team took a twenty-minute break for a quick dinner—and another protein bar for Amanda—she was past the point of being surprised by another three hours of continuous testing after that.

Things didn't start getting bad until the end of those three hours after dinner, when the expressions on every face in the exam room showed nothing but confusion, frustration, complete bafflement, and worry. Even Dr. Caniss looked concerned with whatever results they'd put together from their overeager attempts to *find out what was wrong.*

Great. I either have a magical parasite, or they want me to stay strapped to this chair overnight.

"Do you want to run it again?" one woman asked, lowering her voice as she leaned toward Dr. Caniss and tried not to look at Amanda.

"No. There's no point. We're finished." Caniss briefly met Amanda's gaze, pressed her lips together, then turned to leave the room.

"Okay, what?" Amanda waited patiently for the other shifters to unstrap her from the chair and remove all the devices and wiring. "What did you guys find?"

Nobody would look at her.

"Seriously. You obviously found *something.* What is it?"

"You're probably exhausted after all this, huh?" A smiling woman with the top of a tree tattoo poking up from beneath her shirt collar and climbing up the side of her neck handed Amanda her shoes. "I'll bet Dominique still has something in the mess hall—"

"I don't want food. I want to know what you guys found. Come on. You've been testing me all day, and now you look like someone died." Amanda's weak laugh didn't carry nearly as much weight as she wanted it to. "I'm not dead, so what is it?"

"Come on." The woman completely ignored her questions and

helped the shifter girl out of the chair. "You don't have to eat, but you do have to go back to your room."

"Are you serious?"

"I'm sorry." The woman's weak smile made that part clear as she gestured toward the exam room door and waited for Amanda to exit first.

I can't believe this. They're my test results. I don't even know what the heck they were testing for, but I deserve to know what's making them all freak out like this.

Asking the scientist two more times to give her even a hint about their findings as they hurried through the Canissphere toward Amanda's room didn't get *her* different results either. The only thing her escort told her was that Dr. Caniss would come back to see her if they needed anything else.

Amanda was once again locked up in her cushy Canissphere suite, alone, without her previous freedoms of being able to open the door from the inside and move around the way she wanted.

"This is ridiculous." She paced across her suite again and tried not to lose her temper again.

It shouldn't be this hard. If a bunch of pseudo-doctors won't tell me anything, maybe Fiona will.

When she approached the bed in the recessed sleeping nook, her Coalition phone was gone. Amanda checked under the pillow and the sheets and even under the mattress. Then she checked every drawer in the desk and any other possible hiding spot she could think of, but there was nothing.

"Come on. You had to take my phone too?" With a groan, she climbed onto the thin mattress in the sleeping nook. She couldn't even turn off the lights so she could get to sleep because her Coalition phone controlled the settings in her private room.

If I ever hear Summer say one more thing about feeling like a pris-oner at the Academy, I'll tell her about this. Oh, man. I wanna get back to school...

Amanda was jolted awake by the hydraulic *hiss* of the door sliding open into the wall and Fiona's quick footsteps into her room. She almost launched herself out of bed before remembering that stupid curved ceiling and slowed down to avoid a self-induced concussion. "What's going on?"

"You have some serious explaining to do, kid."

"Come on. There's no way Caniss didn't record our entire conversation yesterday before she turned me into her shifter guinea-pig."

"Oh, she recorded the conversation." Fiona folded her arms and stood in the doorway, but she didn't bother to close the door. "I listened to the whole thing. Which is hard enough to believe on its own, but I know you wouldn't jeopardize your chances of getting out of here by making up a bunch of crap to screw with the doc."

Amanda glanced behind her mentor and into the empty hallway behind her. "You believe me, though, right?"

Fiona shrugged. "Yeah. I believe you."

"Then why does it feel like you're lying to my face?"

Her mentor grimaced and looked away. "There are too many things pointing in completely different directions. Hard to know which ones to pay attention to when you're the only one who had any real experience with that thing in and out of the Villa Puerto Edén kemana."

"You don't believe me at all."

"I'm not lying to you, kid."

"Listen." Amanda stepped forward, feeling like she was about to beg for her life, which was ridiculous.

She's not gonna hurt me. I probably wouldn't believe me either if I were her.

"I know it's weird. Everything that happened is completely nuts, and I'm the only one who was there listening to that creature talk about wanting to rip magic away from Earth. It's not gonna do that. It's gone. I guess I…talked it out of its whole wrath thing."

"Just by talking, huh?"

"Yeah, after I fought an insanely powerful creature that looked like *me*." Amanda scoffed. "Why do you still look so pissed off right now?"

"Because it's not adding up. I don't know what to tell you from here on out."

"Okay. Then how about we drop the creature issue and focus on the wizard."

Fiona shook her head. "Sorry, kid. That's not coming down the pipeline anytime soon."

"*What*? No, Caniss said she'd look into it."

"Then I guess she changed her mind."

"She can't *do* that! I have to find his kind, Fiona. That's part of this whole thing too. The second chance for literally everyone on Earth to convince that thing we can handle magic. Look, I don't know if it can take out every single kemana crystal on the planet, but it wouldn't surprise me at all. That thing told me if we don't start handling the bad stuff in the right way—"

"You're not handling anything right now. Melody took a surprisingly personal interest in this thing, and she's put a hold on almost every other project in this lab so she can focus on sifting through the readings we *did* get from UM-7000 before you…"

Amanda scowled and leaned away from her mentor. "Before I *what*?"

"Got in the way."

"Hey, I saved that kemana from being torn apart! However it happened, the creature's gone. It left. Don't tell me I got in the way!"

"Look, kid. We have no idea what happened, okay? All those

tests? They didn't give us anything useful either. So we've got nothing."

Folding her arms, Amanda looked the redhead woman up and down. "What did the results say?"

"Not much."

"So…what? They were inconclusive?"

"Not exactly."

"Then quit screwing around with me, Fiona. Either they told you something, or they didn't. I've been here long enough to know what *inconclusive* means."

With a heavy sigh, she dropped her chin to her chest and didn't say anything for a long time.

If she's not gonna talk to me, I don't know why she's here.

"Well?"

"Here's the thing. Weird as it is, Amanda, all those test results are… No. They're not inconclusive at all."

"Okay. Then tell me what they said."

Fiona looked up at her mentee from beneath a concerned frown. "Nothing."

"Wait." Amanda huffed out a laugh. "You mean nothing *bad*."

"No, I mean absolutely nothing."

"That doesn't even make sense."

"Tell me about it." Fiona spread her arms in a dramatic gesture of cluelessness. "You had contact with that creature twice. Physically and…psychically, or whatever.

"Then you were radiating the same frequencies and energy blasts as UM-7000, not to mention almost the same *amount*. The only thing that stopped you and put you back together again was forty-eight hours under heavy sedation and…what? An international jet flight?"

Swallowing thickly, Amanda felt suddenly freezing in her fancy suite inside the Canissphere and rubbed her arms. "So there were results, though."

"Yeah. You're not a figment of any of our imaginations, so you have blood cells and a pulse. Congratulations."

"Wouldn't that back up what I've already been telling you guys? You know, that the creature's gone. I mean, it obviously took *all* traces of its magic with it."

"Nope. We still have the samples, and those three kitties you found in the forest are still as messed up as ever. So your theory's a bust. Pack up."

"Maybe it didn't want to leave any evidence behind that I had a conversation with— Hold on." Amanda pointed at her mentor. "Did you tell me to pack my things?"

"Unless you wanna go back to school without your stuff, then yeah. You have twenty minutes, and we're outta here." Fiona turned to leave the room, but the girl darted after her.

"Wait. I can't go until I know someone put that wizard's face through…I don't know. Whatever kind of facial recognition thing you guys have here." Amanda wrinkled her nose. "You do have something like that, right?"

"Not me personally."

"Obviously. Dr. Caniss promised me she'd look into it."

"Yeah, well, you broke a bunch of Omega Industries property, kid. Then you jumped into a private conversation with the only creature in the relatively short history of divergent magical species to give us the slip for five weeks before jumping right off the planet, and we have nothing to show for it. I'm not sure the doc's all that worried about a wizard's ugly face—"

"But *I* am!" Amanda tried to catch her breath and force the angry tears back down again as the redhead turned to face her again.

This time, Fiona's frown was less pissed off and more genuinely, excruciatingly sympathetic. "I know." Her mouth worked open and closed for a moment as if she couldn't decide whether it was a good idea to say something that betrayed how much she didn't like not being able to help. Then she nodded toward the main dome. "Eighteen minutes."

Without another word, Fiona disappeared down the hall, and Amanda closed her eyes.

I can't believe it's all just...ending like this. Fine. They have the guy's face. I'll have to get it back and hunt him down on my own. After I finish school.

CHAPTER SIXTEEN

Despite having a teleportation device and her new blue scooter waiting for her in the entrance tunnel to the Canissphere, Amanda wasn't allowed to make the trip back to the Academy of Necessary Magic all on her own. Fiona had instructions to accompany her. Judging by the woman's scowl as they exited the lab and teleported to the Starbucks train station under Denver, Colorado, Amanda was pretty sure the instructions had come from the top.

She wouldn't do all this because Caniss told her to. Even if the doc said please. Which means Connor Slate probably knows about this whole thing by now too, and now someone has to babysit me like it's my very first time again.

Once they entered the train car and sat—with the Vespa propped awkwardly between them—Fiona handed over Amanda's Coalition phone and sniffed. "Taking this wasn't my idea."

"Okay..." Amanda took her phone and seriously hoped it wasn't dead when she tried to turn it on.

Not dead. Just completely turned off and confiscated. Nice touch.

"It *was* my idea to give it back," Fiona added. "I know that's not a real big consolation, but if Melody called all the shots everywhere all the time, you'd never see that thing again."

"Good thing she doesn't call all the shots," Amanda muttered.

"Yeah." Fiona folded her arms and leaned back against the red velvet cushion of the train cabin's bench before closing her eyes.

In the ten minutes they had until the train sped off at physics-defying speeds, Amanda found four unread texts and two voice-mails on her phone. So she pretended to be completely absorbed by her messages and not feeling the tense, awkward glances Fiona kept shooting her way.

Hey, shifter girl. In case you forgot, it's your damn birthday! This is the only present you get, so don't spend it all in one place.

Despite her frustration with everything that had kept her away from school and her friends and living a normal life as an incredibly abnormal teenage shifter, Amanda couldn't help but smile at Summer's text from her old phone.

Wish I'd seen this earlier. Before they confiscated my phone.

The other three texts were variations of the same Summer-isms.

Happy New Year.

Did the shifter gang let her drink champagne at midnight?

Was Amanda even still alive?

The last text had a very short, obnoxiously cryptic bit added at the end.

Matt's weird. But he won't stop asking about you, so I can't exactly tie him up and dump him in the swamp. Thought you'd like to know.

Matt. What am I supposed to tell him when I get back? What am I supposed to tell any of them?

She listened to the two voicemails next, also from her old phone in Summer's possession. They contained pretty much the same sentiments from Amanda's best friend, but the rest of Amanda's friends had joined her to toss in brief messages before Summer yelled at them to quit trampling her and let her make a stupid phone call in peace.

Amanda's weak laughter cut out instantly when Matt's voice ended the second message.

"Wherever you are, I hope it's better than being stuck here with these whackos. Your friends are insane—"

A round of laughter cut him off, then Summer snarled something and ended the message.

Amanda closed her eyes and held her phone with both hands in her lap.

It wasn't better. Not even a little bit. I don't know how I'm supposed to focus on school or friends or Matt when I'm the only one in the last four years who found that wizard. Now I'm apparently the only one who even cares about catching him.

When the train announced the two-minute countdown to departure, she sent a quick text back to Summer and hoped her best friend wasn't too busy to see it.

On the way back.

She didn't have the energy to write anything more than that because anything else would have felt like an empty lie. For the first time since she'd lost her family and Johnny Walker had taken her in as his ward, Amanda didn't feel like she could keep pretending everything was okay after this. Right now, it wasn't.

It was a small stroke of luck that when Fiona led her up the back staircase of the Everglades City Starbucks and into the parking lot, the woman had no interest in accompanying Amanda the rest of the way back to the Academy. "Focus on school, kid. Everything else is extra at this point."

Amanda didn't bother replying to that but got on her Vespa, strapped on her helmet, and sped south toward the hidden back roads that would take her straight through the middle of the Everglades. School was what felt like "extra." Still, she had to go. She didn't care if Fiona got a little hurt by the lack of goodbye or a thank you for the tense chaperoning.

Wouldn't hurt her nearly as much as her telling me going after that wizard is 'just extra.' She doesn't even wanna help me.

When she made it back to the school grounds and brought her scooter to a wobbly stop in the gravel lot at the end of the drive past the gates, she found Shep already waiting there for her with a giant, gap-toothed grin. "Well, look who it is."

"Hey."

"Now, don't you worry yourself one bit 'bout what to do with that ride, Miss Coulier." The school's driver and resident groundskeeper stared at the Vespa with wide eyes and rubbed his hands together. "I ain't never been on one of these before. How 'bout I take it back to the garage and park it real careful by the pickup van, huh?"

"Thanks, Shep." She left the keys in the ignition and offered him an incredibly weak smile before heading across the central field toward the girls' dorm.

The wizard was too excited by his chance to get on a brand-new scooter to notice the shifter girl's darkened mood. The gentle rev of the scooter's relatively small engine and Shep's whooping laughter followed her across the field.

The only thing she could think about was getting back to her room and being completely alone without being yelled at, interrogated, tested, or locked up with nothing to do but wait until someone decided to come open the door and yell at her some more. She didn't look up at any of the other students milling around the field. None of her friends shouted at her or hurried toward her to bombard her with a million more questions.

Good. They're probably doing something fun right now. None of them have to deal with any of this crap.

Stepping into her dorm room after nearly six weeks of being gone and sleeping on a squeaky cot on the outskirts of the Chilean rainforest brought Amanda the first bit of relief she'd had since waking up at the Canissphere. Everyone at the lab still thought their last mission was a complete failure. No one had believed Amanda's story of convincing the creature now known as UM-7000 to leave Earth alone because there was still good in the world and magicals and that they all deserved another chance.

She dropped her backpack on the floor and flopped face-first onto her bed.

Maybe I was wrong. Maybe I should've let that thing destroy the kemana crystal and keep moving until they were all gone. It's not like anyone would blame me *for letting it happen. They blame me for stopping it.*

Her limbs were so heavy, her eyelids drooped, and even though Amanda's legs still dangled halfway off the side of her bed, she dozed off into an emotionally exhausted half-sleep until a knock at the door startled her awake again.

With a snort, she jerked her head up and tried to tell whoever it was to go away. The only sound that came out of her instead was a garbled groan ending in an agitated growl.

"Yep. She's back, all right. Hey, shifter girl!" Summer pounded much more loudly on the door. "Open up!"

"Hey, maybe she wants to be alone for a while," Grace muttered. "I mean, she's been gone a long time. *Working.* Maybe she's asleep."

"Are you kidding me? *Her?*" Summer snorted and knocked again. "Since when does she sleep in the middle of the day when we don't have class, and her best friends are standing right outside her door? Amanda!"

"Okay, okay." Amanda pushed herself off the bed and staggered toward the door with another groan. "Just *please* stop knocking..."

"See? Told you she's not asleep."

"Not after you've been banging on her door and yelling at her," Grace hissed.

Amanda opened the door and braced herself with a hand on the doorframe. "Hey."

"Hey? *Hey?*" Summer barked out a laugh and spread her arms. "That's all we get? Jeeze, I thought we were harder to forget than that, shifter girl."

Grace's eyes widened as she looked Amanda up and down. "You look awful."

The rainbow-haired witch burst out laughing and pounded the wall beside the door.

"I mean, not that there's anything wrong with that," Grace blurted. "You're tired. Totally understandable. We just... We missed you. You didn't even stop at the cafeteria to say hi."

"Yeah. Sorry." Amanda shrugged. "I'm kind of a zombie right now."

Summer snickered. "Yeah, we all know what *that* looks like. Wasn't from staying up all night with Ladykiller running all naked and furry through the swamp, though—"

Grace elbowed her in the ribs with a warning scowl.

"What? He's been here with *us* the whole time."

"Guys, I'm sorry." Amanda grimaced and started to close the door. "I'm not in the mood right now. For anything. So I'm gonna try to get some—"

"Hold up." Summer slammed her hand on the door to keep it from closing. "What the hell happened?"

"I don't wanna talk about it."

"Uh-huh. Blondie, *you* ask her."

Grace scratched the back of her head and shrugged. "You don't…you know. Look like yourself. Everything okay?"

"Totally. Yeah." Amanda pursed her lips in fake apathy and nodded. "I saved the entire planet from getting all the magic sucked out of it for the rest of forever, and now I'm on probation."

"Whoa!" Summer snorted. "You got arrested?"

"No, Summer. From my job."

"Wait, your shifter gang got you arrested?" The witch looked thoroughly confused. "What happened to 'snitches get stitches?'"

Grace stared at her in disbelief. "It's like getting suspended."

"Except I skipped right over the detention part," Amanda added dryly.

Summer rolled her eyes. "I know what it means. Damn. That sucks, shifter girl."

"Yeah. Like I said, I'm tired, so…"

"We'll let you get some rest." Grace gave her a tight smile and roughly grabbed the sleeve of Summer's black hoodie to haul the other witch away from the door. "Come find us when you're feeling better."

Summer struggled to pull herself out of the other girl's grip. "What are you doing?"

"She can't get any rest with us standing right there and asking her stupid questions, can she?"

"Hey, I can stand wherever I want. She doesn't own the whole third floor."

Shaking her head, Grace tightened her grip and tugged Summer even more forcefully down the hall. "Glad you're home, Amanda."

"Yeah, thanks." Amanda shut her door and braced herself against it with both hands, drawing slow, deep breaths.

Home. No, if I were home, I'd have help finding that murdering bastard. Johnny wouldn't tell me to suck it up and forget about it because my weird test results were more important. He'd be the first one to help me track down that wizard, and he'd probably be the first one to cuff him and take him in if I wanted.

She shook her head and spun dejectedly to shuffle toward her bed again.

The only proof I have of who that asshole is and how to find him is sitting somewhere in the Coalition's giant system, doing absolutely nothing. I should've gone to Johnny first.

The second she flopped down on the bed again and closed her eyes, another knock came at the door.

"Seriously?"

"Miss Coulier?"

Amanda shoved herself off the mattress and turned to glare at the door.

What's Glasket doing here?

"It's Dean Glasket," the principal added with another gentle knock. "Under different circumstances, I would have waited until the official start of the semester to speak with you, but this is something of a time-sensitive matter. Please open the door."

Feeling like she weighed a million pounds, Amanda slogged across her room one more time to open the door and didn't care that she probably looked ready to attack the principal waiting for her on the other side. "What time-sensitive matter?"

Glasket's eyes widened briefly, then she plastered on a completely unconvincing smile and nodded. "May I come in?"

Rolling her eyes, Amanda went back to her bed and sat on the edge of it while Glasket closed the door. It remained open by half an inch, but anyone passing the shifter girl's dorm room wouldn't have any problem recognizing that the conversation was still private.

"First of all, Miss Coulier, I want you to know that Dr. Caniss has already informed me of what you've been dealing with over the last few months…off campus."

Amanda gave the woman a deadpan stare. "Probably the version *she* wants you to hear."

"Is there anything you'd like to add? For clarification?"

Right. Like I'm gonna sit here and complain to my principal about how closed-minded my top-secret employer is or how they won't let me hunt down my family's murderers.

"Not really."

"I understand." Glasket glanced around the room and clasped her hands in front of her. "I'm sorry that the situation forced you to put all that aside for now. Your work with Dr. Caniss and Ms. Damascus, of course. As well as your...more *personal* endeavors."

The girl snorted. "Endeavors. Right."

"I know it must be hard, Amanda."

Being called by her first name made the girl widen her eyes, and when she looked up to meet Glasket's gaze, the woman couldn't have looked more genuinely concerned.

She really is sorry. Unless she's sorry enough to do something, it doesn't help me right now, does it?

"Nonetheless, I'm very glad you've returned to the Academy unharmed and in full health."

"Thanks," Amanda muttered.

"That said, I'm also here to remind you of the meetings I've scheduled for you with your teachers. We expected you back sooner than this, but since classes start in two days, most of them have been pushed back for later in the week once you've had more of an opportunity to...settle back into your routine."

"Most of them?"

The principal looked even more uncomfortable with this part of the conversation than she had at the mention of Amanda's failed mission and the murderer she'd let walk right out of that kemana scot-free. "Mr. Petrov feels it's in your best interest to hold your final sparring session with him *before* classes start. To wrap up the end of last semester, of course."

"In my best interest." Amanda pushed her hands into the mattress behind her to prop herself up and leaned back. "He can't wait 'til I'm in his class on Monday?"

"He was very insistent. Unfortunately, I can't seem to change his mind."

Great. I'm back at school with way too much unfinished business, and I have to kick off my last semester by fighting a teacher who can't wait to get back at me for the last time I kicked his ass.

"Fine." She shrugged. "When am I supposed to fight him?"

"I'm sorry?"

"The...sparring session, I mean."

Glasket pressed her lips together. "Eleven-thirty tomorrow morning. You'll have to postpone lunch until afterward."

"I think I'll be fine."

"I'm glad you understand." Glasket drew a deep breath as though she meant to say something else, then apparently decided against it and turned to swing the door open. Amanda thought the woman was going to walk right out without another word—which she would have preferred—but the principal stopped halfway through the doorway. "I hope you know that if there's anything you need, you can come to me."

"Okay."

"I'm not only talking about alchemy or gardening supplies in lieu of stealing from the Academy storerooms in the west wing. Even if it's more...personal, my office is always open."

Amanda nodded. "Thanks."

"Of course."

After Glasket closed the door behind her, Amanda groaned and dropped onto her back on the bed.

Anything I need, huh? She can't help me with what I need, and the shifters who can, won't lift a finger. I thought senior year was supposed to be better than all the others.

CHAPTER SEVENTEEN

Amanda didn't say much at all during breakfast with her friends the next morning. Jackson and Alex didn't look all that surprised to see her in one of her worst moods yet, which meant Grace and Summer had already told them what little there was to tell from yesterday. No one asked her about the second half of last semester she'd spent away from the Academy or why she hadn't come back when she was supposed to. Much less what she'd been doing for the last six weeks since then.

Her friends joked around like normal, almost as if Amanda wasn't even there. Even if they'd tried to involve her more in the conversations, she wouldn't have been more engaged. It was way too easy to tune out altogether, which didn't help. Because when she tuned out, her mind kept going back to only two things over and over.

The threat UM-7000 made of finishing what it started if "nothing changed" on Earth, and the memory of the sneering wizard turning away from her in the Villa Puerto Edén kemana without an ounce of recognition.

Those thoughts should have been incentive enough to make Amanda focus on her friends or what she still had to look forward to during her last semester of bounty-hunter school, but she couldn't. Not yet.

She left the outdoor cafeteria before anyone else and spent the rest of the morning alone in her room.

By the time she stepped into the training building for her second sparring session that Petrov apparently thought was way too overdue, the rest of the student body had gathered in the central field for Glasket's obligatory start-of-the-semester announcements.

I might be missing lunch, but at least I don't have to stand there listening to Glasket get all sappy about the end of our senior year.

Petrov, however, didn't look any happier to be here than he ever looked standing beside the stage while the Academy of Necessary Magic's principal addressed the students. The bald Combat Training teacher stood in the center of the sparring mats lining the one-room building, his arms folded as he silently watched Amanda remove her shoes and set them in the small available space inside the door.

When she turned to face him, he raised an eyebrow. "Thought you were so special, you could talk your way out of this with a whole bunch of excuses, huh?"

She glared at him as she walked across the mat toward the designated sparring circle taped off in the center, and UM-7000's words raced through her mind again.

"What makes you so special?"

Maybe it's that everyone else wants to tell me I'm not.

Petrov cocked his head when she stopped outside the circle. "Nothing to say to that, Coulier?"

For the first time since she'd started at the Academy, Amanda stopped caring about how Petrov would take anything she said, so she blurted the first thing that came to mind. "Let's

143

get to the part where I kick your ass again so I can get to lunch."

He snorted and raised his eyebrows. "At least you're finally taking this seriously. Let's see what you got."

They both stepped into the circle, and she spread her arms. "You gonna try to take me off-guard again, or—"

"Quit stalling and come at me, Coulier!"

With a snarl, she launched herself at Petrov and did what he'd said.

He blocked her first three punches and narrowly avoided a fourth before she clocked him in the jaw. The wizard didn't have time to recover from the shock of that blow before she brought her knee up into his gut and made him double over with a grunt. Then she shoved him away by the shoulders and stepped back to pace her side of the circle again.

"That's…" Petrov grunted again and slowly straightened. "That's more like it. You should've kept going."

A low growl rose from the shifter girl's throat. "I thought this was supposed to last the whole two-and-a-half hours."

"Yeah, and I think you chickened out when you realized you're ready for this."

"You *want* me to hurt you? 'Cause that's—"

"I want you to quit screwing around!" Petrov spread his arms. "If you can't tell the difference between when to hold back and when to quit stuffing yourself into a shape that doesn't fit you, Coulier, you'll never make it."

"I'm not—"

"If you don't give this a hundred and ten percent, you won't pass my class, and you'll be stuck here another year! Got it?"

All the anger and frustration she'd been bottling up since her overwhelmingly anticlimactic tests at the Canissphere and the Coalition's refusal to help track her family's killer burst through the walls she'd tried to hold up around them. She leapt at him again, and this time, she didn't hold anything back.

Amanda pressed him with everything she had, swinging fists and ducking Petrov's rare attacks when he could get a good shot in. They moved back and forth across the sparring ring, blocking and stepping around each other. He couldn't catch her to pull her in and get her in a deadlock, and she couldn't land another blow like the first one because now he knew she would.

"Let's go!" Petrov barked.

She feinted right and jabbed with her left, but the teacher caught her fist and clamped his other hand around her wrist before jerking her toward him.

"You're better than this," he growled.

"You're not." The second she thought about smashing her head against his to prove her point, a burst of smoky-white light surged out of her, and her ghost-wolf snarled in his face instead.

Petrov reeled backward with wide eyes and almost tripped over his surprise. Amanda didn't give him time to recover. She socked him in the gut, caught the side of his ribs with a right hook, then hooked her left arm around the back of his neck and kneed him in the stomach again.

Grunting, he grappled with the shifter girl, who was much smaller and only a little faster but far more furious. When he kicked one of her legs from out beneath her, and they both tumbled to their knees on the mat, Petrov got in a similar shot to her ribcage before Amanda's magic surged all on its own.

Her ghost-wolf leapt out again—not completely and not with her awareness leaving her body but enough to bring a misty white claw slashing down around Petrov's arm as he struggled to pin the shifter girl down in an armlock.

He roared and released her instantly, but she was already on her feet and spinning around to deliver a roundhouse kick to the side of his head.

Petrov reeled, dropped onto his side, and rolled over onto his back to kick her away from him before he quickly leapt backward and stood.

Apparently, he was over trying to goad her into a real sparring session where fighting as an outlet for anger and resentment wasn't off the table.

For the next half hour, they let each other have it. By then, they were both breathing heavily and stumbling around the sparring ring on the mat.

Only when Petrov raised a hand for her to stop so he could prop his hands on his thighs and take a break did she notice the blood splattered across the circle. She wiped her mouth with the back of a hand and figured it could've been from the split in her lip.

That's gonna hurt tomorrow even more than it hurts now.

"Okay." Clearing his throat, Petrov straightened and stretched out his neck, although he wasn't quite able to roll his shoulders back completely. "We're done."

"Seriously?" Amanda huffed out a laugh, but it was weak and didn't quite get across her agitation the way she wanted. She was too out of breath. "All this crap about not being able to miss one of these sessions. So you schedule it for the day before classes start again, and you can't even go a full hour?"

The teacher shot her a deadpan glare. "Neither can you, looks like."

"I'm not giving up."

"I never said you were, Coulier." Drawing a deep breath, Petrov studied the blood smeared across the mat and probably on both their clothes, then shook his head. "That was good."

"That's it?" She spread her arms and winced at the pain in her shoulder briefly flaring above the pain everywhere else. "That's all you're gonna say?"

"Yeah. That's all I got for you. 'Cause we both know you've got hand-to-hand covered, and there's not a whole lot more I can teach you about fighting at this point."

Amanda blinked in surprise and swallowed. Her throat was raw and dry from however many times she'd screamed and snarled during their short-lived match, plus how heavily she was breathing on top of it. "You're not screwing with me?"

"Do I look like I'm screwing with you?"

A tiny smile flickered at the corner of her mouth and immediately made her split and swollen lip feel like it was about to tear itself open even more. "I guess not."

"Good. But we might have to work on your anger issues."

"I don't have anger issues."

Raising an eyebrow, Petrov lifted his forearm in front of himself to show her the claw marks slashed across his flesh. Blood dripped from his arm to splatter even more onto the mat.

Holy crap. I didn't even shift. Was that...my magic?

She swallowed again, tried to clear her throat, and offered him a half-hearted shrug. "So you got a few scratches. I have a split lip."

"Uh-huh. Just a flesh wound for both of us."

That's his blood all over the mat.

"Okay, fine." With a sigh, Amanda swiped loose strands of hair away from her face and peeled the rest of it off her sweaty cheek and neck. "Maybe I got a little angry. You told me to—"

"Forget what I told you. You were pissed before you got here. *Those* anger issues." Sniffing, he nodded toward the door before grabbing a rag from the shelves full of junk lining the walls of the training building. "You can go."

"Really?"

All it took was one warning stare from the Combat Training teacher to get her moving again. She stumbled toward her shoes and didn't bother to put them on before slamming the door open with one hand and staggering outside into the early afternoon sunshine.

Anger issues. He doesn't even know the half of it, and now he wants to work on them? *Right. That's exactly what I need right now.*

Rolling her eyes, she picked up the pace across the main field and headed straight for the outdoor cafeteria. The noise from the

147

entire student body eating lunch at the picnic tables under the pavilion echoed across the grounds. Then her growling stomach and the need to down at least three glasses of water drowned out everything else.

She knew the other kids would stare at her for showing up looking like she did after her sparring session with Petrov. Somehow, all the stares and whispered speculation made the whole thing worth it.

At least there's still food. They can stare all they want. I'm over it.

Her friends weren't immune either to the shock of seeing the Academy's shifter girl bloody and bruised when she sat at their usual table and dropped her plate in front of her. Amanda chugged the entire plastic cup of water in one breath before hunching over to dig into the baked chicken and green beans piled high on her dish.

Summer winced and pointed at her. "Petrov, huh?"

"Had to get that second sparring session in before classes started. You know, 'cause it's that important." Amanda shoveled more food into her mouth and didn't look up at anyone.

Jackson glanced around the table and wrinkled his nose. "So did he let you out early because he didn't wanna kill you, or..."

"He has nothing left to teach me."

Grace let out a nervous chuckle. "What's that supposed to mean?"

"I don't know. Ask *him*."

The table fell awkwardly silent as her friends watched her eat, and the rest of the student body decided the shifter girl wasn't interesting anymore before they picked up their conversations again.

"You think maybe you should go see Nurse Aiken?"

"I'm fine."

"But your lip's—"

"Grace." Amanda looked up at the blonde witch from across the table, and while she was perfectly aware of how pissed off she must have still looked, she didn't have it in her to try on an expression that didn't match what was going on inside. "I said I'm fine."

"Okay. Sure."

"Shifter healing, Blondie." Summer clicked her tongue. "Don't forget that part."

"So, who looks worse?" Alex crunched down on a double-chocolate cookie and spilled crumbs all over his empty plate. "You or the sergeant?"

Amanda didn't answer that one, and Grace gave the Wood Elf a warning look before he shrugged.

"Just curious. 'Cause last time it was pretty bad."

"Yeah, for *him*." Jackson snickered. "How about when *you* came out of there the last time? Dude, I was so sure he'd broken your arm."

"Nope. Just dislocated."

"Okay, can we stop talking about sparring?" Grace interrupted. "I don't wanna think about what we'll have to do this semester for that class."

"You're gonna have to think about it sooner or later," Summer added as she popped the end of a green bean into her mouth. "We're going right back into that training building tomorrow—"

"So let's stop talking about it until tomorrow." The blonde witch fixed Summer with a tight, irritated smile and nodded. "Thanks."

"I bet it's nothing compared to what Coulier got to do out on her secret missions." Jackson jerked his chin up at Amanda and drummed his fingers on the table. "They train you way better than Petrov, don't they?"

"They never trained me how to fight." Amanda tore the drumstick of the baked chicken away from the attached thigh with a *crunch*. "They're not much better at anything else."

Jackson's smile faded, and he went back to picking at what remained on his plate.

A small, buried part of Amanda felt bad for bringing her bad attitude and even worse mood to the table with her friends, but she couldn't help it.

I need to focus on school. Starting tomorrow, that's what I'll do. They're not gonna blame me for not wanting to talk about anything when I look like this.

"Okay, that's it." Summer pounded a fist on the table. "What the hell happened to you, shifter girl?"

"Summer," Grace chided.

"No way, Blondie. I'm not gonna sit here pretending like everything's okay when she's pissed off and won't even *look at us.*"

Amanda swallowed her chicken, then looked up to meet Summer's gaze before reaching out to grab her friend's water. Summer stared at her until the shifter girl drained that too, then Amanda pressed her lips together and took a deep breath. "Look, guys. I'm sorry I'm in a crappy mood."

"It sucks," Summer muttered.

"I know. I just…I don't really wanna talk about any of it—"

"Bullshit." Summer pointed at her. "The way you're acting right now says you *do* wanna talk about it. I know. 'Cause you're acting like *me* on a bad day, and I hate it."

Jackson and Alex snorted and ducked their heads.

"Yeah, keep laughing, but you jerkoffs know I'm right."

Grace bit her lip and studied Amanda with a concerned frown. "She *is* right, Amanda. This is exactly what Summer does. So why don't you tell us what happened?"

"Fine." Amanda wiped her mouth with a napkin and *hissed* when she handled her split lip too roughly. She tossed the napkin back onto the table and sighed. "Then you guys can't keep asking me more questions about it for the next week or month or however long you can keep it up, okay?"

"Well, yeah." Summer chuckled. "If you tell us right now, why would we need to keep asking?"

"Because that's what you do."

"All right, shifter girl. On my honor." Summer raised her hand, grinned, and flipped Amanda the middle finger.

The guys cracked up laughing.

Grace shook her head and tried to hide a smile.

Amanda couldn't help but smile herself despite how much it hurt her swollen lip. "Yeah. Some honor."

"You know I'm good for it."

So Amanda gave them a very short, very summarized rundown of everything that had happened since the day she'd left the Canissphere on her scooter, thinking she was heading back to the Academy. This time, she didn't bother trying to leave out the details of what the Coalition didn't want her to share with anyone—which for this particular mission was probably everything.

The only thing she didn't mention at all was having smelled and seen, then tried to destroy the wizard who'd killed her family, plus everything related to her desperate attempts to find him again.

So what if they think I broke Mel's machine for fun? I can't talk about the wizard right now. That's too much.

Her friends didn't seem to think there was a giant hole in her abridged story, and it helped a little to see Grace wasn't completely freaking out about UM-7000's threat to return if the world didn't kick itself into gear and shape up with its magic.

All she said about that was, "You *would* be the only one to talk a mind-reading blob out of destroying magicals on Earth."

Everyone was shocked to hear something like that come out of the blonde witch's mouth, but it was broken by Summer's unrestrained cackle and Jackson and Alex catching her contagious laughter a second later.

Amanda smirked and went back to eating her food.

I guess I am. Still doesn't make me special. Still doesn't take away my real problems right now either.

CHAPTER EIGHTEEN

The first week of classes didn't offer nearly as much of a distraction as Amanda had hoped it would. Monday and Tuesday were full of short, fairly useless announcements by all their teachers, reminding the senior class of their self-directed learning for their last semester. The teachers would be available to discuss any hiccups in their projects if needed. Beyond that, it was up to the seniors to figure it out on their own.

Having as much free time this semester didn't help with Amanda's lack of motivation. If they'd had to be in classes all day every day like the last three years, she would've been able to take her mind off how angry and irritable and plain *helpless* she felt. As the week drew out into one long, seemingly endless string of trying not to lose her temper at every little annoyance, she started to realize how pointless being at the Academy of Necessary Magic was.

The only thing that broke up the monotony was Petrov's announcement that he'd canceled their first two classes that week, and he wouldn't have more information for them until they met again on Friday.

"Probably 'cause he's still trying to recover from you clobbering him," Summer muttered.

Amanda had already noticed the bald teacher was wearing a long-sleeved shirt to cover up the dressed gouge wounds on his forearm.

When the seniors finally gathered in the training room to get Petrov's big reveal for what "the fun stuff" in Combat Training was, none of them expected to see three large transport crates lined up across the room. Or the wild look in Petrov's eyes as the class gathered.

"He looks...happy." Grace narrowed her eyes. "That's not a good sign."

"Yeah, what's with the crates?" Jackson whispered.

Alex folded his arms. "I bet it's where he puts the bodies of seniors who don't graduate."

Summer laughed.

"All right, listen up." Petrov paced in front of the crates, blocking their contents from view as he sized the seniors up with the hint of a smile. "I'm surprised every single one of you managed to hold your own with sparring sessions last semester. Honestly, I expected more of you to cry. Since you all survived, it's time to move on to the real gold in this class. You've been working toward this for the last three-and-a-half years, so don't screw it up."

The teacher stopped at the first crate, flipped up the two massive locks, and hauled open the lid to let it drop back on its hinges with a *bang*. Then he did the same with the next two crates. The seniors all craned their necks to get a better view, standing on tiptoes to look over shoulders and peering around their friends.

"You've fought with your magic. I won't say any of you mastered hand-to-hand combat, but it's good enough. You handled relatively dangerous close-range weapons, which didn't completely disappoint me at the very least. Now, we get to see how you do with—"

"Guns." Summer grinned and stepped toward the open crates.

"Hey!" Petrov snapped his fingers and pointed at her. "Get back in line, Flannerty."

"Are you serious?"

"Did she say guns?"

"He didn't say she was wrong."

"I can't see anything."

"Quiet!" the teacher barked. "Yes. Firearms. These in here are as close as you're gonna get at this school to handling real weapons. No bullets in these, but they pack a punch just the same. Upgrades from the fun little snipers set up on the obstacle course, and I know you all remember those."

Another wave of murmuring disbelief filled the training room. Most of the seniors looked as excited as Petrov. Grace looked terrified.

"So here's the deal." The teacher glanced into the open crates and smirked. "First half of the semester, we'll be going off-campus for each class period to test these out at a shooting range. Yeah, it's out in the middle of nowhere so you lunatics won't end up shooting an innocent bystander instead of a target. I expect you to get a handle on these real fast because after spring break, we're taking these with us to the games."

"Um…what?" Tommy asked.

"You got a problem with games, Brunsen?"

"No."

"Good. I'm not telling any of you a single thing about them until you come back from spring break and it's time to get started. Except for you better believe your senior year's about to get real. Mr. LeFor helped me make a few new improvements to the games, so you should count yourselves lucky. Last year's seniors had to fumble their way through the whole thing."

"Well, *that* doesn't make it sound any better," Jackson whispered.

Grace stared with wide eyes at the crates.

Summer rubbed her hands together and looked like she was getting ready to sit down to eat an entire cake by herself.

"Any questions?" Petrov scanned the stunned senior class and didn't leave anyone time to raise a hand. "Good. I'm not answering any. We start this on Monday, so if you have issues with holding a firearm, get over it. Have a great weekend."

For a moment, no one knew if he was messing with them or if he'd dismissed the class. When he turned his back to storm toward the tiny cubicle of an office at the back of the training building, the seniors got the hint and took off in a mob toward the door.

"Coulier!"

Crap.

Amanda caught Grace's concerned glance and shrugged before turning to face the teacher.

He's gonna call me out in front of everybody, isn't he?

"Yeah?"

Petrov waved her forward, then folded his arms and leaned against his office door as the shifter girl wove through the current of seniors hurrying to get outside and start their weekend earlier than all the other students. When she reached him, he looked her up and down and nodded. "I get that you don't always know when you're gonna get snatched up by… whatever you're doing for whoever it is off-campus."

"What?"

"Your…thing. Job or whatever. I don't care. When you're at school, you're coming to meet me here every Saturday night after dinner, and you and I are gonna work on your anger management problems."

Amanda widened her eyes and looked over her shoulder to see the last senior racing out of the building.

155

Of course, he doesn't care if anyone hears him.

"You want me to…"

"It's not what I want, Coulier. It's what you need. Don't tell me you don't have anger issues. We covered that last weekend."

"Seriously?" Her shoulders sagged as she glanced around the room. "I don't need help, okay? And I don't need it from—"

"Glasket approved it. You don't have to like it, but it's happening. Get out."

"I…"

Petrov opened his office door, slipped inside, and shut it again. His head disappeared from view beneath the window in the door. Amanda stood there in stunned silence for another ten seconds before turning away.

Anger management with Petrov? *What the hell is Glasket thinking? That's only gonna make it worse.*

It was a good thing none of her friends asked her why Petrov wanted her to stay after his announcement because she didn't think she could handle having to explain it. That she'd slashed up his arm during their sparring session. That he thought she had enough of a problem with handling her anger that he'd gone to *Glasket* to pitch his stupid anger management idea. Or that the principal had agreed with him and had added it to Amanda's new schedule.

At least if I get called away by the Coalition again, he won't expect me to tune in for anger management *over the phone.*

———

She spent most of that Saturday in her dorm room, searching through her Coalition phone and what little information she had access to on the Coalition network. Of course, there wasn't anything on the surface that hinted at getting into Dr. Caniss' records or somehow finding that image of the wizard the doctor had stored away.

Looking for information on the status of the facial recognition search Caniss had promised her and failed to deliver—or even to start—only made Amanda's mood that much worse as the day progressed.

By the time she got to dinner, her friends had picked up on the fact that she wasn't anywhere close to approachable and didn't look at her. The shifter girl sat at the end of the picnic table's bench, shoveled her food into her mouth without really tasting it, and didn't have to answer questions or pretend to laugh at jokes that weren't funny.

Nothing was funny anymore. Nothing was even *fun*. How could it be?

How could she be herself when she fought off an insanely powerful creature who wanted to destroy all magic on Earth and probably every magical with it? When she had to deal with all this crap at school and in classes and self-directed learning? Much less when one of her family's killers was still out there somewhere in South America, living his life as if no one could touch him?

Without saying anything to her friends, Amanda snatched up her empty dinner dishes and stormed across the outdoor cafeteria to toss everything in the trash and bus bin. She felt her friends looking at her in confusion and concern, but what was she supposed to tell them?

Sorry, guys. I have to learn how to deal with my anger from a guy who screams at high school kids for a living. Be back soon.

She shook her head and trudged across the training field to meet Petrov in the building.

Yeah, right. No one would buy that anyway, and I'm pretty sure I'm not learning shit.

The door to the training building was already open, and Amanda stepped inside to find a completely different setup on the mats than she'd expected.

Two metal folding chairs had been brought into the center

sparring circle, resting six feet apart and facing each other. Behind them stood Petrov, his face a blank mask she couldn't read before he glanced at his watch. "You're early."

"You said after dinner. It's after dinner."

"Uh-huh. Close the door. Then pick a chair."

What is this? How to Throw Chairs When You're Pissed? Fun class.

Frowning, she pulled the door shut with a heavy *thud*, crossed the mats, and stopped behind the chair on the right.

The teacher raised an eyebrow. "You're in a literal mood tonight, aren't you? Feel free to leave that at the door on Saturdays. Or not. If you're trying to get under my skin like this, Amanda, it's not gonna work."

Widening her eyes, she stared at the bald teacher as he removed his other hand from behind his back and sat in the other chair, lowering a single piece of paper into his lap.

He called me Amanda. What the hell is going on?

"Okay. You picked your chair." Without looking at her, Petrov removed a pair of reading glasses from the breast pocket of his shirt and unfolded them with one hand before sliding them onto his face. "Now's the part where you sit in it."

"Just sit?"

"Exactly."

He doesn't even look like he wants to fight. I didn't know he did anything else.

Slowly, she walked around the chair and sank into it. Her hands clammed up immediately because this was all wrong—a calm Petrov, chairs instead of a sparring circle. The guy was wearing *glasses* to look over a paper in his hand and acting like all this was supposed to help her somehow.

When he looked up at her, Petrov's patient smile caught her more off-guard than anything else. It wasn't a grin by any stretch of the imagination, but he suddenly didn't look like nearly as much of a jerk. He didn't look like Petrov at all.

She folded her arms and looked him up and down. "What is this?"

The teacher leaned forward and extended the piece of paper toward her. "My credentials."

"Your what?"

"Take it. Look 'em over. If you have any doubts that I'm the right magical for what we're about to do, that should clear them up. Feel free to ask questions. If you have any."

Amanda took the sheet of paper and *thumped* back in her chair again, fixing Petrov with a suspicious scowl until she finally forced herself to look down and read what he'd given her.

His credentials? What the hell are we doing here?

That made itself mind-numbingly clear by the first few lines making up the header at the top of the page: Marcus Petrov—LCP; C.A.T.S.M.; CAMF.

Below that was nothing short of an impressive curriculum vitae—an entire career over forty-seven years that listed Marcus Petrov, Licensed Clinical Psychologist, as an accomplished professional specializing in acute traumatic stress management and anger management facilitation.

Amanda barked a laugh. "Is this a joke?"

"Nope. But I see how you might think that."

She waved the paper at him. "You teach Combat Training. At a bounty-hunter school."

"Yeah, well…" Petrov removed his glasses and tucked them back into his shirt pocket with a shrug. "Sometimes you have to leave your passion projects behind for the greater good. Which, in my case, means teaching a bunch of adolescent teenagers how to fight. Prepare them for their futures. I know. Seems like a massive jump from one extreme to the other, but sometimes there's a little overlap."

"What—"

"Anger management, Amanda." He stood, leaned toward her, and snatched the paper out of her hands before dropping back into his seat. Then he tossed it aside and let it flutter to the mat before crossing one leg over the other. "I think we both understand that fighting me for class credit won't do a thing to help you with what's going on right now."

She stared at the paper, which had landed face-up with Petrov's name and abbreviated certifications right at the top in large, bold lettering. Like it was mocking her.

"I can't talk about what's going on right now," she muttered, too dazed to look up at him.

This has to be a joke. He's screwing with me. No way is anything on that piece of paper real.

Petrov cleared his throat. "Maybe not the details of your job, but you can talk about how you *feel*."

Hearing those words from her Combat teacher's mouth made her look sharply up at him. He gazed calmly at her with slightly raised eyebrows, as if he knew all she needed was a mandatory therapy session with the last teacher in this school she'd ever want to talk to about anything.

Amanda folded her arms and studied the stuffed shelves behind his head. "I feel fine."

"That's good to hear."

"Awesome. So I'm gonna go now." She started to stand, but Petrov *tsked* and looked at his watch.

"You're here for a full hour every Saturday after dinner no matter what you're feeling or how much you say about it. Sit."

Rolling her eyes, she plopped back down in the chair. "I can't believe this."

"Give it time to sink in. It's real. So. Feel free to elaborate on how *fine* you're doing or whatever else comes to mind. Or not. Either way, we have another fifty-two minutes."

"This is ridiculous."

Petrov nodded. "Probably. It's also mandatory. Look, I'm not gonna stop you from walking right out of here before the hour's up, but I've had four years to perfect my detention game. Which would make the last time you got detention look like a trip to the kemana in comparison."

Amanda leaned as far back in her chair as she could get and let out a bitter laugh. "You can't threaten somebody into therapy. That kinda defeats the whole purpose."

"You're right. I'm not threatening you, Amanda. It's conditional. You hang around for an hour, and you're good to go. Or you can walk right out of here, serve detention with me every day after classes next week, and you'll still be coming back next Saturday to do this all over again. Also with me."

Oh my God, he's not screwing with me.

They stared at each other for what felt like forever. Then she waved dismissively. "Fine. You win."

"This isn't about me. I'm glad you decided to stay. So whenever you're ready, I'm listening."

She couldn't help but laugh again as she folded her arms and stared at the wizard with a mind-blowing second identity from before the Academy students had dubbed him "the sergeant."

I can't believe they think I need therapy. Like that's gonna solve any of my problems. There is no way I'm telling Petrov anything. I'd rather kick his ass again.

However, storming out of here as she wanted would only get her detention for five days in a row. That would only make her angrier. Then she'd have to sit here in front of Petrov again next Saturday, staring at his stupid face and his shiny bald head. She didn't think she could handle that without exploding and proving him right.

This is the dumbest thing they've done at this school.

For the next forty-nine minutes, Amanda sat perfectly still in her chair and glared at Petrov without saying a word. Halfway through, she had to give him credit for staring back at her with a passive, completely nonjudgmental lack of expression without offering to help her get started or barking at her to let it all out.

That would've been worse than him yelling at her to attack him the weekend before.

Finally, a soft *beep* came from Petrov's watch, and he smacked his lips before turning off the alarm. "Hour's up." Then he gestured toward the door. "Great work. Really impressive stuff. See you next Saturday."

Amanda leapt from her chair and stormed out of the training building like it was freshman year again—as if he'd called her a bunch of names and pushed her to her physical limits on the obstacle course. Then took it out on the rest of the class too.

The rest of the class wasn't here. Petrov had been the complete opposite of the teacher she'd thought he was over the last four years. The fact that she didn't have many reasons to be upset about this new arrangement frustrated her that much more.

CHAPTER NINETEEN

It was impossible to calm herself down when she spent the rest of the evening in her dorm room. She either fumed at Petrov and Glasket for forcing *anger management therapy* on her or stopped herself from calling Fiona to yell at the woman about how none of this was fair.

Fiona probably wouldn't have answered her phone anyway. Unleashing her anger on her mentor, who'd probably let her off easy, wouldn't change anything.

Finally, Amanda had to get out of the dorm and away from her thoughts somehow.

She needed to go for a run.

For the first time in her history of sneaking out of the girls' dorm on campus, Amanda didn't try to be quiet. She threw the door to the back stairwell open before her stomping footfalls down the stairs echoed all around her. The dorm's back door shrieked in protest when she shoved it open with both hands. Then she booked it in a furious march across the open grounds of the campus toward the eastern edge of the grounds and her favorite shifting spot in the reeds.

She hadn't taken five steps with her head down and fists

clenched before Matt's voice made her whip her head up and stop.

"I figured this would be the best way to get your attention." He stood a few yards away, directly in her path, with his hands in his pockets and a hopeful smile bringing out those dimples like always.

Amanda blinked furiously and scowled at the grass again because she didn't want to scowl at him. "It's not. Sorry."

Then she took off again, trying to veer around him as quickly as possible. Of course, he stepped quickly into her path again, both hands lifted. "Hey. I'm not trying to make you mad. I just... I mean, I guess I wanted to say hi. You were gone a long time."

"Yeah, I was." She didn't slow down, but when he stepped out of her way and turned to walk beside her, it released a surprising amount of the pressure building behind all her irritation.

I really can't deal with this right now. Not on top of everything else. I'll say the wrong thing, and he'll think I don't care, then everything that happened between us will be wiped clean. I can't...

"Amanda." Matt's hand slipped around hers, and that one simple, gentle action made her stop again. He stepped toward her, dipped his head closer to hers, and lowered his voice. "Are you okay?"

She closed her eyes to focus on drawing a deep breath. When she opened them again to look up at him, there was nothing she could do to stop the stinging tears from welling in her eyes.

Don't cry. Don't even think about crying. Not now.

"Whoa. Obviously not." Matt frowned as he studied her face and gave her hand a gentle squeeze before releasing it. "I'm sorry."

Amanda couldn't tell what surprised her more—that he'd apologized or that he followed it with wrapping her up in his arms and hugging her right there in the middle of the grass between the dorms and the swamp. She swallowed the lump in her throat and didn't know what to do.

"For what?" she whispered.

"I didn't know you were feeling it this much."

When she clenched her eyes shut against the mix of relief that he wasn't asking her more questions and the weirdness of being totally okay with him invading her personal space, the first few tears spilled from the corners of her eyes, and she let out a shuddering breath.

"I mean, not that I know what *it* is," Matt added, "but I definitely would've given you more space if—"

"No." Finally, she got her arms to move and wrapped them around his middle to hug him back. "I don't think more space is gonna do anything for me right now."

"Oh." He let out a nervous chuckle and scanned the empty grounds in the darkness around them. "Okay. But, so you know, if you *do* need to be alone, I get it."

Sniffing and forcing the tears way back where they belonged, Amanda stepped away from him and quickly wiped the tear stains off her cheeks. "Thanks. I'm good."

Matt stared at her, his crooked smile dimmed by the concern behind his eyes as he slowly removed his hands from her shoulders and slipped them into his pockets again. "Sure. Can I, uh… ask one question?"

"You mean besides that one?"

He huffed out a laugh and scuffed the bottom of his sneaker against the grass. "Yeah."

"Sure. Go ahead. I don't know if I'll be able to answer it, but hey. Take a shot."

Tilting his head, Matt narrowed his eyes and looked like he couldn't figure out whether or not to smile. "Sad or seriously pissed off?"

"What?"

"Or something else?" He shrugged. "I don't know. Normally those are the two big ones, but I guess there's always a third option."

Amanda choked out a bitter laugh and tilted her head back to look at the stars. "If option three is 'all of the above,' it's probably that."

"Gotcha."

"I don't know how I'm supposed to handle it because Petrov's apparently the school counselor now, and Glasket forced me into therapy, so…"

A knot of dread tightened in her gut, and she froze.

Why? Why did I say all that? Oh my God, that was the dumbest thing I could've done right now.

"Therapy." Matt bit his lip and slightly turned his head away from her. "With…Petrov?"

She couldn't look directly at him anymore, but now it was more out of humiliation than not wanting to hurt *his* feelings. "Yep. It's okay, Matt. I know what you're thinking. Crazy shifter girl needs therapy, and it's way too much for you to handle. It's way too much for *me* to handle, so I'll… I'm gonna go over—"

"Whoa, whoa. Hold on." He shook his head, laughed, then shook his head again. "Sorry. I'm not laughing at *you*. It's not too much for me to handle. Trust me. I just… *Petrov*? Really?"

Amanda barked a laugh. "I *know*. It's like the whole world turned upside down and reality doesn't exist anymore."

"Uh, yeah. That's one way to put it." They both laughed. Then Amanda looked up into those bright blue eyes turned a light, colorless gray in the darkness and had to remember to breathe again. Matt's crooked smile had fully returned, and its usual charm was a million times stronger after not having seen him for almost two and a half months.

"Not that…" Amanda cleared her throat. "I mean, there's no way in hell I'm talking to *Petrov* about anything. Ever."

"Yeah, then I'd tell you that's too much to handle."

"Ha. Funny."

The corners of Matt's eyes crinkled even more when his smile widened. "Well, *I'm* here. If you wanna talk to *me* about what happened. Or whatever's going on. Just to get it off your chest, maybe. I won't ask a bunch of crazy questions or anything. I'm just—"

"I know." Smiling at this shifter boy standing here with her now made her painfully aware of how long it had been since she'd smiled about something.

How is he so nice all the time? I don't get it.

"Thanks, Matt. Really."

"Yeah. Anytime. I just…" A small, self-conscious laugh escaped him as he gazed around the grounds again.

"Okay, this probably sounds insane, but I missed you. So, we can do whatever you want. Or *not*…do whatever, and that didn't even make sense, but I'm trying to say I don't wanna bother you. I don't wanna make this weird, so stop me at any time because I feel like I'm making this—"

"You're not."

"What?"

"It's not weird." She couldn't help but flash him a grin. "We can *not* do whatever together. It's cool."

"Okay…" He gave her a playful frown. "I feel like you're messing with me now."

"A little." This time when she laughed, it felt like a laugh. Matt joined her, and the shifter girl stepped around him to head toward the edge of the swamp. "Wanna take a walk?"

"Yep." He caught up to her, his hands thrust into the pockets of his jeans.

Neither of them said a thing, both wearing not-so-hidden smiles until they reached the water's edge. For some reason, being out here in the swamp again, with Matt, destroyed the hesitation she'd carried around the one thing she didn't think she could talk about.

"I found him," Amanda blurted. "In South America."

"Okay." Matt shot her a sidelong glance, then dropped his gaze to the ground as they walked north along the bank. "Might be a dumb question, but who are you talking about?"

Really? I'm gonna open this can of worms right now?

She swallowed and looked out over the dark water shadowed by draping branches and cut by the occasional reflection of stars.

I have to talk about it to someone. *Even if he can't do anything to help me find the guy, at least he won't tell me to forget about it.*

"One, of, um…" Her eyes stung again with tears, but she forced them back again went for it. "One of the magicals who… killed my family."

"Whoa. Amanda." Matt touched her arm, and she turned away from the river to look up at him. "That's…"

"Yeah. I know."

"What happened? Wait, you were in South America?"

"Yep. Way down there. Can we keep walking?"

"Totally." He stared straight ahead for a while longer, then reached out to slip his fingers through hers and gave her hand a gentle squeeze. "So, do you take off to different countries every time you leave, or is that a—"

"It was a one-time thing. So far." She stepped closer to him as they walked, smiling because that was all she could do now that they were talking and he was holding her hand. Also that after spitting out a random, vague mention of the wizard in the kemana, it felt like she could finally stop thinking about him.

"That's pretty cool." Matt looked her up and down again and wrinkled his nose. "How's the food down there?"

"Well, it was crap, but we basically camped out in the jungle the whole—you know what? I don't wanna talk about the Coalition or the job or all the crazy stuff that…" She puffed out a sigh. "Sorry."

"It's okay." He nodded and squeezed her hand again. "Seriously. You don't have to talk about anything."

"Okay." Apparently, she *did* have to talk about it because she couldn't stop herself from going right back to the one thing they'd both tried to avoid. "He got away."

"Oh." With a sharp inhale, Matt met her gaze head-on and shook his head. "That must've been…the worst thing ever. I'm so sorry."

Tears stung Amanda's eyes again, and she rapidly blinked them away. "Yeah, it was. I figured out a way to get a picture of him, though. Sort of."

"Okay…"

"I mean, I saw him, and the lab has this crazy machine that can translate brainwaves into images, so I got the bastard's face down into the Coalition's system, and that's how I'm gonna find him." A sharp laugh burst out of her, and she shook her head. "If the Coalition even lifts a finger to help me with this. They're *supposed* to be looking for him, but I don't think they've done anything."

"Really? Why not?"

"I've been back here for over a week now. They've had *days* to find him and figure out where he is. Maybe find the other dirt-bags who were with him…that night." Amanda ran her other hand over her hair and puffed out a sigh. "It's like they don't even care."

"That sucks. Any chance they haven't told you anything 'cause they want you to…I don't know. Focus on school? Or not *him*?"

"Ha. Yeah, everyone wants me to focus on school." She snorted. "They would've sent me *something*. They haven't even started looking."

Neither of them could think of anything to say after that, but they kept walking in silence along the riverbank.

I can't believe I feel better. Not a lot. It still sucks, but I think I can breathe right now.

An owl dove silently from a tree branch up ahead and swooped down into the reeds. The plants rustled, then the bird darted back up into the darkness with a small snake writhing from its beak before both creatures disappeared into the thick foliage over the swamp.

"Whoa." Matt stared at where the owl had disappeared, his smile flickering. "You saw that, right?"

"Yeah. I didn't know owls ate snakes."

"Me neither."

"Hey, Matt, everything I told you… Nobody else knows about this stuff. Nobody here, anyway. So don't tell anyone, okay?"

He turned toward her and looked her right in the eye. "I promise. I won't tell anybody."

"Not even my friends. If they ask."

"Got it. Trust me, I've had a lot of practice telling your friends to quit asking me about you. If you ignore how weirdly annoying Summer is sometimes, they're pretty cool."

Amanda laughed and stared at him. "A lot of practice? What, like, you hung out with them while I was gone?"

"Uh…yeah. Is that a bad thing?"

"What? No. No. I just didn't expect *that*. I mean, I got that voicemail from everybody. And you. I guess I thought that was a one-time thing."

They kept walking, and Matt shrugged. "They let me tag along with them a few times. To the kemana. And the kemana. And another time they wanted to go to the kemana—"

"Okay, I get it. They like going there, I know. They weren't, like, jerks to you or anything, right?"

He grinned and studied the edge of the water up ahead. "Just Summer."

"Ha. Yeah, that's a given."

"No, like I said, they're pretty cool. I mean, Grace was a little weird to be around at first. Then she got over it. I don't know if it's because Summer's insane or what, but I think she's the only girl I know who isn't a shifter and doesn't…you know."

"Go crazy when you're around?"

Matt grimaced. "Yeah."

"Yeah, Summer has weird tastes in just about everything. I'd go with it's 'cause she's insane. That's my best guess."

They both laughed at that, and Matt seemed like he was finally loosening up a little too the more he kept talking. "You're probably right. Or it might have had something to do with their whole perception of me changing when I told them what I am."

"Huh. That's—wait." Amanda leaned away from him to fix him with a playful but still completely confused frown. "You told them?"

"Yep."

"Wow. How did *that* come up?"

"I was hanging out with them a lot after you left. Then the Halloween party kinda got a little weird. I had no idea Grace is that terrifying when she's mad."

"What did you do?"

"Oh, come on." He wrinkled his nose. "I didn't do anything. I usually don't have to for girls to… You know, any way I say this is gonna make me sound like a tool."

"Oh my God." Amanda's mouth dropped open when she put the pieces together on her own. "Grace fought a bunch of girls off you, didn't she?"

"Well, *fight's* a strong word."

"She *did*."

"Okay, kind of. It got cleared up. Eventually. Then I figured it was time to quit trying to bury it, you know? What I am and what my dad is and how that makes things weird most of the time. So yeah, I told your friends about the Lorikor thing. My magic. That none of it works on shifters. And, uh…they handled it."

Amanda burst out laughing.

"It's not that funny."

"It kind of is, though." She tried to hold it together but had to let it all out of her system before she could say anything else. "Not that you told them. Sorry. I'm glad you could talk about it. It's just… Grace fighting anyone is hard to imagine, and it shouldn't be because we've been in Combat Training together for the last four years."

"I guess a Halloween party's different." Matt chuckled. "She might've tried to fight *me* when I told them what was going on."

Another snorting laugh made Amanda double over before she straightened quickly and shook her head. "Sorry. I tried to imagine that."

"Yeah, it wasn't as funny at that moment."

"So she got pissed when she figured out she was like everyone else. Not immune to the whole...Lorikor thing."

Matt grimaced again, but this time it was tinged with a smile. "Yep. Once she eventually stopped trying to avoid me, she's been pretty cool about it too. Then everything was fine."

"Cool. That's good to hear." Imagining her friends sitting around their regular picnic table under the pavilion and listening to Matt spill the beans about his magical heritage—their eyes widening and mouths dropping farther open by the second—almost made her crack up again.

Except for Jackson. Oh, man. That probably didn't go over well.

"How did Jackson take it?"

Matt pressed his lips together and looked back and forth across the water. "I know he likes you. Not exactly a secret."

"Yeah, that's been a thing for a while. Not that me and *Jackson* are a thing. He's an amazing friend. He's not...I don't—"

"I know." He grinned at her and lowered his head. "It's okay."

"Now I kind of feel bad, you know?"

"I don't think you have anything to worry about. I mean, it's not like Jackson and I sat and talked about *you* or anything, but he's been totally cool. It wouldn't matter if he did have an issue with me."

Matt stepped closer and grabbed her other hand now too as he leaned down toward her and studied her gaze. "I really like you. Your friends are a bonus, I guess. Well, except for Summer."

"Ha!" Amanda immediately clamped her mouth shut and tried so hard not to keep laughing. "You know, she's helpful sometimes..."

"Probably." Biting his lip, he lowered his head and stared at their clasped hands. "You know, so we're clear, I wasn't only trying to be nice when I said I missed you."

Her heart leapt up into her throat, but she couldn't stop staring up at him. "I know."

"Good. You don't think you're gonna leave me stranded at another school dance and take off on a scooter again like that, do you?" He couldn't finish the question before laughing at it himself, and Amanda grimaced half in amusement and half in a weird embarrassment.

"I don't *think* so?"

"Okay. I'll take that."

Now he's looking at me like that, and I have no idea if I can handle any more than this right now. Why does that even matter right now?

Matt leaned slowly closer, making it hard to think he was trying to do anything other than kiss her again, and Amanda had no control over her reaction when she leaned away and drew a deep breath.

"You know what I really need right now?"

"Um…" He laughed and shook his head. "Don't make me guess."

"I need to go for a run."

"Right. Sounds good."

Amanda let go of his hands, backed away, and didn't realize it was the first time she didn't need to hide behind a wall of reeds before shifting in the middle of the night. Other than when an angry magical spirit or a singular of wild boar attacked the school, or divergent mermaids brainwashed Academy students.

She didn't think about anything but racing away through the swamp with the wind in her fur and Matt's black wolf loping into the water behind her.

It was exactly what she needed.

CHAPTER TWENTY

After that night, things started to feel a little easier to handle. Amanda spent the next few weeks thinking maybe she could deal with the balancing act of schoolwork, her friends, Matt, and the Coalition. Plus all the unknowns that came with whether or not Dr. Caniss would use the wizard's image to pave the road to finding the Coulier family justice finally. Still, it was easier to focus on trying to enjoy herself while she had nothing else to do but work on her solo projects for class and spend time with her friends.

The only thing that bothered her—and continued to worsen each night—were the dreams.

They were all variations of the same thing—memories of her interactions with UM-7000 and its ultimatum, or a mashed-up replay of watching her family get killed and seeing the wizard with the white striped hair at the kemana. Sometimes, she dreamed about her family's deaths set *inside* the Villa Puerto Edén kemana. Waking up before the 5:00 a.m. alarm bell blasted across the campus, covered in a cold sweat and gasping, became part of Amanda's new routine for the semester.

She started taking showers before any of the other girls

stirred in the morning, but the dreams somehow became a release for everything she didn't want to think about during the day. When she had them every night, she could stop thinking about the Coalition and UM-7000 and her family while she was awake.

That didn't stop her from checking her Coalition phone at least twice a day to make sure she hadn't missed any attempts to contact her. Still nothing, but Amanda didn't expect to hear from the shifters who'd written her off as an anomaly and a liability and not worth their resources to help with her "personal matters."

Things got exciting during Combat Training once Petrov finished his more instructional classes with the modified firearms. Every class period with their bald teacher, who moonlighted as a therapist on Saturday nights, the seniors crowded onto the Academy airboats. Their trips took them out to an island three times larger than the entrance to the Everglades kemana to practice their new skills.

By the second week of making the trip and repeatedly demonstrating that they could disengage the safety, aim, shoot, and hit something without freaking out, some of the seniors started to develop a knack for long-range weapons.

"How come you're not racing to those crates like everyone else?" Blake asked Amanda as the girls stood away from the surge of other kids trying to find their favorite weapons.

The shifter girl shrugged. "I'll use whatever's left. How come *you're* not over there?"

"I'm not…" The witch sighed. "I'm good at fighting close up. I know that."

"Yeah, everyone knows that, Blake."

The other girl grinned, but her pride quickly disappeared again when she frowned at the crates of firearms. "I'm not good with guns. I guess I have to accept that."

"We've only been doing this for a few weeks. You'll get it. It's fine."

"I don't think so. Everyone else picked it up. You're...really good."

"Oh." Amanda rolled her eyes and snorted. "That's because I've spent the last four years shooting guns in the middle of the swamp. This is basically like being back home. I wasn't amazing at it when I started. So keep practicing."

Blake wasn't the only one who had a hard time warming up to weapons. The senior class hadn't expected to be using them before they graduated and got jobs where guns were part of the territory. Amanda wasn't the only senior who already had a knack for firearms, either.

After a month, Jackson had risen to the top of the class with his consistency in hitting whatever mark Petrov set for them. When he shot a perfect bullseye from the farthest distance any of them had tried—and not with a bullet but with the painful, jolting bursts of orange energy they all remembered from the obstacle course—the entire shooting range went silent.

"Holy crap." Tommy's jaw dropped open. "Did you *see* that?"

"He's better than Summer!"

"He's better than everyone."

Jackson grinned and let his buddies jostle him around but didn't say a word as he waited for Petrov to return with the target for proof. Summer laughed and looked the wizard up and down. "No shit. Look at that, huh? Romeo *does* have a skill."

She punched him in the shoulder, and his grin morphed into an irritated grimace. "You gotta cut it out with the nicknames, Summer. It's not as cool as you think it is."

"Aw, come on." She shoved him a little harder, and he took a staggering step away from her. "Don't be so uptight. You've been Romeo *forever*. I can't change your name now."

"It's not my name."

"So?"

"So, I'm telling you to stop. Pick something else, or don't pick anything at all. It's not that hard."

"I was trying to compliment you, okay. Damn. Somebody eat all your cereal this morning or what—"

"Just shut up!" Jackson whirled toward her and slightly raised the modified pistol from where he'd been holding it pointed safely at the ground. The sharp *bang* of his finger pulling the trigger and the burst of orange light striking the dirt an inch away from her shoe made everyone else jump and scramble away from them. All conversation stopped, and Jackson glared at the rainbow-haired witch, clenching his jaw over and over.

"Are you kidding me right now?" Summer muttered. "You missed."

"I didn't miss. I wanted you to stop talking."

"Pris!" Petrov stormed toward the tables laid out with weapons, the tin can Jackson had shot dangling from his hand but no longer the focus. "What the hell is going on?"

"Sorry." Jackson engaged the pistol's safety and set the weapon gently on the table beside the others. "I got angry."

"So you thought it was a good idea to fire a warning shot at Flannerty's foot?" Petrov slammed the tin can onto the table and widened his eyes. "That wasn't a rhetorical question!"

The boy blinked quickly and puffed out a sigh. "Yeah. I guess I thought it was a good idea at the time."

Amanda wrinkled her nose as she watched the tension rising with the rest of the class.

Great. Summer pushed him too hard, and now he's the one getting in trouble for it. Romeo was a bad choice in the first place.

Petrov exhaled heavily through his nose and pointed at Jackson. "I'm only gonna say this once. You don't fire warning shots into the ground unless you have bullets in a clip. Shoot her in the foot next time. Maybe then she'll get the hint."

"What the hell?" Summer turned toward Petrov and spread her arms. "Are you serious?"

"You've been hit with those things before. You all have. It's no big deal. Pris, here, knows exactly what he's doing. Nice shot, by the way. You hit the can dead center.

"Listen up, everybody! You could all learn a thing or two from what Pris did. He has enough handle on himself to consciously choose *not* to shoot Flannerty even though she would've been fine. He has damn good long-range aim too."

Some of the boys chuckled and started to congratulate Jackson, but Petrov pointed at them and barked, "Hey! That doesn't mean you zipperheads can start shooting each other with these things because you think it's funny. If anyone else feels like testing these weapons out on anything that *isn't* the designated target out there, you'll be spending the rest of the class sitting on the sidelines. Like you're doing for the rest of the class, Pris. Take a seat."

With a confused smile, Jackson turned away from the table and scratched the back of his head as he walked through the students crowding around the weapons table.

"That doesn't seem like an awful punishment," Blake muttered. "You think he'd make *me* sit out if I accidentally shot somebody?"

Amanda stifled a laugh. "Probably not. You're at the top of the class for hand-to-hand."

The other girl groaned. "Shit."

"And you." Petrov nodded at Summer. "If you can't learn when to push somebody's buttons and when to let a thing the hell alone, you're gonna find yourself hit with real bullets out on a job somewhere instead of almost getting shocked by an electric blast. Got it?"

Summer rolled her eyes and grabbed one of the open weapons on the table before raising it and firing three quick shots. "I'll be fine."

Petrov snorted and shook his head. "Uh-huh. It's everyone else I'm worried about."

The other projects for the rest of Amanda's classes couldn't have been any more boring. She'd chosen a random name from Ms. Ralthorn's list of "infamous modern bounty hunters"—Angus Fletchen—and couldn't focus on reading enough to write her report for more than five minutes at a time.

No spark of inspiration had hit her yet for how she was supposed to complete Mrs. Zimmer's "alchemical scenario," so she kept putting it off, hoping the idea lightbulb would go off eventually. Even her time spent in the greenhouse had lost its usual appeal, but she still carefully nurtured the two Fatethistle plants in the cellar beneath the trapdoor. She made sure all the plants she had to harvest for Nurse Aiken were still doing what they were supposed to as well.

Beyond the bare minimum, when it came to her school-work, Amanda was going through the motions. At first, she thought it had something to do with being in her second semester of senior year—her last semester of high school. That she was getting itchy like everyone else to be done with this and branch out beyond what the Academy of Necessary Magic had to offer.

When she started dozing off at lunch and leaving dinner early at least every other day to go back to her room and climb into bed, she knew it was because of her dreams. She couldn't keep ignoring the fact that if she kept going like this on so little sleep, she'd end up doing something stupid.

So after six weeks of meeting Petrov in the training building every Saturday after dinner and saying absolutely nothing for an entire hour, Amanda finally decided she might as well start talking.

"Okay." She plopped into the chair facing his and puffed out a sigh. "This might sound stupid to you because you have a bunch of degrees or whatever, but it's a serious question."

"Huh." Petrov folded his arms and nodded. "And here I was thinking I should start bringing a book to our hour of silence."

Amanda rolled her eyes, leaned forward and propped her forearms on her thighs, and tried to look serious without coming across like a desperate teenager asking the last person in the world she'd expected to go to for answers. Because she was both.

"How do I get rid of my dreams?"

Petrov blinked, leaned back, and tilted his head. "Well, they're part of the process, Amanda, so the fastest way to get rid of your dreams would be to get rid of sleep altogether. Which you need."

"No, I know *that*." She shifted back in her chair, rubbed her palms on her thighs, then folded her arms. "Never mind."

This was a dumb idea. He's not gonna help me.

"How bad are they?"

"What?"

"Your dreams." The teacher spread his arms. "Or at least the ones you're trying to get rid of."

"Well, that would be all of them right now. They're...pretty bad."

"Okay. You losing sleep?"

"A little." When she looked up at him, he raised an eyebrow, and she caved. "Okay, a lot. I can't get more than, like, four hours. Five tops, but that hasn't happened for a while."

Petrov crossed one leg over the other and tilted his head from side to side. "If you were anyone else, I'd ask if you've tried this and that, blah, blah, blah, dream-related therapist stuff. We both know that's a waste of time, so why don't we get down to the real crap."

Amanda snorted. "If I'm wasting your time so much, why do you keep making me show up to these stupid things?"

"Right. First of all, I don't make you do anything. No one's holding a gun to your head. Only detention. Second, I didn't say *you* were wasting my time. I said going through the usual list of questions and recommended 'quick fixes' would be a waste of time. I meant for you."

"Why? You don't think I can handle trying out a *quick fix*?"

The corner of Petrov's mouth twitched, and he looked like he was about to burst out laughing. "No, I *know* you can handle it. I'm guessing you've already tried everything I would've recommended anyway because I also know you're only talking to me about anything at all as a last resort. So you're out of options. Am I wrong?"

Okay, he gets points for being creepily accurate on that, I guess.

"No." Amanda stared at the shelf behind Petrov's head. "You're not. You know, you don't even talk like a therapist."

"No, I talk like myself. If someone else can't handle *me* being real, they don't do very well when pitted against being real with themselves. It's effective for separating people who are ready to do real work and people who want me to throw 'em a pity party."

"Ha. You don't do pity parties."

Petrov's smile widened enough to show actual teeth. "No. I don't. Now quit changing the subject. Back to dreams."

Amanda grimaced and shifted again in her chair. "Do I have to tell you what they're about?"

"No. But you don't ask for help unless you're ready for answers you already know you won't like."

"Don't do that. It's creepy."

"What?"

She wagged her finger at him. "That...telling me what I do stuff. Like you're trying to mess with my head."

Petrov chuckled. "They don't call us shrinks for nothing."

With a half-serious groan, Amanda tipped her head back and stared at the ceiling. "Fine. I only have two dreams anymore. One's about this seriously messed-up creature I was hunting for the Coalition of Shifters and how I managed to convince it not to suck all the magic out of Earth because we're not all lowlife pieces of shit who steal and lie and start wars and kill people.

"The other one's about the night I watched my whole family get killed, which I thought I'd stopped dreaming about at the very least. But apparently not, because I saw one of their murderers at the same kemana in South America where I fought that creature who looked like *me*, and the bastard's still out there. The shifters I thought were on my side won't lift a finger to help me catch him or any of the others who shot my sister and my parents in the back of the head."

As soon as the giant string of what felt more like a confession than anything else finished unraveling from her mouth, Amanda instantly clenched her eyes shut and gritted her teeth.

That was way too much. You were supposed to talk about the dreams, dummy. Not spill your guts like that.

"Okay, then." Petrov drummed his fingers on his thigh and studied the opposite wall of the training building behind Amanda. "That pretty much explains everything."

"No, it doesn't. It explains my dreams. I'm not gonna talk about anything else."

"Yeah, please don't." When she glared at him, his small smirk returned. "I'm kidding."

"Awesome. Glad you're having fun with my nightmares."

"All right, listen. That is, if you *want* to listen. Because it sounded like you've been holding that in for a while, so if all you wanted was to get that off your chest—"

"I want the dreams to stop."

"Sure. First, I already know about your work with the Coalition, but I gotta admit I haven't heard anything as detailed as *that*. So thank you. For saving the planet, apparently."

Amanda scoffed. "Again, not the time to make jokes."

"That was me being completely serious. I don't thank many magicals for a lot of anything, so don't expect a repeat occurrence. It's more meaningful that way."

Wrinkling her nose, she couldn't help a tiny smile. Everything coming out of Petrov's mouth was delivered with a perfect matter-of-factness that from anyone else would have sounded sincere. But Mr. Petrov didn't do sincere, and she couldn't figure out if he was trying to say nice things in a jerky way to lighten the mood or if he was still messing with her.

I guess it doesn't matter. As long as he tells me how to fix this.

"So, your creature dream makes sense. That's why you were gone. Still fresh in your mind." The teacher sniffed and let out a heavy sigh. "I did *not* know about your family. Specifically. With that level of detail."

"Yeah, I don't talk about it that much."

"Huh. I wonder why."

She fixed him with a deadpan stare. "So, how do I stop dreaming about this crap?"

Petrov looked her directly in the eyes. "What do you want right now? I'm not talking about here in this building, so don't tell me it's to get the hell out of here and find better help somewhere else."

Amanda stifled a laugh and pressed her lips together.

"I'm asking you what your top priority is, Amanda. The bigger-picture stuff."

"Um…" She shook her head and stared at her lap. "I mean, right now, it's to find the assholes who killed my family. I thought that was pretty obvious with all the dreams."

"Right. So when you wake up from those dreams and can't go back to sleep, it's not because you're scared."

"Are you kidding? No. It's 'cause I can't stand the fact that one of them got away *again* because no one wanted to listen to me."

"It's because you're pissed."

"No shit!"

Petrov narrowed his eyes, and Amanda let out a long, slow breath to calm herself down again.

"You're doing that on purpose," she muttered.

"Yep. So are you. The kid who came straight out of Johnny

Walker's swamp-side shanty to attend the Academy of Necessary Magic. I got a chicken-or-the-egg question for you."

"Fine."

"Did your guardian fund this school because you wanted to be a bounty hunter, or do you want to be a bounty hunter because he funded this school?"

Amanda cocked her head. "That has nothing to do with my dreams."

"Answer the question."

"I have no idea why Johnny does most things he does, okay? I came here because this is the only school for magic I could go to that would take me when I was twelve, first of all, and it's the only school anywhere that trains kids how to do what Johnny does. And all the other bounty hunters."

Amanda shrugged. "I'm here because *I* want to do what he does. And I want to do it better."

"Because of your family."

"Obviously." With a frustrated sigh, she spread her arms. "It's been four *years*, and nobody's found the magicals who killed them and kidnapped me to sell on the black market. You'd think that'd be kind of a big deal. Top priority.

"Nobody cares. None of the professionals. No FBI, no police, no private contractors or investigators or anything. Not even the Coalition. But I *did* find one of them in South America. And now…"

Now I'm talking way too much. Dang. He knows what he's doing.

"Now you have to decide whether what you thought you wanted is still what you actually want," Petrov said flatly.

"What? Of course, it's what I want."

"Okay. You sound pretty convinced."

"Is this you trying to change my mind? Because I'm not gonna change my mind. They have to pay for what they did, and if nobody else is gonna do it, I'm the one who has to."

He nodded, then leaned slightly forward and met her gaze

again. "Right now, Amanda, you're closer than most magicals ever get to doing things the right way. Getting justice. Finding those responsible for doing terrible things and holding them *accountable* instead of storming in to kick ass and maybe feel better. That's what you need to remember."

Doing things the right way.

It was the same thing she'd said to UM-7000 during their little mind-reading chat. The same thing Johnny had told Amanda a little over two years ago after dinner when he'd been feeling chattier than normal about his personal stuff.

Somehow, the topic of families and how they change had morphed into what both Johnny's and Amanda's families had been like before they found each other. The dwarf had finally, for the first time, told her about unraveling the case of his daughter's murder and going after the Red Boar for justice.

"You're damn straight I wanted to kill the bastard," Johnny had said with a glass of whiskey in hand. "I sure as shit had the chance, too. I didn't take it. You gotta do this kinda thing right, kid. *Especially* when it's personal. Not the way they killed Dawn, not the way your folks and sister went. Ain't nothin' to make us better'n the assholes who took 'em if we don't do it right."

It was an odd memory to have right now as she sat on a metal chair in the middle of a sparring mat with her Combat Training teacher turned surprisingly blunt therapist, but Johnny's story had stuck with her. His words had stuck with her enough to repeat them to UM-7000, and now Petrov was saying pretty much the same thing.

"You haven't, uh…been contacted by some kinda crazy creature from Oriceran that talks fire-and-brimstone shit about getting rid of magic on Earth because magicals don't deserve it anymore, right?"

Petrov snickered. "Why do you ask?"

"Just double-checking."

"Uh-huh. You sound crazy, Coulier."

Amanda quickly grabbed her mouth to wipe away a smile. "Yeah, one of us is."

"You wanna know how to get rid of your dreams?"

"Seriously? I thought we were jumping right past all that."

After a short, clipped laugh, Petrov pointed at her and fixed her with a milder version of the "don't screw with me" frown he'd been giving her the last four years during class. "You think you're useless, helpless, incapable of doing something right without screwing up in every way imaginable first, and only then stumbling on the right answer without knowing why or how."

"Wow." She widened her eyes. "Ouch."

"Doesn't make it easier when everyone else is telling you the same thing. Fuck what everybody else says. You need to quit lying to *yourself*. Soon as you do that, poof." He popped open his fist and swept his arm out to the side. "Dreams gone."

"Really? That's your answer? *Believe in myself,* and I can do anything?"

"Nope. Get out of your own way. You said it yourself. If nobody else is gonna step up and do what needs doing, you're the one who has to. So find a way to do it." Petrov glanced at his watch and shrugged. "Or find some kinda side project, finish it, and get a significantly lower amount of satisfaction out of making yourself useful for something that doesn't really matter to you. Your choice. Our hour's up."

"Hey, great. All my problems are solved." With a smirk, Amanda stood from her chair and headed for the door. "Good thing I'm not paying you."

"Well, you saved the world, so I guess we're working in trade."

She barked a harsh laugh and shoved open the door before stepping out into the dark, breezy night.

Instead of heading right back to the dorms as she normally did, Amanda went in the opposite direction toward the edge of campus grounds and the riverbank of the swamp. She needed a little extra time to let everything Petrov had told her sink in—his odd comments and otherwise insulting demeanor aside.

Stop lying to myself, huh? Okay. So I need to finish a project. Do what I have to do to find that bastard wizard on my own.

She reached out to brush her fingertips along the tallest fern leaves and the rustling reeds at the water's edge as she walked.

I already have everything I need right here. A freaking school for bounty hunters. I don't need anything else from anyone else. If I have to wait until I graduate to go out and track him down, fine. I need to stop wasting my time while I'm still in school.

A new plan formed in her mind, and as the shifter girl made her way along the empty northeast boundary of the Academy grounds, she realized what she had to do.

Even if they didn't know it, her teachers had already given her the building blocks of everything she'd need this semester to prepare for her first actual bounty. Sure, the client was herself this time, and she wouldn't be getting paid, but that didn't matter one bit. That wasn't why she was doing this in the first place.

CHAPTER TWENTY-ONE

Most of the building blocks for Amanda's new plan had come from all her research reading about the bounty hunter she'd chosen for her History of Oriceran report due at the end of the year.

Angus had been a big deal before magic's reveal on Earth, even before Johnny Walker had entered the game. The Light Elf was known for his insane accuracy in tracking down his targets and apprehending them, but only after months of researching them, studying them, knowing his bounty's strengths, weaknesses, and history. It took him a lot longer to bring in his bounties than any of the other independently contracted professionals of his time at the end of the twentieth century. That was because he was meticulous, exact, and left no room for error.

A nearly perfect track record with contracted jobs had made Angus *the* most successful bounty hunter, which made up for his comparatively long timeline of months or even years. If a client wanted someone found, and they wanted the job done right, the Light Elf was the guy. His fees were through the roof, of course, but they paid for a guarantee of capture and return of literally any magical by Angus Fletchen himself.

Until the first and only time he failed, which happened to be the last job he ever took. And his last day among the living.

Because while Angus had been so precise in his planning and studying and careful observation of his targets, he left no room for error. The guy was *horrible* at adapting to new situations and improvising on the fly. So he'd spent an entire career focusing on controlling every variable imaginable in going after his contracted bounties. That inability to reorient himself and try new tactics when plans changed ended up killing him in the end —the one bounty who was unpredictable enough.

Amanda pored through every book on Angus Fletchen she could find in the Academy library. Discovering exactly *how* the Light Elf had met his end made her burst out laughing. It got her some dirty looks from the four other students trying to focus in the silence and solitude of the library, but she ignored them and kept scribbling her notes.

The guy had no ability to think on his feet. Yeah, that's not a problem I have at all. Pretty sure I've picked up more than a few things about how to improvise from Johnny. Might even be better than him at that part. Who knows?

The necessary skills, supplies, and methods Angus Fletchen had used to track his quarry—conveniently cataloged in Angus's notes with meticulous detail until the day he died, now published in public magical texts—were the only parts Amanda was interested in. The shifter girl had an opportunity to cherry-pick what worked from the two greatest bounty hunters she knew.

Angus's ability to plan, Johnny's ability to jump in any direction at the drop of a dime if the situation called for it, and Amanda's lifelong habit of pouring all her energy into something with laser-like focus until she got the thing done. As long as it was something she wanted.

She wanted this more than anything.

Unfortunately, without a sliver of physical evidence from the wizard she'd be hunting—no hair or fingerprints, no leftover bit of magic confiscated to then use it to track him down, no dossier from a larger organization—she had to improvise from the very beginning. She didn't even have the guy's name, let alone who he worked for, where he lived, or where she was most likely to find him at any given time.

The greenhouse she'd all but neglected for anything beyond growing the plants required for Nurse Aiken and the Academy store of herbs, however, turned out to be her greatest asset after all.

Glasket hesitated only a little when Amanda gave her the list of new seeds she wanted and asked for an emergency order.

"Overnight shipping would be awesome," the girl said as she stepped away from the principal's desk and clasped her hands together. "You know, if they do that with magical-seed orders."

After perusing the list, Glasket removed her reading glasses and looked up at Amanda with a dubious frown. "I'm not sure I understand why it would be in this school's best interests to order *another* round of Dreamscape seeds, Ms. Coulier. Not to mention, allow you to grow those plants again on school property. You do remember what happened last time, don't you?"

"Yeah. I know what it is and what it does this time. Plus I know what I'm doing."

The principal read over her student's writeup one final time and sighed. "Why the rush almost halfway through your second semester?"

"Um…because it's almost halfway through the semester?" Amanda wrinkled her nose, then pointed at the paper on the desk. "I promise this is legit, Dean Glasket. I need the Dreamscape to help me alchemize something I need to use for my scenario thing in Zimmer's class. I wrote it down. It's all right there."

"Yes, and you seem to have left out the specific alchemical equation you're trying to replicate for that project with fully mature Dreamscape. I have no doubt you can grow that plant in only half a semester. I won't ask how because I choose to take you at your word when you promised to come to me if you needed any more of the school's supplies for your various projects."

"I already have everything I need. Except for the Dreamscape."

"As I recall, those dusty blue flowers are grown and harvested to manifest nonphysical traits into reality. I'm a little concerned, and quite frankly, at a loss as to how a plant like this will prove beneficial for an alchemy assignment. Can you guarantee there won't be another outbreak of emotional confessions running rampant in this school if I order these seeds for you?"

Amanda snorted. "As long as nobody tries to break into the greenhouse to play around with glittering blue flowers."

Glasket raised an eyebrow and clearly didn't find that funny at all.

"Yes," the girl added, then quickly cleared her throat and tried to look as serious as possible. "Absolutely. I promise that won't happen again."

"All right. There's also a safety concern here. Last time, you weren't alchemizing the Dreamscape flowers. There's a chance whatever non-physical quality you're trying to draw out with that plant could prove physically dangerous once manifested."

"Not with this. Trust me."

"I still have to ask what you're attempting to bring to fruition with this."

Amanda pressed her lips together and tried not to fidget.

Why can't she sign off the stupid seeds? This is important, and I made it work for school too. What's the holdup?

"Miss Coulier?"

"A memory."

"I'm sorry?"

The girl spread her arms and plastered an eager grin on her face. "I need the Dreamscape to alchemize a memory."

"I do hope it's completely benign."

"Trust me. This kind of memory never killed anybody."

Glasket winced at that, but after another ten seconds of studying her student's pleading eyes, she picked up a pen and scribbled something at the bottom corner of Amanda's writeup. "All right. I'll put in the order."

"Yes!"

"I can't guarantee overnight shipping. End of the week at the latest."

"That's totally fine. I can wait that long. No problem."

"Good."

"Thanks, Glasket. Seriously. You won't regret it." Grinning, Amanda spun and practically skipped toward the door to the principal's office.

"Miss Coulier."

"Yeah?"

When she turned, she found Glasket staring at her with another raised eyebrow, her head tilted in irritation. "What did you call me?"

"I… Dean. Dean Glasket." Amanda amped up what she hoped was a working charm in her smile and let out a self-conscious chuckle. "Thank you."

"Good luck."

After that, it was a matter of waiting for the seed order to arrive. Then Amanda could get to work accelerating the natural growth process for the Dreamscape to bring everything together.

Glasket's promise of the seeds arriving by the end of the week at the latest was completely accurate. The packet was sitting on the worktable at the end of the center gardening trough that Friday morning when Amanda stepped inside the greenhouse. She spent the entire morning and the rest of the afternoon after lunch clearing out space at the far end of the trough closest to the curving wall of windows, away from all the other plants so it wouldn't contaminate them. Mostly so they wouldn't contaminate the Dreamscape in return.

She didn't even have to ask for more alchemy supplies—not to mention a centrifuge—because she still had a tiny bit of the accelerant left over from last year's illegal science experiment with her friends. She'd kept that in the cellar beneath the trap door, in case, and now she had the perfect reason to use the rest of it.

I'm even more excited about this than I was for the Fatethistle.

It only took her two weeks with the accelerant to get those beautiful, dangerous blue flowers to bloom on the Dreamscape. By the time she was ready for the last part of her plan before harvesting the blossoms, the Spring Fling dance was only a week away.

Amanda didn't have any space in her mind whatsoever for school dances and parties and the last of any of it she'd be experiencing as an Academy student. She wanted to get this done, get it done *right*, and use her finals as an opportunity to test out her theory. Which, of course, she was ninety-nine percent sure would work for exactly what she wanted to achieve after graduation.

Still, that one percent of being wrong would mean she might have to start all over from the beginning.

Don't think about that now. Think about how awesome it is that you already know how to do this. Kinda.

She'd waited until that Friday night a week before the dance to return to the greenhouse and set everything up. With the Louper match in full swing and most of the student body gathered in the main field to watch the game through the projection, it was the perfect time to sneak away without anyone wondering where she was.

Not that many people wondered about her at all lately. Her friends had accepted that she was onto something big and didn't want to be distracted, so they mostly saw her only at meals. Even then, Amanda had been wolfing down her food faster than ever.

She used the added time to double-check her theories against the research on Angus Fletchen, gather supplies from Zimmer's storeroom—with the Alchemy teacher's approval of her request list, of course—and map out everything she meant to create and build. Her goal was to finalize all her class projects and make sure they'd all add something to her real focus.

Finding that wizard, tracking him down, and bringing him in. Even if she had to do it all on her own.

Amanda pulled a folding metal chair up to the end of the last trough where the Dreamscape flowers glowed with an alluring blue light and settled into it. The cheers and shouts of the students watching the Louper game were constant background noise, but she tuned it all out as she closed her eyes and drew a deep breath.

Okay. Intention is everything. Being aware of what I'm trying to do takes care of the rest of it. So here we go. If I can talk to vengeful Oriceran blobs in my mind and find every other hidden divergent critter, I should be able to do this. *Then Mel's machine won't matter. Who needs a machine anyway when I have plants?*

That thought made her laugh, and she shook her head to pull herself back into focus.

Here we go.

The second her ghost-wolf drew away from her, and she reached toward the Dreamscape with only one thing in mind, someone knocked on the greenhouse door.

CHAPTER TWENTY-TWO

Amanda's magic snapped right back into her, and her eyes flew open. "Seriously?" she whispered.

"Amanda?" It was Matt.

"Uh...yeah?" She turned in the chair to stare at his dark silhouette through the frosted glass window in the door.

He chuckled. "Okay, well, now I know you're in there, so..."

"Yeah, hold on." Wrinkling her nose, Amanda stood and left her project to answer the door.

Best reason ever to have a lock on that door. If he'd walked right in, I'd end up alchemizing some Lorikor-shifter magic boost instead of the only memory I need to make real right now. Close call.

She opened the door and found Matt standing there with his hands in his pockets and a wide grin. The second he met her gaze, his smile faded.

"Crap. I interrupted something important, didn't I?"

"Kinda." She couldn't help but smile back at him, not even a little frustrated by the interruption now that she stood there looking at him and those dimples.

"Sorry. I thought you were trying to avoid the whole screaming match out there too. I'll go find something else to—"

"No, it's totally fine. You can come in."

"Really?"

"Yeah. I should probably take a break anyway. Kinda been at it hard for a while."

"I noticed."

Amanda opened the door even wider and stepped aside to let him in. Matt entered the greenhouse, and his eyes widened as he took in the one room in the entire school where Amanda had complete privacy and control.

Well, there's my dorm room, but he's not coming up there.

"Whoa. I had no idea this was so…"

"Full of plants?" She shut the door and watched Matt amble down the closest trough as he studied the product of her green shifter thumb.

He huffed out a laugh. "Just because I don't have a greenhouse doesn't mean I don't know what it's for."

"You still look surprised, though."

Matt turned at the edge of the first trough and walked back down the line beside the next one. "I mean, when I heard this place existed and that you spent so much time here, I guess I imagined more of a…closet filled with little pots."

Amanda snorted and folded her arms. "I kinda have one of those too."

"What?"

"It's… Never mind."

I showed all my other friends the cellar. I could show him too. Then I'd have to explain everything else about the Fatethistle down there, and he already knows what it does, and I have no idea how that stuff interacts with all the Lorikor parts… Just no. Not right now.

"Okay." Matt shrugged and reached toward a pale yellow leaf of the Flowering Arrowberry growing in the second trough. "What's this—"

"Don't!"

He instantly retracted his hand and froze.

"Just…don't touch those. Please."

"I feel like I should be surprised they let you grow poisonous plants in here, but I don't think I am."

Amanda laughed and shook her head. "No, they're not poisonous. I got rid of those a while ago. Well, except for the Underweaver." She pointed at the flesh-melting greenery growing as far away from the Dreamscape as space allowed.

Matt swallowed. "I don't even wanna ask."

"Don't worry. That's the only one that hurts. For the most part. But the Anchorbloom keeps it tame, I guess."

"Then what are these?" He stepped away from the yellow-leafed plants and slipped his hands back into his pockets.

"Oh, that's Flowering Arrowberry. For Nurse Aiken. I have to wear gloves with those because if they're touched before they get processed, it completely ruins their ability to…" She paused when he raised his eyebrows, and she could almost see the interest seeping out of him by the second. "Sorry. Just a bunch of nerdy gardener talk, I guess."

"Don't be sorry. It's cool that you're so into this stuff. Honestly, I end up killing everything I touch." Matt's smile disappeared, and his mouth dropped open. "I mean plants. Obviously. Not like small animals or people or, you know…*you* or anything."

"Yeah, we covered the part where you don't torture small animals last semester, remember?"

He let out an airy, relieved laugh and lowered his head as he hurried down the row between troughs to join her again. "Trust me. I won't forget that conversation anytime soon." When he turned to scan the full troughs again, he noticed the chair beside the Dreamscape and nodded toward it. "Cool flowers. What were you doing with that one?"

"Oh. Um…I was working on my final assignments."

"With plants?"

"Yeah, it's… Okay, do you want me to explain it all to you, or were you being polite?"

"I definitely wanna know about that one. What is it?"

"Dreamscape." Amanda headed down the final wider row between the fourth and fifth troughs and stopped in front of her newly matured manifestation plant. "It takes thoughts and intentions and kinda…makes them real, I guess."

"Seriously?" Matt leaned closer toward the plants, maybe to smell the flowers, but Amanda grabbed his hand and pulled him back.

"Can't touch those either. Or get too close. Sorry."

He grinned at her and laced their fingers together. "Not too sure about what kind of intention I'd be making real with these things, right?"

What's that supposed to mean?

The question normally wouldn't have bothered her, but they were standing here in her greenhouse, alone, holding hands, and she couldn't figure out if he was talking about *that* or something that had absolutely nothing to do with her.

"Pretty much." Amanda forced herself to look away from him and nodded at the shimmering blue flowers instead. "This is the stuff that made the whole school break out into confessing all the things they were thinking and feeling but would *never* say out loud. You know, private, secret stuff."

Matt's mouth fell open again, but it was buoyed by a wide smile this time. "*This* stuff? You're the one who gave it to everybody."

"No, I'm the one who grew it. Then it got used as party favors at the dance, and it…it didn't go well. I didn't know it was Dreamscape then. I thought it was something completely different and way less chaotic."

"Good story, though."

"I guess." They stared at each other, and the butterflies in Amanda's stomach went haywire when Matt's blue-eyed gaze roamed around her face before dropping to her lips.

I don't need to end up alchemizing this *instead, either. We should leave.*

He drew a sharp breath, then looked back at the plant. "So, what are you growing it for this time?"

"Um…" She blinked quickly and tried to recover, but the butterflies weren't exactly good listeners. "I told you it's for class, right?"

"Yep. I mean specifically. Kinda hard to picture how you'd use a confession plant for any of our projects. Even Zimmer's weird *scenarios.*"

With a short burst of laughter, Amanda shook her head. "*Intention* plant. I'm using it to…"

She paused, wondering now if it was the right move at all to blurt out all her plans.

He knows about everything anyway. The wizard. The Coalition not helping me. It's not like I'd be spilling any more secrets.

"You don't have to tell me if you don't want to," Matt muttered. "It's still cool to look at. I promise I won't—"

"The Dreamscape's gonna help me pull out the wizard's scent. From my memories. If I can lock onto that with these flowers, I can alchemize the whole thing into a device that tracks magical frequencies, and it'll lead me right to him."

After a thick swallow, Amanda drew a deep breath. "I mean, if it works the way I think it will. Which it should, based on everything I know about how all the other parts work. So…"

She studied his wide blue eyes and waited for him to say something.

I can't tell if he's impressed or thinks I'm insane. Not like either of those is better when I don't know if this will work.

"So that's it. I know it's a longshot, but—"

"It's brilliant."

"What?"

Matt's crooked smile returned as he turned back toward the Dreamscape and all the glowing, glittery blue flowers. "I mean, *I* could never come up with something like that. Maybe if I knew everything you know about what you can do. Not saying you have to tell me, by the way."

"You've mentioned that a few times." Amanda huffed out a laugh and frowned playfully. "It doesn't sound crazy to you?"

"I'm a little surprised that you even think you need someone else's opinion, but no, Amanda. This is…" He puffed out his cheeks and exhaled. "This might be better than that weird machine you said makes pictures out of your thoughts."

"Brainwaves. But yeah, I was thinking the same thing."

Running a hand through his hair, Matt backed away from the trough. "And here I come, interrupting the whole thing because I don't like crowds."

She squeezed his hand and looked up at his profile. The boy still stared at the plants, his eyes wide and a smile of disbelief lifting the corner of his mouth. "I have the rest of the semester to do this. Being interrupted one night isn't gonna ruin the whole process. I'm glad you did."

"Yeah?" He looked down at her—half-hopeful and half-wary, like he couldn't believe she was serious.

Amanda shrugged. "I don't like crowds either."

"Right. I can't, uh…stay and watch you do the whole memory-plant thing, can I?"

"The last time I had Dreamscape in here, I wasn't very careful at all about the intentions I was putting out there. I thought I was talking to myself for fun, which turned out to be a major disaster. So…probably not."

"No, I get it. The last thing I wanna do is get in your way. Or get inside those flowers somehow so you end up alchemizing something totally different, like how much I—" Matt stopped, opened and closed his mouth, then puffed out a sigh.

"How much you what?"

"Nothing." He laughed. "You'll tell me how it went after, though, right?"

"Definitely."

What was he about to say? Maybe we should get out of here before we end up contaminating every single flower by standing next to each other holding hands.

She pulled her hand out of his to grab the metal chair and folded it up with a *clang*. "You wanna sit?"

"Okay." Chuckling, Matt followed her down the row until they reached the open space between the troughs and the green metal cabinet. He grabbed the second chair from against the wall as Amanda unfolded hers and sat.

She didn't expect him to set up the other chair right next to hers with the metal sides touching, but she wasn't about to tell him to move farther away, either.

"So all the extra work you've been doing," Matt started as he rubbed his palms on the legs of his jeans. "It's all to find that wizard. Then it happens to work out for our final projects?"

"Pretty much." Amanda studied the healthy plants growing in neat lines out of the troughs and tried to ignore Matt's arm pressed against hers and how warm it was.

Just don't move. It's fine.

"Lately, it feels a little too convenient, you know? Like somebody planted all this stuff and wrote out the whole senior year so I'd find all the pieces and put them together myself."

Matt hummed in thought. "That's one massive conspiracy."

"I don't think that's what's going on. It only feels that way."

"Or maybe you're really good at finding all the pieces on your own. You know, without somebody having to dish it up to you."

"That's what I thought too." Amanda frowned. "Until I started questioning how good I knew I was."

"I don't know why you'd ever question it."

She tried to smile at him but ended up having to look away again. "Kinda hard to keep believing something like that when a massive, top-secret organization that runs pretty much all things shifter keeps telling me I'm too young, too inexperienced, too stubborn, blah blah blah.

"I mean, an internship's one thing, I guess. But they *hired* me last year. Told me to pick a team and that they'd let me call the shots on a bunch of things. Then as soon as I try to call the shots on something they can't understand and aren't willing to accept that I *know* what I'm doing, it's all over. They send me packing like I'm the one who started all the problems in the first place. Not the one who fixed them."

"That was a pretty stupid choice on their part."

"Ha. Tell that to the Coalition."

Matt pressed his lips together and lowered his head, leaning forward to catch her attention. "You still haven't heard from them about finding the guy?"

"Nope. Not even that they're working on it. Even if they've already started looking for him, I'm pretty sure at this point they wouldn't tell me on purpose. You know, to still hold something over my head so I'll jump the next time they think they need me."

"That's messed up."

"Oh, yeah. I mean, it's par for the course with these guys, and that's not even the worst part. Apparently, I'm the only shifter ever who tries to do something different than everyone else even though what they've always been doing *doesn't work*. Like trying to figure out what a creature wants and how we can help it instead of hunting it down and shooting first to bring back a science trophy."

A bitter laugh escaped her. "Better yet, how about *talking* with an ancient Oriceran creature intent on stripping magic out of Earth and every single magical on this planet if we don't prove we can use magic the way we were supposed to use it. For good. I mean, how hard is it to say, 'Hey, good work, Amanda. No idea how you did it, but that doesn't matter because you saved the world, so thanks'? Simple. And way too hard for a whole lab of scientists to admit they don't have all the answers."

She drew a deep breath and blinked at the worktable in front of them.

Crap. I wasn't supposed to say all that. Man, I was doing such a good job not dumping my Coalition crap on anyone. Petrov doesn't count.

"Wait a minute." Matt turned his body to look at her more directly and slung his arm over the back of her chair. "*That's* what you were doing while you were gone?"

Amanda grimaced. "Yeah. Since the end of November, at least. I mean, I left school to go find a bunch of magical turtle-bomb babies, but we solved that whole issue. Also because I was there to look at things differently. Then UM-7000 showed up and... Hey, I shouldn't be telling you all this. It's pretty, like, top-secret stuff."

"No, I get it. I won't tell anyone." He studied her face, then frowned. "What kinda name is UM-7000, though?"

"Oh, jeeze. Dr. Caniss doesn't like naming the creatures. So everything gets a *number.*"

"They have seven *thousand* different creatures?"

"I don't think so. It's closer to almost six, I think. Pretty sure she wanted to make it stand out. Or her favorite number's seven. Or maybe she doesn't like six. I honestly have no idea."

Matt burst out laughing, and Amanda couldn't help but join him.

"It sounds ridiculous, right?"

"A little."

"Trust me, hearing about it isn't anywhere near as ridiculous as what goes on in that lab half the time. And they still think *I'm* the one who needs to 'figure out how the world works.'"

"Because you saved the world?"

"No. It's because I kinda...commandeered their super expensive equipment without asking. Then blew it up."

"*What?*"

"That part was an accident, okay?" She couldn't help but laugh again at Matt's growing smile and how it was so much easier to talk to him about this stuff without him freaking out or telling her what she should do next. He looked at her like she was some famous magical telling stories about the old days.

"So they won't help you find that wizard because you blew some stuff up?" Matt chuckled. "I always thought that was part of the whole process. You know, science. Right?"

"Not when it's a sixteen-year-old girl trying to get something done. What do you do with a sixteen-year-old girl who breaks your rules 'cause she knows they're stupid? Take her stuff. Duh."

"They can't do that if they're not your parents." Matt pursed his lips in confusion. "I think."

"Well, they could take everything *they* gave me. Plus everything I got from using their system. Like the image they confiscated. And the phone they gave me, but I got that back. Pretty sure I'm still locked out of the system, though, until they decide to 'grant me access' again. It doesn't make sense. I think I'm starting to understand why *Johnny's* so pissed off all the time, though."

"Huh. I haven't met the guy, but from what you told me, he doesn't seem like someone who'd get mad at you for saving the world."

"Ha! No, I'm talking about him being… Well, he's kind of a jerk to everyone else on the outside. Not me. Not Lisa. But I think I get it.

"I'm pretty sure a whole lot of people have told him *he* can't do something, and nobody believes him either when he says he knows what he's doing. Until he proves them wrong. Which he pretty much always does."

"Right. Didn't you say something about him blackmailing the FBI, or is that wishful thinking?"

Amanda grinned and stared at the plants. "No, that happened. I think. He won't tell me one way or the other, but he's terrible at hiding when he's proud of something most people would have a heart attack thinking about."

"That's…" Matt laughed and slumped back in his chair again, making Amanda highly aware of the fact that he hadn't removed his arm from around the back of her chair. "That's awesome. I know he's not, you know, your actual dad or anything, but you guys sound a lot alike."

"Yeah, I've kinda tossed that idea around a few times. I guess now I have to prove people wrong enough times that they start taking me as seriously as they take Johnny."

For a moment, neither of them had anything else to say. When Matt straightened in his chair and removed his arm from *almost* around Amanda's shoulder, she thought she'd said something wrong. Then he looked at her with a deepening frown. "You said they locked you out of the system. The Coalition, I mean."

"Yeah."

"I guess your phone's connected to it, right?"

"Everything's connected. I couldn't even turn the lights off in my room at the lab 'cause my fancy upgrade came with smart lights. And they took my phone."

"What else can it do?"

"Um… I mean, I can send voice commands. That's not super special, though. We have all our gear hooked up to the system. Send files back and forth. When I still had access to everything, at least."

"Okay. Good. That's actually really good."

Amanda wrinkled her nose. "That I don't have access?"

"No, that your phone still does."

"Matt, they locked me out."

This time when he grinned at her, he looked like he'd stumbled upon the meaning of life. "Yeah, but every lock has a key. You gotta know where to look for it."

"You mean, break into the Coalition mainframe?"

"Why not? Or at the very least see if they've started looking for that wizard. If they have, awesome. You get your information, and they don't have anything to hang over your head anymore. If they haven't started, you still found another way to find him without the Coalition's help. Just a quick break-in to take a look. Hack into the system, poke around, get right back out again."

Amanda burst out laughing.

"What?" His smile didn't falter at all as he watched her crack up over his suggestion. "Why's that funny?"

"I'm sorry. It's a good idea. But... I mean, I'm good at a lot of things, Matt, but teenage hacker isn't on the list."

"Okay. Well, maybe I can give it a try."

"I don't know..."

"You don't have anything to lose, right? Not if they're holding out on you."

She stared at him and almost laughed again.

He wants me to hand over my Coalition phone so he can try to break into it? I don't even think that's something Johnny *could do. Maybe Matt knows something I don't, right?*

Taking a deep breath, she stood abruptly from her chair and reached for her back pocket. "I'm not even supposed to be *talking* about this stuff, let alone handing over advanced tech that doesn't belong to me."

Matt looked up at her in concern. "Okay. I get it. It's totally fine, and I'm *not* trying to pressure you into anything. I thought maybe you'd want to—"

"Here." She held her sleek, nearly transparent Coalition phone out to him and nodded.

"Really?"

"You're right. I don't have anything to lose. At this point, if they're hiding information from me that I *deserve* to have because of what that wizard did, maybe they deserve to be hacked."

Matt stared at the phone and reached for it. "Can't argue with you there."

"It's pretty advanced stuff, though. So we probably shouldn't get our hopes up."

"Sure. Doesn't hurt to try." He glanced at her before sitting back in his chair and scrolling rapidly through the rows of apps and files on her phone.

Right. Trying won't get us anywhere because the Coalition has everything locked up way too tightly for a couple of shifter kids to get into.

CHAPTER TWENTY-THREE

By the time Amanda sat back in her chair beside Matt and tried to get a glimpse of what he was doing on her phone, the boy's fingers were flying across the screen.

Which didn't look anything like the screen she saw every time she opened her phone.

"Whoa. What's that?"

"Just bypassing a few security steps. They set this up fairly well, but it's kind of a half-assed job."

Amanda snorted. "Oh, yeah?"

"I don't think they expected you to do any digging on your own like this. Hold on. I gotta…" His words petered out, and now he was fully immersed in all the symbols and command codes and whatever else scrolled across the screen. Matt's eyes grew wider by the second, and he snickered before turning the phone sideways and typing away on the touch-screen keyboard lining the bottom.

I didn't know it could do that.

His smile flickered in and out. Even when he muttered to himself about firewalls or access codes or some kind of network something-something Amanda didn't recognize at all, he didn't look up at her. She couldn't follow most of what he was doing, but less than ten minutes later, Matt sucked in a sharp breath through his teeth and tapped the screen.

"Kicked you out, huh?"

"What? No way. We're in."

Amanda tilted her head and stared at his profile as he grinned at the black backlight behind her screen. "In? As in—"

"The Coalition system." He looked up at her and raised his eyebrows. "That was almost as hard as I expected. Where do you wanna look first?"

"Holy shit." She laughed, then had to think about where the Coalition's greatest scientific minds like Dr. Caniss would file away something like the image of an unidentified murderer pulled out of a teenager employer's head. "Okay...I mean, have you tried looking up my name?"

"They have a file on you. Of course, they do. Hold on." Matt typed some more, then tapped an icon and leaned toward Amanda so they could stare at the screen together. "Hey, look. It's your face."

"It's my file..." Amanda scrolled down and skimmed the content, looking for anything remotely connected to her "borrowing" Mel's machine. "It's not in here."

"Okay. Um..." Matt tapped in another lightning-fast command and nodded. "Here. All the files connected with you. I guess these are...reports?"

"Missions, probably."

"What?" He looked at her with wide eyes. "Like, you call them actual missions?"

"Yeah, and we're looking for the wizard, remember?"

"Uh-huh." The boy went back to diligently scanning the file names. "Okay, here's South America. Man, I bet there's some crazy stuff in here—"

"Don't read the reports. Please."

"Confidential. Got it. I'll pull up another hidden search to…" His ability to speak and type madly away on her phone at the same time still didn't exist, and he was at it for so long that Amanda sat back in her chair again with a sigh.

Why do I even care if he reads anything or not? He hacked into the Coalition mainframe. On my phone. If that's not already in too deep, I don't know what is.

"I got it!"

"Seriously?" Amanda jolted away from the back of the chair. "Like, you found their search results or—"

"This him?" Matt showed her the screen, and there was the rendition of the wizard's face she'd pulled from her mind, painted in glowing blue pixels. The pixels weren't visible when the picture was the size of her phone screen, but the image was still perfectly recognizable.

Her gut twisted on itself looking at the wizard's smug sneer again, and she swallowed. "That's him."

"Piece of shit," Matt muttered before typing again.

Despite everything, that one little comment made her smile.

"Yep. Yep. Yep." The boyo's eyes darted back and forth almost as fast as his fingers. "And… Aw, man."

"What?"

"Well, they started running the search."

Amanda clenched her fists in her lap and stared at him. "And?"

"Nothing yet. No information. I can't tell when they started the search, but all it pulls up is that it's still in progress and 'analysis pending.' Whatever that means. I don't know why anyone would try to analyze a picture like this, but I can't get anything else out of it."

With a low growl, Amanda stood from her chair and paced toward the wall of windows. "I knew it. I *knew* they'd start this without telling me a thing."

"Want me to look for anything else?"

"No. I'll end up smashing that thing."

Matt entered another command that didn't take nearly as long as others, then puffed out a sigh and set the phone gently on the empty chair beside him. "Okay, well, we're out of there now. Your phone didn't explode or anything, so I'm pretty sure it's safe. You okay?"

"Not really." She spun to pace in the other direction toward the door, gritting her teeth as she tried to stop thinking about the wizard's face and concentrate on what she had to do next. "I mean, it's not like I'm surprised. I knew they'd do this. But *seeing* it?

"If they're already running the stupid search, it means they still believe me. They *know* it's better to listen to me than ignore everything I tell them, but they can't admit they were wrong and tell me. Jesus, it's like everybody has their head shoved so far up their own—"

Matt let out a startled cry and leapt out of his chair, which flew backward away from him and toppled to the floor with a loud clatter. Amanda spun toward him to see none other than Fiona Damascus standing there in front of the worktables, her arms folded as she scowled at the shifter girl.

The woman opened her mouth. Then a giant cheer rose from the main field as the student body cheered for what sounded like an epic play by the Florida Gators.

Fiona glanced at the ceiling and smirked. "Kind of a nice entrance, don't you think?"

Matt tugged the bottom of his shirt down and cleared his throat.

Amanda glared at her mentor. "I don't know why you felt like you needed to make an entrance at all."

"Oh, you don't, huh?" Fiona stormed toward the shifter girl and thrust a finger toward her, completely ignoring Matt as the boy stepped backward out of the way. "Well, *I* don't know why you still feel like the rules don't apply to you. They're there for a reason, kid. It's pretty simple."

"The rules? You break the rules all the time—"

"I have the track record to back that up! What part of *probation* do you not understand?"

"Mostly why I'm on it in the first place." Amanda didn't so much as flinch when Fiona lunged toward her and got all up in her face.

The woman snarled. "So you thought that was a good enough reason to go poking around places you're not supposed to be? Don't even think about giving me some kind of clueless excuse, kid. I got an alert that you were trying to hack into the system."

Amanda swallowed.

How the hell did she figure that out so quickly?

Matt snorted. "It's not *trying* if it was a success, though, right?"

Fiona's eyes widened before she turned slowly to look the shifter boy up and down. "I don't know who you think you are, buddy, but this doesn't have anything to do with you. Why the hell are you…"

The woman growled and shook her head. "Damnit, Amanda. Were you trying to show off for this guy, or did you get it in your head that being *locked out* of your system access was the best opportunity to piss me off?"

Amanda shrugged. "Probably a little of both."

"Jesus Christ, kid. You can't whip out technology like that and go scrolling through with a friend. We already *covered* this!"

"I did it." Matt lifted his chin. "*I* broke into the system. Amanda only gave me the phone."

"That's even *worse!*" Fiona whirled on the shifter boy again and spread her arms. "Do you know how many magicals I've had to lock up or seriously injure for *thinking* about classified information?"

"Fiona—"

"Don't Fiona me, kid. I can't believe you'd do something so stupid—"

"Hey. It was *my* idea." Matt stepped toward the furious shifter woman. Although he didn't take any kind of aggressive stance or point in her face as she'd done to Amanda, he was clearly furious. "She wouldn't have done it on her own, but I told her I could find what she was looking for. What *you* have been keeping from her."

Fiona snickered. "Are you for real? You don't even know half of all the—"

"I know you and Caniss took that image from Amanda." Matt narrowed his eyes. "I know you locked her out of the system because nothing she told you made sense, and you figured it was safer to make her think she's going crazy. I know it takes a serious lack of morals to keep this kind of information from her when she already *told* you what that wizard did to her family."

Fiona raised her eyebrows, but Matt hadn't finished.

"You know what? Forget a lack of morals. You're all assholes *and* morons if you think Amanda won't keep doing whatever it takes to find this guy and put him away." He folded his arms and shook his head, wearing much the same look as every other adult in Amanda's life who had no problem expressing how much they disapproved of the shifter girl's choices. "She doesn't *need* you."

Blinking quickly, Fiona tilted her head and gave him a pert smile. "You done?"

"Unless you want more."

"Let me guess." The woman turned toward Amanda and pointed at Matt. "This is your boyfriend."

The girl widened her eyes and froze. She could barely look at Matt.

Jesus Christ. Why does she have to bring that up now? *I never said he was my anything, and now he's gonna think I've been running around calling him my boyfriend.*

"I'm right, aren't I?" Fiona looked Matt up and down again. "Because this makes everything else make total sense."

"Fiona, this isn't—"

"I'm whatever Amanda wants me to be, okay?" Matt cut in.

Barking out a sharp laugh, the woman shot him a sidelong glance and jerked her chin up at him. "So, what does she want you to be?"

He folded his arms. "I don't know. It doesn't matter. *You're* still the one who's failing her."

The smile disappeared from Fiona's face, and her lip twitched in the first attempts at a snarl as she stared him down.

That really pissed her off. Amanda looked back and forth between the two shifters verbally duking it out on her behalf, and bit her lip. *I can't believe he said all that right to her face. For me. He probably wouldn't if he knew who she is.*

When Matt showed no sign of backing down, Fiona pulled herself together and snickered instead. "Get a load of *this* guy, huh? I should still be furious with you, kid, but honestly, I'm more impressed than anything else. You teamed up with a decent juvenile hacker—"

Matt scoffed. "Decent."

"And it turns out he's a hell of a cheerleader too. Way to start building a backup team that doesn't suck."

"Thanks." Amanda's anger slithered back into her awareness now that Fiona's had petered out. "At least now I know how to build a team that stands up to help me instead of turning their backs when I need them the most."

"Oh, give me a break. What is this, high school?" Fiona frowned, gazed around the greenhouse, then sighed. "Okay. I get it. Listen, kid. No one's trying to keep the information from you. We all needed a break after what happened down in…" She eyed Matt and grimaced. "Well, I don't have to say it."

"South America," he muttered. "I already know."

"Well, isn't that *swell?*" The woman rolled her eyes. "We thought it was better to let you settle back into classes, and

Melody took her sweet time going over every single report with a toothpick. We're running the search on your wizard right now."

"It's too late to tell me something like that and expect me to stop being angry." Amanda shook her head. "I already saw that you're running the search. And you didn't tell me until you saw somebody breaking into the system."

"I…" Fiona hissed through her gritted teeth, raised her clenched fists, then drew a deep breath. "How about this? We move past this whole hacking kerfuffle and focus on what comes next. If the system pulls up any information about that paint-by-brainwaves face—"

"It'll find him."

"Uh-huh. Whatever information we get, kid, I'll make sure somebody pings you with an update. Until then, *both of you* are gonna knock it off with this secret hacker business and stay out of the system. You know, I'm not a fan of training teenagers, but trust me, I enjoy *arresting* teenagers even less."

"Can you even do that?" Matt asked.

Fiona spun toward him and pointed at his face. "You don't wanna find out."

Then a blue light flashed around her, and the next second, she was gone.

The greenhouse was completely silent before another cheer from the Louper match raced across campus and reached the room as a muted roar. Amanda pressed her lips together and slowly looked up at Matt, who was staring at the spot where Fiona had been standing.

"That's incredibly weird."

"Sorry about her."

He met Amanda's gaze and grinned. "No way. Don't start apologizing for somebody who won't take you seriously." Casting another glance at the empty air where there had been an angry shifter woman, Matt walked toward Amanda and lowered his head with another self-conscious laugh. "I'm the one who should be apologizing. To you."

"What?"

"I kinda feel like I stole your thunder on that one." He rubbed the back of his neck and grimaced. "You know, telling her how shitty of a move it was to keep all this stuff from you. You probably wanted to let her have it, but I…I couldn't help myself."

"It was pretty awesome." She bit her lip when he looked up at her in surprise. "I don't find myself in a lot of situations where I have someone with me who's *always* on my side. Even when I do stupid stuff. Especially with the Coalition, so… Thank you."

"Any time. Although I'm not sure if she believed me when I said I was the one who hacked into your phone."

"She believed you. We both know I couldn't have done that. At all. But hey. *That's* a cool secret to know about you."

"Ha. Yeah…" Wrinkling his nose, Matt scuffed the sole of his sneaker against the greenhouse's linoleum floor with a *squeak*. "That's a thing I do. It's why I got sent here in the first place. To the Academy."

She snorted. "To learn how to be a professional hacker?"

"I wish. No, I kinda got into some trouble for jumping into the wrong corporation's back data. I mean, I did it on purpose, but they weren't all that excited about it.

"I think my dad assumes finishing high school at a school for bounty hunters will scare me straight or something. Honestly, I have more resources here to use my…*talents* than I'd ever have anywhere else. Probably even with a cushy job in cybersecurity."

"Resources? At the school?"

"Just a bunch of tech. You can use half the stuff in LeFor's workshop for *way* more than he's teaching us, and I'm pretty sure he has no idea."

Amanda laughed and quickly covered her mouth. "That's crazy. And you're a *hacker*."

She nudged him in the shoulder, and he let out a hesitant noise that was half-laugh, half-groan. "I guess it fits."

"I think it's super cool."

"Thanks." He fixed her with a playful frown, then grabbed her hand and stepped closer. "That's not the *only* thing I am, though."

Amanda stared at her hand in his and swallowed.

No. He's not gonna bring that up again, is he?

With another self-conscious chuckle, Matt looked up at her and looked like he was somewhere on the line between laughing and grimacing in discomfort. "It was kinda weird that she called me your boyfriend, though."

Crap. He's bringing it up.

"Okay, for the record, I did *not* tell her you were."

"But you did tell her *something* about me."

"Yeah…you came up a few times." She wrinkled her nose and looked over his shoulder at the plants lining the greenhouse. "Fiona thinks going out for runs with you makes us…you know. Whatever. Which is totally stupid. It's only going for a run."

"Right. She's crazy."

They both laughed, but Matt still didn't let go of her hand. Amanda couldn't look up at him as he leaned closer because if she did, she knew what would happen.

"I meant what I said, though."

"Which part?"

He swallowed and broke into that famous Matt Hardy smile— crooked, careless, and a little self-conscious. "All of it. But I'm talking about me being whatever you want me to be."

"Are you…" Despite her heart racing and the butterflies throwing bombs now in her stomach, Amanda finally had to look up at him and tried to smile back like this wasn't a big deal. "Are you asking me to…"

"I don't know." Matt laughed. "I mean, I know I said it's what- ever you want. But I *really* don't care what you call it as long as—"

Amanda stopped him the same way he'd stopped her from her

rambling beside her new scooter during the Homecoming dance. This time, kissing the shifter boy inside the Academy's greenhouse felt like a way better move, and he didn't seem as surprised by it now as she'd been back then.

Maybe he is, and I don't care.

The next thing she knew, her arms were around his neck, and he'd pulled her closer to hold her against him gently. It couldn't have lasted more than twenty seconds, but compared to their quick goodbye before Amanda raced off to the Canissphere and disappeared for the next three months, it felt like forever.

When she finally pulled away, Matt blinked and puffed out a quick breath. "*Or* you could do that."

Okay, now he does *sound surprised. Crap, maybe I shouldn't have done that.*

Amanda bit her lip. "Was that not—"

"Literally whenever you want, Amanda."

"Oh." She finally caught her breath and grinned. "Okay. So, I don't...really know what I'm doing. Or what *we're* doing, I guess. I mean, if you want to be—"

"I like you. I *think* you like me."

"Wow. It's not obvious enough, huh?"

Matt snorted. "Now it is. Honestly, I only know what it's like to have girls think they're in love with me for doing absolutely nothing. So this is new to me too."

"Right." She bit her lip and couldn't think of anything to say.

So we're a thing. Maybe. Oh my God, how does anybody ever figure this out?

"Hey, so, not that I hope it takes forever for you to get the information you're looking for, but if you haven't heard anything by next weekend, do you..." Matt cleared his throat. "You wanna go to the dance with me?"

"You mean, like, a date?"

"I think so."

For the first time, Amanda understood what all the craziness in the girls' dorm was about in the days leading up to school dances. Because right now, she wanted to scream.

"Okay."

"Okay?

"Yeah, I'll go with you. To the dance. Where everyone else will be there too."

Matt burst out laughing. "It has to be better than the last one, right?"

"It sure as hell better be."

CHAPTER TWENTY-FOUR

Having a date to the Spring Fling dance—not to mention a date she liked—finally gave Amanda a reason to dress up. The only problem was she hadn't told any of her friends about what had happened between her and Matt. That was mostly because she'd been busy successfully reaching out to the Dreamscape with her magic and filling up all those blue flowers with what she seriously hoped was the memory of the wizard's scent and nothing else.

So by the time the Spring Fling came around, she couldn't ask Grace or any of the other girls she knew who understood how to do makeup and hair if they'd help her with hers. Fortunately, she ran into Blake Lively at the kemana the night before the dance, and neither of them could ignore the reason behind why they'd bumped into each other in a dress shop.

"I didn't think you were into this whole thing." Blake's eyes widened as she eyed the plain but shiny silver dress Amanda had randomly tugged off the rack.

"Last dance before we graduate, right?" Amanda tried to keep a straight face. "I guess I might as well go all-out at least once."

"Awesome. Hey, if you need any help getting ready—"

"Yes. Yes, I need serious help, Blake. Please tell me you know what you're doing."

The witch laughed and tucked her hair behind her ear before sifting through the other dresses. "I got you. Just need to find a dress first that doesn't cost more than all our semester 'budgets' put together."

Amanda grinned. "Pick whatever you want. I'll get it for you."

"No. That's… You don't have to—"

"Trust me. This makes us even."

On the night of the dance, Amanda got yelled at by Blake at least once every ten minutes because she wouldn't sit still enough for her last-minute hairstylist and makeup artist to do what she was trying to do.

"We're almost done, Amanda. You seriously need to chill out."

"I don't know what you're talking about. I'm totally fine."

"Hey, if I didn't have awesome reflexes, I would've drawn eyeliner down your nose. Quit moving!" They both laughed, then Blake leaned in again to continue her work and shook her head. "Jeeze, I feel like I'm talking to a toddler."

"Thanks."

By the time they finally finished, all the other girls had cleared the dorm to join the boys in front of the veiled archway marking the entrance to the dance.

Good. I'm glad nobody's gonna see me like this until I get out there because I probably…

Amanda stepped in front of the mirror in Blake's room and froze.

"What?"

Blake finished tying up her hair and hummed in approval. "I'll take that as a compliment."

"I don't even *look* like me."

"You look…" Blake shook her head. "Are you sure you're only doing this for fun? Or for somebody else?"

Amanda turned sideways and frowned at her reflection. "I'm doing it. Or you did it. So that's all that matters, right? Thanks."

"Uh-huh." With a laugh, Blake grabbed the shifter girl's hand tugged her out of her room. "I don't wanna be late, but hey. Either way, *you're* making an entrance."

"Wait, I don't wanna *make an entrance.*"

"Too late. Everybody's gonna lose it when they see you."

That's not even remotely what I'm trying to do.

The butterflies thumped around in her stomach again as Amanda let the brown-haired witch pull her down the stairs, across the common room, and through the dorm's front doors. They headed toward the outskirts of the main field. The entire student body had gathered in front of the curved archway blocking the dance's mystery theme from view.

"Please don't start shouting for everyone to look at me," Amanda muttered and slowed as Blake let go of her hand.

"Trust me. I won't have to." The other girl grinned. "See you inside."

Blake wasn't wrong at all. It only took a minute of Amanda standing there at the very back of the crowd, all by herself, before students glanced her way and did a double-take at the shifter girl in the sleek silver dress and her hair piled on her head. Then the whispers started.

Oh, come on. I'm not wearing that *much makeup.*

Once Summer saw her, though, it was impossible to keep hiding.

"Holy *shit!*" The rainbow-haired witch ran toward Amanda with her mouth hanging open. "What the hell did you do?"

"Summer."

"No, no. It's amazing. You don't even look like *you*, shifter girl. All fancy and… Damn."

"Thanks. Blake helped."

"She probably didn't even need to." Summer puffed out her cheeks, then burst out laughing. "You look like you're about to puke."

"I kinda feel like it." Amanda grimaced. "Everybody's staring."

"Screw them. Hey, do you have a *date* for this—"

"*Amanda.*" With a gasp, Grace headed toward them, her eyes bulging from her head. "Whoa!"

"Okay. Thanks. We can stop talking about how I look now."

"No, we can't. You look amazing! Summer, doesn't she look—"

"Getting me to copy everything you say isn't gonna make her feel any better, Blondie." Summer snorted. "I already told her."

"Oh my God. I didn't think you would ever... Wait. Did someone ask you to the dance?"

Amanda heaved a massive sigh. "So because I dressed up this time, that automatically means I have a date?"

"I mean, I don't know why else you would do this. That's the only thing that could've changed, right?"

"Okay. Yeah. Somebody did ask me, and it was—"

"Whoa. Coulier, is that *you*?" Jackson stepped up behind the girls, and they all turned to see him shaking his head, his eyes wide. "I...didn't recognize you. Ha."

Summer and Grace exchanged a glance. Then the rainbow-haired witch smacked her lips. "I'm gonna go find Woody. I think he got hold of something that explodes, and even if he didn't, it's probably way less awkward than this."

She took off into the crowd, and Grace opened her mouth to say something before Annabelle and Jasmine called her to join them. "See you in there." With a tight smile, Grace waved and hurried to join her other friends.

Leaving Amanda and Jackson alone at the back of the crowd.

Yep. This is awkward. Where's Matt? Not that it would make this any less *awkward, but still.*

223

Jackson shoved his hands into his pockets and rocked forward. "You do look pretty."

"Thanks, Jackson. I like your…corduroys."

The wizard snorted. "You're not gonna tell me I'm pretty too."

"Oh, right. Sorry."

"You're going to the dance with somebody, aren't you?"

Amanda blinked quickly and searched the crowd of students. Matt was nowhere in sight.

Please don't let this be one of those things he regrets doing so he doesn't show up, and I look like an idiot.

"Yeah." She turned toward Jackson with a small smile. "I'm, uh…"

Then she saw him hurrying toward the crowd from the boy's dorm in gray dress slacks, a royal-blue shirt, and incredibly shiny black loafers.

Wow.

"What?" Jackson asked.

"Sorry. I'm going with Matt. He asked me last week, so…"

That was the moment Matt looked their way and saw Amanda in her dress and an only slightly dejected-looking Jackson standing beside her. His eyes widened, then he met her gaze and grinned before heading toward them.

Great. Now it's gonna be even more awkward.

"Huh." Jackson jerked his chin up as Matt finally reached them. "Yeah, I always knew it was a long shot."

"Wait, what?"

"Hey, guys." Matt stopped short and caught his breath before fixing Amanda with that crooked smile. "I didn't think you were gonna dress up, but you look…"

"Thanks." Amanda blushed and cursed her decision to go buy a dress. "You too."

"Cool." Jackson clapped and looked back and forth between them. "I'll let you two make vague compliments at each other in private. I'm gonna go eat all the brownies."

The wizard grinned at them, then playfully socked Matt in the shoulder. "Listen, dude. I don't know *what* you did. Just don't screw it up."

"Wasn't planning on it."

"Good. 'Cause if you do anything to hurt her, I'll kick your ass." The wizard glanced down and pointed. "Nice shoes, by the way."

Matt laughed. "Thanks, man."

"Yep. Have fun, shifters." Clicking his tongue, Jackson raced off to join everyone else as the veil opened and let the students through onto the dancefloor.

Amanda stared after the wizard and couldn't believe what had happened. "Did he threaten you, then compliment your shoes?"

Matt slid his fingers through hers and pulled her forward. "Yep. See? I told you he was cool about it."

"You did. I just…I'm glad my friends are so awesome."

"Yeah, me too. Come on."

They filtered through the archway and onto the dancefloor as the last students to enter. Amanda hardly paid attention to the decorations, the music, or all the floating lights. The only thing she could focus on was Matt's hand in hers and the scathing stares coming her way from almost every single girl there.

"Wow. I think I made myself an *easier* target than the last time."

Matt turned toward her and grabbed her other hand too. "We can leave if you want."

"Mm…not yet. I can ignore them if you can. It's hard to take it seriously when they can't help it."

He laughed through a grimace and gazed briefly around the dancefloor. "Sorry."

"Don't be. I didn't wear a dress for them anyway."

"It's a great dress."

"Ha. Thanks."

"You, uh…want some HardPull or something?"

"Yeah, let's go get some—what the…" Amanda stared over Matt's shoulder and couldn't believe what she was seeing.

"What? Did Glasket wear another weird costume like Homecoming?" Matt turned and didn't see anything until Amanda repeatedly smacked his arm and pointed at the refreshments table. "Uh…"

"Right?" She barked out a laugh. "When did *that* happen?"

Shoving his hands into his pockets again, Matt tilted his head and shrugged. "I have no idea. Didn't know that was a thing."

"Well, it's blowing my mind right now."

Standing behind the refreshment table were Summer and Alex. Neither of them was remotely interested in the snacks or the giant punch bowl of HardPull because they were way too busy making out with each other.

Jackson stood at the far end of the table with a brownie halfway raised to his mouth and stared at them in shocked disgust. "Dude!"

When that didn't work to untangle the odd couple, Jackson looked down at his brownie, then chucked it at the back of Alex's head.

"What the—"

"Do you *mind*? Some of us are eating over here."

Alex turned without any expression at all and jerked his chin up at the wizard. "Nothing's stopping you."

"Except for that."

"Well then *maybe*," Summer said as she peered around Alex and pointed at the wizard, "you should quit staring. I don't like watching *you* eat half the dessert every single day, but all I have to do is stop looking at you, Jackson."

"Yeah, but you throw stuff at me all the—" Jackson froze, then broke into a wide grin. "*Hey*. You stopped with the—"

"Nobody cares." Grinning, Summer grabbed Alex's hand and pulled him with her as she walked backward into the crowd of students on the dancefloor.

Jackson sighed through his grin and piled an overflowing handful of brownies onto one hand.

Amanda didn't think her best friend had noticed the school's only two shifters staring at her until Summer and Alex were almost right in front of them. "What are *you* two looking at?"

"Um…" Amanda glanced back and forth between Summer and Alex, who twisted his pursed lips to one side and didn't say a word. "You guys are—"

"You know what, shifter girl? You didn't tell me either. About this whole…wolfy setup you and Ladykiller got goin' on. So we're pretty damn even."

Alex snorted and cracked a tiny smile.

"Yeah, I know, but—"

"Wait, Ladykiller?" Matt wrinkled his nose. "You didn't pick something better after I told you guys why that happens?"

"Why would I do that?" Summer laughed. "You should see your faces right now. Seriously. That's the best part."

Glasket stepped up onto the stage, and LeFor's floating microphone squealed as it followed her before she finally got the thing under control again.

"Welcome to your Spring Fling dance this year." The principal grinned and spread her arms. "Unfortunately, I didn't have much prepared to say tonight—"

"So turn the music back on!" Evan shouted, followed by an eruption of laughter.

"Yes, Mr. Hutchinson. That's the plan. I want you all to enjoy yourselves tonight. Safely. Whoever started that rumor about fireworks needs to start another one about how any student I catch with any type of explosive, magical or otherwise, will spend the rest of the night in my office dusting every surface imaginable. Have fun."

With that, Glasket stepped off the stage, and the music cranked up again with a cheer from the students.

Amanda burst out laughing. "That was totally not a Glasket speech."

Matt shook his head. "Nope. I haven't even been here a whole year, and even *I* know that was weird."

"Summer, I'm pretty sure she was talking about you. And fireworks."

"What? Get real, shifter girl. That was *last* year. I'm not stupid. Hey." She elbowed Alex in the ribs and smirked. "Wanna dance?"

"Sure."

The witch grabbed his hand and hauled him away through the dancing crowd. She glanced over her shoulder to give Amanda a comically exaggerated wink before disappearing.

"She totally brought fireworks."

Matt leaned toward Amanda and muttered, "I won't tell anybody if you won't."

"Are you kidding? I didn't get to see them last time. No way am I missing out on those again."

CHAPTER TWENTY-FIVE

After such a complete success of her last school dance—including the fireworks, for which Principal Glasket hadn't been able to find the culprit—Amanda dove back into her projects with a lot more excitement and dedication than she'd expected. Somehow, being able to let loose with her friends and not worry about anyone seeing her and Matt together had lifted a giant weight off her shoulders.

Over the next few weeks, as the end of the semester drew nearer, Amanda spent her days perfecting Angus Fletchen's methods and creating her alchemized "scent tracker." It so happened that she was able to use the same thing with her scenario for Mrs. Zimmer, who approved the write-up and told Amanda how impressed she was with such a unique application of a common formula.

The real test would come when she had to put her theory to use with the actual scenario during her finals, but every day, she felt more confident that her plan would work. If it gave her a passing grade for her finals, the rest of the solution she'd created would do what she needed. The mix of crushed Dreamscape leaves, a bunch of alchemy, and a completely different memory soaked up by the blue flowers would find the wizard who'd narrowly escaped her in South America.

The only real change in schedule for any of them was that Petrov had now switched their Combat Training with firearms at the makeshift firing range to what he'd called "the games," and the seniors very quickly found out what that meant.

LeFor had repurposed the virtual reality technology from an older collection of Louper headsets to pair the system with the firearms that shot painful orange darts of electricity instead of bullets. The class split up into teams, and they were left to their own devices for two and a half hours every other day to assign tasks to each other and strategize before Petrov sucked them into a virtual reality not unlike the Louper field to begin.

Summer rolled her eyes as she disengaged the safety on her rifle. "This is so stupid. We're basically playing capture the flag with guns. Why can't he call it that?"

"Because then we wouldn't have been near as worried about what *the games* were." Amanda crouched behind a neon-orange boulder and scanned the virtual forest in front of them. "If you don't stop talking, we're about to—"

Orange pellets cracked against the boulder, then Jackson shouted, "You two suck at hiding!"

"Crap. Why did *he* have to find us?"

Summer snorted. "Because he's trying to take out the best shot in the class. Typical."

"Wait, wait, wait. Summer, don't—"

The rainbow-haired witch leapt out from behind the boulder and shoved the empty clip into the magazine of her semi-automatic magic-rifle for effect. "You're going down, wizard."

"Summer! Get back—"

"Say hello to my little friend!" Summer's scream and the rapid fire of her not-so-deadly weapon echoed madly through the virtual woods, joined by random shots from the other team whenever they could get them in.

"Come on…" Amanda propped her back against the other side of the boulder and couldn't help but laugh when the shouts of the other team—some of them in anger but most of them in pain— rose above the roar of gunfire.

The shifter girl shook her head and didn't even try to help Summer out with what would have otherwise been a bloody battle with only a single victor.

Petrov should've never given her a gun. As if everyone didn't already find her annoying enough.

———

At night, Amanda and Matt went for runs, or visited the kitchen pixies together, or sat by the water's edge in the darkness. Yes, there was a fair amount of kissing too, but most of the time, they talked—about life before the Academy, about Johnny and Lisa or Matt's parents, about what they wanted to do after graduation right around the corner.

Most importantly of all, Amanda's dreams had stopped.

She hadn't even realized it until two weeks before the end of the semester when she sat across from Petrov in the training building, and he asked her about them point-blank.

"The dreams?" Amanda stared at him, then jumped in her chair. "Oh, *those* dreams. Yeah. I, uh…I haven't had one for a while."

"Huh." Petrov cocked his head. "You didn't think that was something to mention between the last time we talked about them and now?"

"Well, I guess I forgot about them." She gave him a pitifully unconvincing smile. "I'm cured. Yay…"

"That's not how this works, but nice try."

"Oh, come on. I'm doing good. Haven't had a rage freak-out in a while. I'm busy. School's almost done—"

"You have a boyfriend."

"Seriously?"

He spread his arms. "Or is that not important either?"

Amanda scrunched up her face and folded her arms. "I know what you're trying to do."

"What's that, huh?"

"You're trying to piss me off. Because you know I'm not gonna talk about something like that anyway. And you know I know that."

"And you know I know you know." Petrov wiggled his head as he said it all in a mockingly high-pitched voice. "You wanna know what else I know?"

She snorted. "Not really."

"Good. Get outta here."

"Wait, for real?"

Petrov heaved a massive sigh. "Do I have to spell it out for you?"

"Do I have to come back next weekend?"

"Out."

"Yes!" Amanda leapt from her chair and tore across the training building. "If anyone ever asks, Mr. Petrov, they should totally pay you more!"

"What the hell is *that* supposed to—" The door banged shut, and the shifter girl was gone.

He scoffed and kicked the empty chair in front of him. Then a laugh burst out of the bald Combat Training teacher, and he stood to fold the chairs and put them away. "She has no idea how much they're already paying me for this crap. Never thought I'd say it, Coulier. You're gonna be just fine."

At the beginning of finals week, Glasket showed up at the outdoor cafeteria during breakfast to announce that the special guest they'd all been so eagerly waiting for was finally coming in that afternoon.

"I expect all of you to be out in the main field after lunch. No exceptions. This guest of ours has come a long way to speak to us, and I don't want to give the impression that we're not grateful. I expect everyone to give our guest the attention and respect this magical deserves, and you might learn a thing or two. Enjoy your morning."

Amanda groaned and slumped her chin into her hand propped up on the table. "I don't know how she does it, but Glasket has the *worst* timing."

"Because you have so much work to do during finals week." Grace laughed, but when Amanda rolled her eyes and stared at her, the blonde witch's smile faded. "Seriously? You haven't finished all your projects? What have you been *doing* this whole time?"

"Huh." Summer stuck a forkful of eggs into her mouth and raised her eyebrows. "Somebody has a serious issue with other people's procrastination."

"No, I don't understand how Amanda could leave everything for the last minute when she made us think she's been working on her projects as hard as we have."

"Speak for yourself," Jackson muttered. "I ended up slopping a few things together and hoping they stick."

"Wow. You're really taking this seriously."

"I haven't been putting it all off, Grace." Amanda straightened with a sigh. "I…have a timer on my alchemy setup in the greenhouse, and if I'm supposed to be at this guest-speaker thing or whatever, I'll miss the transfer of all the—"

"Amanda, if it's for your Alchemy scenario, you can't *tell* us about it," Grace interrupted.

"Yeah. Jeeze." Summer blew a raspberry. "What a horrible shifter you are."

"Okay, well, the details don't matter." Amanda tried not to laugh when Grace glared at the other witch, and Summer took a violent bite of bacon in response. "Except for the fact that I have to be in the greenhouse instead. If I'm not, my whole project is screwed."

"Maybe Glasket'll let you go anyway," Jackson offered. "I mean, she let you leave school for three months for a *job*."

"Jackson, she said no exceptions." Grace shook her head. "I'm pretty sure that applies to Amanda too this time."

"*Everyone's* supposed to be there, right?" Alex asked. "Even the teachers?"

"Probably."

The Wood Elf shrugged. "Then sneak out."

"Really?" Grace stared at him. "That's your answer. On the *last* week of school."

"Nobody's gonna see her leave. Probably. Nobody's gonna leave to find her if we all have to be there. Or don't go in the first place."

Amanda perked up a little. "That's perfect."

Alex smirked. "I know."

"I would've thought of it all on my own eventually."

Grace threw up her hands. "Why do I even try?"

"Because you worrying your witchy little brains out over every single thing is how you show us you care, Blondie." Summer leaned forward and patted the tabletop between them. "We still don't appreciate it."

Grace stared at the other witch's hand. Then the entire table cracked up laughing.

When Amanda stopped laughing enough to clear the rest of her plate, she looked around at her friends ribbing each other over breakfast, and grinned.

Okay, fine. I came to the Academy to be the best bounty hunter on Earth, and I will be. Having friends like this made it all worth it.

So she wouldn't gather in the central field with everyone else after lunch and would sneak behind the back of the girls' dorm to wait until the coast was clear.

———

As the students filed into the rows of seats stretching out across the central field six hours later, Matt found Amanda's friends already sitting at the end of one row, but Amanda wasn't with them. So he pushed his way into the row behind them and sat.

"Hey, guys."

"'Sup, Ladykiller?" Summer turned and slung her arm over the back of her chair to nod at him.

Grace rolled her eyes.

"You guys know where Amanda is?"

"Uh...do *you*?"

Grace elbowed Summer in the side. "Stop."

"I'm only asking. I mean, wouldn't that suck if I blabbed my mouth about something I wasn't supposed to?"

"You do that anyway," Jackson said.

"I'm trying to make a point here, okay?"

"She's in the greenhouse," Alex said flatly.

Matt grinned. "Thanks, man."

"Oh, come on." Grace shook her head. "Now if anyone finds out, we're all accomplices."

"No one's gonna find out, Blondie. Chill out."

"She's not coming to this speaker thing, right?" Matt asked.

"Nope." Summer rolled her eyes. "Anyone even know who we're supposed to be getting our minds blown by? Or whatever."

Grace widened her eyes as she stared at the stage. "Yep. Just found out."

A tall, lithe woman had stepped onto the stage with Glasket. Long dark hair fell over her shoulders, the pointed tips of her ears barely showed, and her smile made all the denim and leather look a little out of place on her. But she shook the principal's hand and chuckled at some joke Glasket made.

"We supposed to know who that is?" Summer asked.

"Uh, *yeah*. That's Izzy Berens."

"And?"

"Wait, isn't that the name of one of the other bounty hunters who started this school?" Jackson asked.

"You guys don't pay attention to anything, do you?" Grace pointed at the stage. "That's Leira Berens' *daughter*. I couldn't find a lot on her when I was doing my report on Leira for Ralthorn, but what I did find is…pretty intense."

"Great. She got her mommy to get her speaking gig."

"Summer, I don't think that's why she's here."

"Some bounty hunter gets another bounty hunter to come talk to a bunch of kids. It's all the same. 'Stay in school, kids. Don't do drugs. Always check the safety on your electric-shock revolver.'"

Jackson and Alex snickered.

"Whatever." Grace folded her arms. "You'll see what I'm talking about once you listen to her. You know, like we're *supposed* to be doing."

"All right. Senior year didn't loosen you up *at all*."

The dark-haired elf on stage cleared her throat into the mic. "Hey. Can everybody hear me?"

The students didn't say a thing, but a few of them in the back nodded.

"Cool. My name's Izzy Berens. First, I want to thank Dean Glasket for inviting me out here to talk to you guys. I'm happy to be the first guest speaker, so hopefully, they keep getting better after this."

The teachers chuckled, but none of the students joined them.

"It was kind of surprising to be asked to do this at a school that trains bounty hunters. A school funded by bounty hunters who've had their fair share of government contracts over the years. Then there's me. I don't work for anybody but myself. I definitely don't work with the government."

Summer snorted. "All right. She's not horrible."

"I guess the most important thing I can tell you guys," Izzy continued, "is that it really, *really* doesn't matter where you come from or what you've been through, or even what *school* you went to. If this is what you want to do, you'll figure out a way to make it work. That's what I had to do too. Of course, I wasn't at a bounty hunter school, but I did spend a few years at the School of Necessary Magic."

The woman shook her head and scanned the crowd with a coy smile. "Didn't have a chance to graduate, though. Still, I figured out a way to make the obstacles work for me. I'm *definitely* not telling you guys to drop out of school and not graduate, and everything will be okay. You'll all have a lot more opportunities than I did that way, and if you can stick this out to the end, that's what you should do."

Summer nudged Grace in the side. "See? Just because you get kicked out of SoNM doesn't mean you're worthless."

"I never said you were worthless, Summer."

"I'm making sure you heard me."

"So I guess I can kick this off with a few stories of my own from back in the day," Izzy continued. "Maybe that'll wake some of you up."

As their guest speaker continued, Summer spun in her chair. "Hey, Ladykiller. You ever hear of a—hey. Oh, come on. Where'd he go?"

Jackson turned to scan the central field and smothered a laugh. "Looks like he had some emergency in the main building."

"*What?*" Grace looked toward the building in time to see Matt slipping through the glass front doors. "Why? Why would he do that?"

Summer snickered and turned back around to fold her arms.

"My guess? Perfect time to go suck face with the shifter girl in the greenhouse."

"Stop." Grace smacked her arm, and the other witch grinned, waggling her eyebrows.

"I bet she finished that alchemy project *weeks* ago."

"Summer, shut up and pay attention."

CHAPTER TWENTY-SIX

Amanda got it from her friends that night at dinner, and none of them believed her when she said she had no idea Matt would show up in the greenhouse and that she'd been working on her Alchemy project. The fact that they were more supportive of her and Matt than they were about the secrets they thought she was trying to keep from them made her realize she owed them a real explanation.

Not that Matt and I didn't do anything when I finished the last part of making the solution, but that's not the point.

"Guys, listen. I have a lot to tell you, and it's not an over-dinner kind of thing. Wanna meet me out here tonight? I'll explain everything."

That got her weird looks and a few snickers. Still, her friends agreed to join her back at the cafeteria that night, when there was a much higher chance of no other students being up and about on campus to overhear the whole thing.

The conversation that night started with a few more jokes about her and Matt, then Amanda finally had to spit it all out so her friends wouldn't be any more embarrassed by their lack of knowledge when they finally did hear it all.

That didn't mean they weren't pissed off when she finished telling them everything about her expedition to South America, UM-7000, and seeing the wizard who killed her parents. Then doing everything she could to start looking for him before the Coalition cut her off from all access and resources and sent her back to school with an indefinite suspension from work.

Amanda wasn't surprised to see her friends' faces morphing into horror and disgust as she finished her story, but she *was* surprised to find they weren't mad at her at all for not having told them sooner.

"How *dare* they?" Grace snarled. "That's like… You don't ex-communicate the one person who knew how to handle the problem!"

"Forget handling problems, Blondie." Summer pounded a fist down on the table. "She saved the fucking world, and nobody gives a shit."

"Nobody even knows," Jackson muttered, his face pale and his eyes wide. "Oh, man. Nobody's *ever* gonna know. *We* didn't even know."

"You can't tell anybody, guys." Amanda fixed them all with a pleading look. "Please. It's bad enough as it is."

"Who's gonna believe us even if we *did* tell them?" Alex asked. "I mean, yeah. We believe *you*. But still."

"Want me to go back to that stupid boardroom and smash in that shifter-mafia don's face?" Summer pounded her fist into her opposite hand and nodded. "Because I will."

"What, you mean Connor Slate?"

"Sure. Him too."

"Summer, he's the director of the Coalition. You can't walk in there and start beating him up."

"The hell I can't. I remember exactly how to get back there, and this time, he won't be able to see me *or* smell me. That baking soda really works."

"Okay, no. No." Amanda shook her head. "Seriously. I don't

want you guys to try to fix this for me, okay? There's nothing to fix. I got it."

"Amanda, they tried to keep that picture from you, and they didn't even tell you they were looking for him." Grace's wide eyes shimmered with tears. "That's basically saying they don't care that the wizard who...who *murdered your family* is still out there walking free."

Amanda swallowed. "I know. I figured out how to find him on my own. You know, after graduation."

"Then I'm coming with you." Summer clapped a hand on the shifter girl's back. "Nope. You don't have a say in this. I'm coming."

"Yeah, we'll probably all end up telling you the same thing," Jackson said. "If the Coalition won't help you, which is seriously messed up, then somebody has to. You can't do this by yourself."

Amanda wrinkled her nose and tried to hold the tears back from welling in her eyes. It didn't work, but at least she didn't start crying. "Thanks. That's...that's great to hear. Seriously. But you guys shouldn't put yourselves in that kind of danger to help me out. I mean, no offense, but you haven't exactly gone out to catch a criminal before."

Alex scoffed. "Neither have you."

"No, but I've been hunting divergent creatures for the last year. You guys have been here. I don't want any of you to get hurt."

Summer laughed. "This is hilarious. You're so deep in this that you don't hear how stupid you sound right now."

"What?"

"Amanda." Grace set her hands on the table, then glanced around their circle of friends and tried to hold back a laugh. "You're right. You were out hunting creatures, and we've been here the whole time. At a school for *bounty hunters*."

"I know, but—"

"If they didn't think we could handle stuff like this right out of high school, why the *hell* would they put us through the torture of taking our finals in front of all those scouts for employers on Friday? Huh?"

Amanda stared at the blonde witch and felt all her other friends staring at her. Then she huffed out a laugh and pushed herself away from the table. "Shit."

"*Now* you put your brains back where they belong." Summer slapped her on the back again. "Like it or not, shifter girl, you're stuck with us. You better like it."

"That doesn't even make sense. Stop hitting me."

"Just watch. We got your back!" The witch thumped Amanda again, and the shifter girl shoved Summer off the picnic bench. She toppled backward and landed with a *thud* before the entire table burst out laughing.

Including Summer.

"See? We're ready!"

"Looks like you're ready to get your ass kicked," Jackson said.

"Hey, if I can't take it, I shouldn't be dishing it out."

Chuckling, Amanda offered Summer a hand up, and the witch dusted off her pants before pointing her finger at everyone around the table. "We survived bounty-hunter juvie, okay. We can handle one asshole wizard who thinks he can fuck with the wrong shifter girl and get away with it."

"Maybe don't say that to his face, though," Grace added. "I don't want you to get your guts splattered all over the ceiling right when I finally started to like you."

Amanda stared at her friends with a confused smile. "Jesus, when did you guys get so…violent?"

Alex shrugged. "Probably when we met you. Personally, I'm pretty happy with it."

"Ha. Okay, then. We graduate this weekend. Then we go take that son of a bitch down."

"Now you're *talkin'*, shifter girl." Summer almost slapped

Amanda's back again, but the door to the back of the kitchens opened with a soft *squeak*, and light spilled out onto the grass.

No one moved as Fred's hulking form emerged from around the back corner of the kitchens with a giant tray in both hands. "Now, I can't say I wasn't eavesdropping because then I'd be lying, and that's not something I do. But I do have two pies that *someone*"—the giant pixie raised his voice and turned slightly back toward the open door—"decided to bake with lemon zest instead of orange, and that wasn't the plan. But it tastes better. So…"

"You've gotta be kidding me." Grace gestured at Fred. "*This* is what we've been missing out on for four years? Entire pies?"

"Um…yeah." Amanda stood from the table and headed toward the grinning pixie. "Not too late to get in on it, though. If Fred says it's good, it's probably the best thing you've ever tasted."

When she met the pixie's gaze, Fred nodded.

So he knows the plan. What happens in the kitchen stays in the kitchen, right? Or the cafeteria. Same difference.

CHAPTER TWENTY-SEVEN

On the last day of finals, Amanda had passed all her final project exams but one. The seniors got to choose which final they wanted to showcase on the last day. That meant presenting it in front of all the private company scouts looking for newly graduated Academy students to offer them their first job.

Amanda received praise from Ralthorn for her report on Angus Fletchen. Calsgrave gave her a guaranteed pass for basically not letting plants die. LeFor's stare held both approval and what looked a lot like jealousy for having put together her magical-frequency tracker added to her "DIY tech kit." Petrov rolled his eyes when she'd scored an eight out of ten on the shooting range and during the final game of Capture the Flag with Guns.

Now, all she had left was to execute her plans for Zimmer's Alchemy scenario, which she'd built on all her work in her other classes. However, she had to wait half the morning until it was her turn to "perform."

She and Matt sat next to each other in the side field on the northwest side of campus outside the greenhouse's curving wall of windows. This was where the seniors finished their finals together, one right after the other, and this was where the scouts had also gathered to watch and take notes on their top choices for new hires.

"This is the weirdest way to end high school," Amanda muttered as they watched Blake Lively beat the crap out of Petrov in front of an audience.

"I mean, it's better than sitting in a stuffy room all day and taking a two-and-a-half-hour test, right?"

"Slightly, yeah." They laughed, and she gestured at the tables set up for the scouts on the other end of the field. "I mean it's weird that they're here to watch us. Like, are these our finals to pass so we graduate, or is this a job interview?"

"Saves us a bunch of time having to do them separately."

"Right. That's one way to look at it."

"Hey." Matt grabbed her hand, and when she looked at him, the corners of his eyes crinkled above his reassuring smile. "It'll work."

"I already have a job."

He playfully rolled his eyes. "You keep reminding me of that like it means something."

"Ha."

"I'm talking about your tracker, Amanda." Matt squeezed her hand. "You did everything right. I saw it. It'll work for your scenario, and it'll work finding the wizard. Watch."

"Thanks." She drew a deep breath and held it before puffing it all out again, but it didn't make her feel any better. "I guess I won't know until I try it out. Sink or swim, right?"

"Right. Hey, if you start sinking, I'm a *really* good swimmer. So…you know, I'll probably come help you."

Amanda laughed and didn't try to stop him when he leaned in to kiss her.

"Miss Coulier," Zimmer called from the center of the field.

The young shifters instantly pulled away from each other.

"I hope you remembered your final scenario is *today*."

"Crap." Amanda grabbed her backpack and leapt to her feet. "I guess I'm up."

"I can't wait to see how awesome it is." Matt gave her two thumbs-up before she turned and raced across the field.

Zimmer stood with her arms folded in the area where she'd set up Amanda's unique Alchemy scenario. She'd done it while Blake had been beating up their Combat Training teacher—for a high score of ten out of ten, which Petrov wrote down with a smear of blood left behind. She raised an eyebrow as the shifter girl hurried to join her and muttered, "You have everything else you need?"

"Yeah."

"Good." Looking the girl up and down one more time, Zimmer winked before turning to face the audience of scouts. "Miss Coulier's scenario involved a common obstacle encountered during any number of investigative cases. During her freshman year, she had a unique experience with a number of grubs we discovered were highly attracted to the wards set around this school."

Amanda knelt in the sectioned-off area and unzipped her backpack to take out all her supplies.

"The details of that situation don't matter, but for her final exam, the only information Miss Coulier has is that the item she has to find to pass this exam relates to those grubs in some way. That's it.

"Now, she and I have discussed her plan for finding this unknown item where I've placed it on campus, and I approved her...unique execution of it. However, she performed all the alchemical processes and the design of whatever else she includes in finding this item on her own time without supervision. So we'll see if this works."

Zimmer turned to watch her student, and Amanda opened the single wooden box laid out in the grass in front of her. Inside was the clue Zimmer had given her even though she didn't need it. She took it out and looked up at Zimmer.

"A picture?"

"That's not the item you're looking for, but I figured a visual aid couldn't hurt."

"Okay." Amanda dropped the photo of the orange grub with purple polka-dots and pulled the vial of crushed and boiled Dreamscape flowers—the ones she'd filled with her intentional memories of the grubs from freshman year. "Um…do I have to say what I'm doing, or?"

"If you want to."

"Not really." After uncorking the vial, Amanda grabbed the magical tracking device she'd made herself and held the potion over the small panel that would hopefully read the magical frequency of her grub memories.

This is as close as I could get, and I really hope this works.

She poured five drops onto the panel and corked the vial while she waited for the device to do its thing.

Nobody said a word as they watched the shifter girl kneeling in the grass.

Come on, come on. It has to work.

The seconds felt like days until the tracker let out a soft *beep,* and a wobbly line of blue light illuminated on the screen.

"I got it!" Amanda leapt to her feet and looked up at Zimmer. "Yeah. Okay. I got it."

The teacher didn't say a word.

Amanda stared down at the screen and turned back and forth. The blue light turned across the screen with her, and she grinned.

It's picking up something. *So follow the trail.*

It didn't take her long at all to walk across the field, looking down at the screen to make sure she was going in the right direction. She only stopped and looked up when the end of the blue line came into view, and she found herself standing in front of Shep.

247

"Um…are *you* the item?"

The wizard let out a wheezing laugh. "Not as far as I know, Miss Coulier. But, uh…" He looked at Zimmer, who nodded. Shep reached into his baggy pocket and pulled out a small black jewelry box before whispering, "I reckon you passed your last final."

"Really?" She took the box and opened it.

Inside was the broken-off tip of one of the grub-catchers she and Summer had spent hours collecting freshman year. Amanda laughed and turned toward Zimmer. "It worked."

"That seems to be the case." Zimmer offered her a small smile and nodded. "Congratulations, Miss Coulier."

"Oh my God. Holy crap. It worked." Amanda's eyes filled with tears, and she couldn't catch her breath before she dropped the box right there in the grass and took off toward Matt. Her friends had joined him at some point during her scenario, and now they stared at her in apprehension.

"Well?" Grace shrugged. "Say something. Because your face right now is telling me nothing."

"It works." Amanda stared at her friends with wide eyes, and Matt pushed himself to his feet. "It's gonna work. I did it. I'm gonna find him. I can't—" She choked on her attempt to hold back her tears again, and her friends watched her mutely with a mixture of pride and the same terrified determination she felt.

Matt was the first one to move, and he wrapped her up in a big hug before whispering in her ear, "See? You don't need anybody to get this done."

"Thanks."

"You're still not doing the rest of this on your own." He released her, and Amanda blinked back more tears before she realized what all the looks on her friends' faces meant.

"Wait, you guys all talked about this together?"

"Yeah, and you told Ladykiller before us." Summer snorted and folded her arms. "Go figure."

"I...I can't believe—"

"Jeeze!" Jackson leapt behind Grace and thrust her in front of him like a witch shield when a burst of blue light flashed right beside Amanda. "Stop doing that!"

Fiona studied the five soon-to-be Academy graduates standing around her mentee and smirked. "Maybe you should stop being so jumpy."

"What are you doing here?" Grace hissed, trying to keep her voice down as the next senior walked out onto the field for their last final. "You can't be here."

"Actually, I can."

"You *shouldn't*." The witch pointed at Amanda. "After what you did to her? She doesn't want to see you."

"That so?" Fiona glanced at Amanda sidelong. "You're getting chatty with the locals, kid."

"Building my team that doesn't suck." Amanda stepped away from the red-haired woman to stand beside her friends. "And they don't."

"That's cute. Glad to hear it. Listen, kid, we need to make a decision right now."

"She doesn't have to do anything for you," Summer said.

Fiona pointed at her. "Don't say another word. I'll get to you later."

"What's going on?" Amanda and Matt shared a glance. Then the shifter girl stepped forward. "What decision?"

"Kid, I need to know if what you saw in that kemana is the real deal. The actual guy. Are you a hundred percent on that?"

"Five hundred." Amanda swallowed. "Why?"

"Okay. I'm breaking the usual protocol for this stuff, and your principal's gonna kill me, but I'll deal with her later. Grab your boyfriend."

"Fiona."

"Do it."

Matt grabbed Amanda's hand and gave it a reassuring squeeze.

"And you. Baking Soda." Fiona pointed at Summer next. "Let's go."

"Nope. You're crazy. I'm not going anywhere with you."

"Oh, for the love of—I can't believe I'm still gonna do this." The woman leapt toward Summer, who tried to slap her hand away, but Fiona was faster and clamped a hand around the witch's wrist before tugging her toward Amanda and Matt.

"Hey!" Grace tried to step in front of her. "What are you doing?"

"I'll make sure they get in touch with you. Congratulations on graduating and being adults and everything. It's super fun."

"Fiona, what's—"

The woman clapped a hand on Amanda's shoulder, then everything flashed with blue light, and they all disappeared.

Summer gasped, coughed, and stumbled forward across the bright green grass of the hidden valley in the Rocky Mountains. Matt made a sound like he was going to be sick but fortunately wasn't. He still didn't let go of Amanda's hand.

The shifter girl stared at the place where the invisible entrance to the invisible Canissphere lay right in front of them. "What is this?"

"Don't play dumb, kid. You know exactly where you are."

"I mean, why are we here. Why are Summer and Matt here?"

"Take me back." Summer swallowed thickly and clutched her stomach. "You're psycho."

"You'll puke if I teleport you again right now. Suck it up." Fiona marched toward the entrance. "We found your wizard, kid. Pinpointed all his major contacts too. Right now, he's in Rio de Janeiro, living it up. That won't last very long."

"You...you *found* him?"

"You're not hearing things. I promise." Fiona turned again to eye the three completely stunned teenagers standing in the middle of an open field. "Hey, because you *technically* weren't wrong about anything else, Dr. Caniss agreed to lend you the use of Omega Industries' resources for this whole bag 'em and tag 'em thing.

"All the lowlifes who, well…you know. So it's pretty much an overlap with your current job. Seeing as these idiots have gone from kidnapping twelve-year-old shifters to hunting divergent whales for fun. Go figure."

"Wait, wait, wait. I still have my job?"

"Uh-huh."

"And…Caniss is helping me with this whole thing."

"Yeah, kid. But we're kind of on a time crunch, so let's move."

"Oh my God. This is happening right now."

"So why do *we* have to be here for this?" Summer groaned.

Fiona growled and tipped her head back to glare at the sky before spinning around. "It sure as hell isn't for moral support. It's not because *I* like you. You're damn near impossible to smell now that you know how to cast a real illusion, let alone invisible. We're gonna need somebody who can slip into a few tight places unnoticed."

"Why would I do that for *you*?" Summer finally straightened and took a deep breath. "I don't like you either."

"Well, you like bombs. I saw your little stunt on the field when you were taking your test this morning. Nice stuff. Kinda looks like an explosion or two I've seen from a certain dwarf bounty hunter I know."

Summer and Amanda exchanged a wide-eyed glance.

She used the accelerant she stole from Johnny to make bombs for her finals. Holy crap. How did I not see that coming?

Fiona grinned. "So yeah, you'll help us, Summer. Because I'm gonna let you build all the bombs you want, and you get to set them. Unless you're not interested in that anymore, then—"

"Done." Summer nodded with a perfectly straight face. "I'm in."

MARTHA CARR & MICHAEL ANDERLE

"Thought so."

"And I'm...what?" Matt frowned at the woman. "Coming in to say sorry?"

"I mean, you can apologize if you want." Fiona shrugged. "You're here because we've been having a little trouble pinning an exact location on this guy. You hacked into our system. So I figured you'd be cool with using it to hack into someone else's."

"You..." Matt's eyes grew wide. Then he laughed sharply before clearing his throat. "I don't work for free."

Summer and Amanda stared at him, and Fiona winked. "None of you do. Now hurry the hell up. I don't do babysitting."

The woman turned, and after three more quick strides, disappeared.

"What happened?" Summer muttered.

"The lab's invisible, and she walked inside," Amanda replied.

"We all got hired by the Coalition of Shifters." Matt grabbed his head with both hands and puffed out his cheeks. "And you're a witch."

Summer threw her head back for one of her maniacal cackles. "Yeah, but I'm a badass witch. Don't forget it."

"My dad's gonna *kill* me."

Amanda frowned at Matt, still unable to believe this was real herself. "Why?"

"Because being hired as a hacker means I was right." The boy snorted and laughed. "I got a job doing what he wanted me to stop."

"Screw what your dad thinks, Ladykiller." Summer punched his shoulder and headed past the shifters toward the place where Fiona had disappeared. "Mine never helped me."

"Well, *that* explains a lot."

Amanda's phone buzzed in her pocket, and she drew it out with a frown to find Johnny's name on the screen. "Um...hold on a sec, guys."

Matt waited patiently for her while Summer reached out with

both hands to feel along the invisible outer wall of the Canis-sphere. "What is this? Who doesn't have a damn door?"

Amanda pressed the phone to her ear. "Hey, Johnny."

"I heard from Fiona 'bout an hour ago. Don't think I ain't already figured what you're fixin' to do."

"Um...good to hear from you too." Amanda shrugged when Matt gave her a questioning look.

"So I'll say what I gotta say, then you go do your thing."

"Okay..."

"I've been in your shoes, kid. I know what this feels like. Just remember what I told you, huh?" Johnny cleared his throat. "You do *whatever it takes* to get the job done. The right way. Then hell. The rest is up to your damn preference, understand?"

"Yeah, Johnny. Thanks."

"Good. Now quit wastin' your time talkin' to me." He ended the call like that, and Amanda looked down at her phone, unable to keep her smile from growing wider by the second.

My preference. I'm the sixteen-year-old monster hunter, and I'm about to go after one hell of a monster with two of my best friends.

It was pretty weird to spell it all out like that, even in her mind. Still, the way this had turned out wasn't that much weirder than anything else she'd done in the last four years.

As far as Amanda was concerned, that was how she preferred it.

Get sneak peeks, exclusive giveaways, behind the scenes content, and more. PLUS you'll be notified of special **one day only fan pricing** on new releases.

Sign up today to get free stories.

Visit: https://marthacarr.com/read-free-stories/

AUTHOR NOTES - MARTHA CARR
AUGUST 19, 2021

On Sunday I leave for vacay for a week to a spa resort. The last time I took a vacation longer than a weekend was in 2016 when I took the Offspring to the west coast of Ireland. I didn't intend for so much time to slip by, but it did and it's something I mean to change.

There was time off for trips for weddings and funerals and moving from one house to another and surgeries – and somewhere in my head I associated that with vacation because I was taking time off from work.

The grooves in my brain for middle class worker bee run deep and I'm cautious about taking time off – for anything.

But going through cancer again – and chemo this time – has left me determined to make a change or two.

In Ireland, away from the news and TV and social media I stopped thinking so much. I became more present and noticed every little detail around me. Even now, I can still feel the peace in the middle of my chest. Imagine if I had done something similar every year since then. What would my stress levels look like?

Right now, they're kind of high. Despite meditation and long walks and CBD oil and sitting out in the garden – and maybe they'd be higher without all of that – I can feel the tension running through me.

Plus, I've never been to a spa resort before. Again, what took me so long? I'm going to a place in Monterey, the Post Ranch Inn, that has no TVs in the rooms and sits on a cliff overlooking the ocean. There's even a redwood forest on the property and a skylight over the bed to see the stars. I plan to look at my phone as little as possible and hug a tree every morning and night.

I'm going with one of my best friends, Dhyanna who's more like my big sister – part of my family I created around me.

The goal is to let all the worries go for just a week. Leela will be in good hands, Lois will be in boarding at her favorite place on the planet with all her buddies and work will be all caught up for just a week. The very capable and crafty assistant, Grace will be at the helm just in case.

There's an art museum with local art on the grounds, meditation, yoga, gardens to roam… And the Monterey Aquarium, plus dinner at a restaurant that serves eight courses and takes two and a half hours. There will be pictures, of course in my Fan group on Facebook and probably author notes. But for that week, I will let all of that melt away and just be.

It took me till nearly 62 years old to figure out that – in life – if you're not having fun, ask why. More adventures to follow.

AUTHOR NOTES - MICHAEL ANDERLE
AUGUST 19, 2021

Thank you for not only reading this book but this entire series and these author notes as well.

HATS and my Wife

When I first started writing, I would tell stories of my wife (Judith) and some of the shenanigans that occurred. Especially when she really didn't know about and/or pay much attention to this author life of mine.

(She didn't know anything about my writing until I had already published two books and paid little attention to it for a while after that.)

We are presently renting a house for a week in Cabo San Lucas and (hopefully) closing on Casa Anderle this week.

I'm not holding my breath for it to happen. We shall see.

Both of us brought an LMBPN hat down with us. Mine is black, hers is white.

She started with the 'I've lost my black LMBPN hat' comment yesterday in the Phoenix airport. We had arrived on an American Airlines flight to Phoenix from Las Vegas and were getting ready to get on the American Airlines Phoenix to San Juan Del Cabo leg.

I figured the answer to "who owns the black hat" was in question at this point.

Sure enough, my ownership rights continued slipping off the runway later last night when I pulled out the black hat (along with her white hat…luggage issues) and set them on the dining room table.

Judith made another comment.

The tentacles of acquisition were sneaking their way up the legs of the table towards the hat… I could picture the scene. Hopefully, you can picture the scene as well. If not, think about tentacles growing up from the floor, snaking around gray wooden table legs, and then arching over the top corner to stretch, beckoning, toward the black hat about two feet from the corner.

Can you picture the scene now?

Move to this morning. Both of us woke up with bedhead and a complete lack of desire to do anything hair problems first thing upon waking up. So, I took a meeting this morning and slipped on ~~MY~~ her black hat.

Judith (who wakes up later than I do) came stumbling down the stairs in a fog (complete lie…mostly on the fog comment.) Somehow, she grabs ~~MY~~ her black hat and throws it on her head while I'm working from the couch.

I roll my eyes. She's so obvious.

After her meeting, she starts looking at the size of the hat. The hat is a S/M (but the hat has elastic bands for size.) This black hat was and has been in MY office for a while. I have owned black LMBPN hats, so me having a black hat is not in question.

Apparently, who lost their black hat is now in question.

Somehow, the logic is now that if I own a black LMBPN hat in S/M, that must then mean this hat is Judith's.

So, apparently, I brought ~~MY~~ her black hat down as well as her white hat, and I'll have to ask to use ~~MY~~ her black hat while we're here in Cabo San Lucas.

It's not worth the trouble to argue since we have two or three more of the black hats back in Las Vegas, and she can only use one of the hats at a time.

It is, however, worth the trouble to mention it in my author notes, and I will snicker for days about writing this.

Sometime in the future, this will come back to bite me in the ass, I'm sure.

But until then...

Anyway, stay safe and sane out there, and I look forward to talking to you in the next book!

Ad Aeternitatem,

Michael Anderle

Solve a murder, save her mother, and stop the apocalypse?

What would you do when elves ask you to investigate a prince's murder and you didn't even know elves, or magic, was real?

Meet Leira Berens, Austin homicide detective who's good at what she does – track down the bad guys and lock them away.

Which is why the elves want her to solve this murder – fast. It's not just about tracking down the killer and bringing them to justice. It's about saving the world!

If you're looking for a heroine who prefers fighting to flirting, check out The Leira Chronicles today!

AVAILABLE ON AMAZON AND IN KINDLE UNLIMITED!

BOOKS BY MICHAEL ANDERLE

Sign up for the LMBPN email list to be notified of new releases and
special deals!

https://lmbpn.com/email/

For a complete list of books by Michael Anderle, please visit:

www.lmbpn.com/ma-books/

CONNECT WITH THE AUTHORS

Martha Carr Social

Website: http://www.marthacarr.com

Facebook: https://www.facebook.com/groups/MarthaCarrFans/

Michael Anderle Social

Website: http://lmbpn.com

Email List: http://lmbpn.com/email/

https://www.facebook.com/LMBPNPublishing

https://twitter.com/MichaelAnderle

https://www.instagram.com/lmbpn_publishing/

https://www.bookbub.com/authors/michael-anderle

Made in the USA
Las Vegas, NV
01 March 2024

86414785R00163